# In A Place Apart

## Phil Young

**Wordsonthestreet**

First published 2009 by
Wordsonthestreet
Six San Antonio Park, Salthill, Galway, Ireland
Web: www.wordsonthestreet.com
Email: publisher@wordsonthestreet.com

The moral right of the author has been asserted.

A catalogue record for this book is available from the British Library.

ISBN        978-0-9552604-9-0

Cover Design: Wordsonthestreet
Layout and typesetting: Wordsonthestreet
Printed and bound in the UK

# In A Place Apart

## About the author

Phil Young is a native of Dunmanway in West Cork, and now lives in Dublin. She graduated from Trinity College, Dublin with an MPhil in Anglo-Irish literature, and has had a number of short stories and articles published in various magazines. She has also been featured several times on the RTE Radio programme *Sunday Miscellany.*

Phil Young is the author of the first ever biography of children's writer, Patricia Lynch. This biography was launched in Cork as part of the Cork European City of Culture celebrations in 2005.

*This novel is dedicated
To my friends in our creative writing group*

# PART ONE

# MARGARET

# CHAPTER ONE

It was cold in the boat. Margaret sat upright, her body rigid beneath her heavy wool coat. If she moved, if she bent to remove her shawl from the trunk by her feet, she would get sick. The boat rocked gently as the waves slapped against its sides. She had never been on a boat before, and had not realised it would make her feel like this. She stared straight ahead, trying to ignore the sensations in her stomach.

The island was just a dot in the distance, a dark shape against the pale dawn sky. It seemed farther away now than when they had set out, and all around her the sea heaved. Opposite her, Owen's body moved in smooth rhythmic sweeps, as the oars cut through the water. He had not spoken since they had left the harbour, his energies directed at guiding the boat through the channel and out on to the open sea. This was a journey that was familiar to him, but for Margaret it was all new and strange.

As she became more accustomed to the swaying motion, the sick feeling eased and Margaret could relax a little. She drew her coat more firmly about her, and tightened the headscarf beneath her chin.

'Are you cold?' Owen didn't break the rhythm of the rowing.

'I'm alright.'

'Why don't you get your shawl from the trunk? Your coat is too thin.'

'I'm fine, really.' Margaret smiled to reassure her new husband. He nodded, and did not speak again.

Her husband ... was this man really her husband? It had all happened so fast. This time yesterday she was Margaret of the Shop in Ballymona, and now she was Mrs. Owen McDowell. She was about to become a woman of the Island. She, who knew nothing of the sea, who had never been outside her own townland. Suddenly the enormity of what she had done hit her. Up to this, she had buffeted her way through the many opposing forces, determination closing her mind to what might lie ahead. Her battle was with her parents, her friends, her priest – all united against her. But she had ploughed through their opposition. She wanted Owen so badly. She was so desperate to become his wife that cutting herself off from her past to embrace the very different life which would come with marrying Owen seemed of no consequence.

'They're different ... primitive and backward.' Her mother's voice was tight with anger. 'They never marry outside their own. Inbred and closed. Do you want to become part of that? Do you, do you?'

'It's a hard life, girl. They know no better, but you'll never stick it. Why would you want to do something like that? And you brought up knowing every comfort?'

Her father's voice could not disguise the hurt he felt. She was letting them down and bringing shame on them She knew that. But she didn't care. Not even when they brought in old Father Sweeney to talk sense into her. Her mulish silence in the face of all his arguments finally defeated him. And, to avoid a greater scandal, he agreed to marry her.

They were nearing the island now. She was so cold, she had ceased to notice it, and a tremor of excitement ran through her as the white rocks caught the morning sun. These were the rocks which had fascinated her ever since she was a small child. Her bedroom was in the attic of their three-storey house in Ballymona, and on sunny mornings the glow from those distant shapes threw channels of light across the water. They were the only part of the island she could see, though she had heard tell that the sand there was as white as snow, and that beyond the rugged coastline, the land was green and fertile. Inishbawn, the white island. A strange land, as alien to the mainlanders as Australia or America would have been.

'We're almost there.' Owen relaxed on the oars. The shape of the island was now spread across her vision. A rugged coastline, white sandy beaches, and the vivid whiteness of the rocks. Beyond that she could not see, but as the boat drew near, she could see a small harbour with a wooden pier, a low, grey building, and groups of men standing nearby.

Owen guided the boat alongside the pier, where a number of other boats were tied up. A stooped man moved with surprising speed down the pier, to take the rope thrown up by Owen. He held the boat steady, while Owen passed up the box of provisions and Margaret's trunk, and then Owen himself jumped up. The two men exchanged words in a rapid dialect that was incomprehensible to Margaret, and then Owen turned to her, his arms outstretched.

'Are you ready? Just put your foot on the side of the boat, and I'll haul you up.' Terrified, Margaret did as she was told, her heart pounding as she felt the swell of the sea beneath her. Owen's arms came around her, and she was hoisted up. It was an ignominious introduction to her new island home. It was not the sort of entry she would have liked to have made, especially as she was being stared at with great curiosity by the men standing around the harbour.

'There, you're safe now. You're on dry land.' Owen released his hold on her, and turned to the man, who was already loading up the provisions and the trunk on to a wooden cart.

'Thomas, this is my wife ... from the mainland.'

Margaret smiled at the man, but he merely nodded and continued with what he was doing.

'Thomas helps me at Derryglas,' Owen explained. 'I couldn't manage without him.'

Owen took her arm, and they followed Thomas around the side of the building. The men grouped around the building greeted Owen, and a few shouted a welcome to Margaret. The buzz of their talk grew louder as Margaret and Owen moved away, and Margaret reddened in the knowledge that she was the topic under discussion.

Thomas had loaded the trunk and the box of provisions from the hand-cart on to the pony and trap which was waiting on the other side of the building. He watched in silence, one hand propping up a rusty bicycle, as Owen helped Margaret to step up into the trap. It was a nice trap ... the sort of trap which brought the well to do farmers and their wives into Mass on Sundays in Ballymona. It was well -sprung and well -upholstered, with a fine looking pony to pull it. Along the side, the name of Owen's place, *Derryglas* , was printed in neat gold lettering. Owen tucked the tartan rug around his wife's knees.

'Are you comfortable? We'll be at Derryglas in about an hour. It's on the other side of the island, but the pony will make short work of the journey.'

Owen looked at ease, now that he was back on Inishbawn. On the mainland there was always a sense of awkwardness about him ... a stiffness that Margaret had wondered at. But now he seemed a natural part of his surroundings.

'I can't wait to meet your mother and your sister. Will they be at Derryglas when we get there?' Margaret burrowed into the rug, and leaned her head against Owen's shoulder, feeling the warmth of his body and the comfort of it.

'Of course they will. They want to meet you, don't they?'

'Isn't it a shame they couldn't have come over to the wedding? I wish they had been there. It seems strange coming here as your wife, and never having met them. I hope they'll like me. Do you think they'll like me, Owen?'

Owen, holding the reins with one hand, put the other tightly around her shoulder and pressed her to him.

'How could they not like you? And it's no matter whether they do or don't. Aren't you my choice? My woman? Don't you be worrying now.'

'I'm going to be such a good wife to you, Owen. I'll learn all about the farm and everything, so that I'll be able to help you.'

In her mind's eye, Margaret could see them working together, partners, side by side.

Owen laughed. 'You won't need to be bothering yourself with farming ... there'll be plenty for you to do inside. Sure, what would a little townie like you know about the land?'

'I can learn, can't I? And won't Hannah show me? Isn't it a wonder she never married, Owen? Maybe she will now, since I'll be there to look after your mother.'

'Maybe she will at that. Paudie Barrett has been long enough trying to persuade her, God knows. Maybe this is what she's been waiting for.'

Owen clicked at the pony, who broke into a brisk trot, the brasses on his harness making music to the clip- clopping of his hooves. Margaret, pressed closely against her husband's side, looked around her with interest.

The little harbour village was now behind them, its huddle of white cottages and lime fronted houses strung out as far as the church. The church stood in isolation on a slight incline, separated from the parochial house by an untidy-looking graveyard, its headstones barely visible above the growth of scutch grass and weeds. Dry stone walls marked the boundary of the road, and divided up the rock- strewn land into parcels of cultivation. Scrawny cattle grazed here and there, and raised their heads curiously as the pony and trap went by. Away from the shoreline, the white cliffs merged into rugged rocks, the April sunshine highlighting the pale covering of green which was gradually softening their outline. The cottages became more and more sparse. Sheep and goats now replaced the cattle, and bunches of newly- born kids bounced sure-footedly on the higher slopes.

The road began to climb more steeply, and the pony slowed to a walk. Margaret thought she had never seen such emptiness. Now there was hardly a house to be seen. Just black bog and the occasional stunted tree, its branches cowering leeward, away from the Atlantic winds. It was so still and quiet that even the creak of the pony's harness seemed an intrusion. Far below them the sea glittered, and rose here and there in a flurry of white.

It was almost mid-morning, and they had now reached what appeared to be the highest point on the island. Owen pulled the pony over, and loosened the reins.

'You can see Derryglas from here.' He took Margaret by the hand, and led her off the road, across some scrub-land. Margaret gasped when she looked at the other side of Inishbawn. The contrast was total. She could see a soft green valley: fertile squares parcelled off by low walls. White cottages, smoke drifting from their chimneys, were dotted here and there. Hardy, black cattle grazed in clumps. Fringing the green fields, a shingle beach stretched to meet the Atlantic, the white of its stones just as startling as the white of the cliffs on the other side of the island.

'Which house is Derryglas?' Margaret shaded her eyes against the glare.

'See ... over there. Right at the most westerly point.'

The house pointed out by Owen was sunk behind a shelterbelt of low trees, and Margaret could just make out the sheen of its slate roof, and the tall narrow chimneys. It did not look like an islander's house.

They stood there in silence, looking down on Derryglas. The wind wrapped Margaret's coat in flapping folds around their legs, and spread her loosened hair across their faces. She could hear it whistle through the gaps in the nearby walls, and sigh as it lifted the sedge at their feet. The steady boom of the waves on the shore echoed across the island to the cliffs on the other side, and Margaret felt as though their entwined bodies were merging with the land and becoming part of something as old as time. This was now her home, where she belonged. This place, she felt, was where her spirit had always yearned to be. When Owen drew away from her, she was conscious of the tears on her face, but she could not explain why she was crying.

It was downhill all the way now to Derryglas, and the rested pony strained to put the road behind him. Owen pointed out his land to Margaret, explaining to her why some crops thrived and others wilted in the face of the harsh island climate. They turned in through an open gateway, and the last hundred yards was along a sandy path. Margaret's eyes were fixed on her new home, as the pony and trap drew up outside Derryglas. It was a fine, solid, stone-built house, long and low, its slate roof frowning over the upstairs windows. Two lace-curtained windows shone on either side of the door, and a porch, green with potted geraniums, sheltered the entrance. A lean-to and what looked like a stable jutted from one side of the house, and behind them Margaret could see the tops of several outhouses. A well-stocked vegetable garden, protected by fuchsia hedges, led to the drilled potato patch.

'Well, what do you think? Will you settle?' Owen was beside her, her trunk on his shoulder.

'I love it ... it's not a bit like I'd expected.'

'What did you expect? A thatched cottage? Or maybe a fine mansion? It's comfortable, but you'll have no frills here.'

'I wasn't expecting frills ... I wasn't expecting anything as fine as this. And I can't wait to meet your mother and Hannah.'

'Come on then. They're probably having their dinner. With luck, they'll have a bite ready for us.'

The front door opened straight into a large, dim room. Margaret's eyes took a moment to adjust, but she got the impression of sparse furniture, a huge chimney piece, a turf fire burning in the grate, and a table set with blue and white crockery.

Two women stood by the table. They were dressed in black. The older, her frame as tall and angular as a man's, had Owen's sallow colouring, his high cheekbones, even his deep-set, slate blue eyes. Her white hair, scraped back into a tight bun on the nape of her neck, stretched the skin across her face, and made her nose appear even more prominent. The younger woman was short ... shorter than Margaret. She must have been pretty at one time, but now, though Margaret knew that Hannah was still in her twenties, she had a sloppy, careless look about her which made her seem middle-aged. Her hair was streelishly hanging around her face, and the pale blue eyes which met Margaret's were suspicious and hostile.

Margaret smiled nervously, and advanced towards her new family. Julia, the older woman ignored her, and turned to Owen.

'You came on the small boat? Why couldn't you have waited for the steamer?'

'We'd have had two more nights on the mainland. You'd not have managed on your own here, with only Hannah and Thomas to help you with the cattle and everything else.'

'We'd have managed fine. That boat was no way to bring ... to bring her to the island.'

'Her name is Margaret. And she'll have to get used to the boat sooner or later. It's as well to make it sooner.'

'I didn't mind the boat, really I didn't.' Margaret looked from one to the other, but she was still ignored.

'She's not dressed for the open boat ... nor even for the island.'

Hostile eyes ran up and down her body, making Margaret feel like a schoolgirl being scrutinised in front of the class. Her fine wool coat, her lisle stockings, her soft narrow shoes, suddenly seemed silly and frivolous. They had looked so beautiful when she had bought them for her wedding. She had felt good in them, as she stood in front of the priest, her new husband by her side. She had seen the admiration and the pride in Owen's face. But now she just felt awkward.

'I can get some warmer things ... Hannah can tell me what. I wish you could have come over for the wedding, Hannah, and you too Mrs. McDowell. I wanted very much to have you both there, but Owen explained that you haven't been well, and wouldn't have been up to the journey.'

'There's nothing wrong with me.' Julia addressed Margaret directly for the first time. 'Nothing at all. And why Owen couldn't have stayed nearer home when he went looking for a woman, when he thought to get married ... well, it's not for me to say.' She turned to her daughter, and gestured towards the pot by the fire.

'Give them a bit of stew Hannah, and then you'd better see to the calves.' She pulled her shawl across her shoulders and went out through the back door. Hannah, having scooped some of the warm food onto two plates, soon followed her.

'What did I do wrong, Owen? Why were they like that to me?' Margaret struggled against her tears. This was not at all the welcome she had been expecting. Opposition from her own parents was bad enough – after all it was considered a terrible come-down to marry an island man – but she had expected a welcome from her in-laws. She had come, ready to adapt and to fit in, and become part of Owen's family. She loved Owen, and all her life it seemed that she had loved Inishbawn from afar. Rejection had never entered her head.

'Don't worry about it.' Owen squeezed her hand across the table. 'It's just their way. They'll come around. They'll come around, in their own time.'

He continued to eat his dinner in silence, while Margaret poked about with hers. Her hunger had faded, and yet she was afraid of antagonising the women further by not eating the meal which had been put in front of her. When Owen had finished, he cleared the scraps into a bucket, and left the plates on the table in the scullery. The women had still not returned, and Owen took her upstairs to show her their bedroom.

'You'll like the view, whatever you think about the room,' he said as he opened the door at the top of the stairs. 'You can make any changes you want ... nobody will bother you up here, and I'm not particular.'

The room was large, full of dark, cumbersome furniture. The brass bed took up the full of one wall, and opposite it were a washstand, a wardrobe and a wooden blanket box. The window, with its deep-cushioned window seat, looked out across the ocean – sea and sky as far as the eye could see. Clouds dipped down to meet the water, and the pale April sunshine made the white shingle beach below them sparkle like jewels.

'Well, what do you think?' Owen drew her body against his, and together they looked out at the vastness of the scene. It was as if they were alone in the world, just the two of them and Inishbawn.

Later, Owen had his work to attend to, and Margaret unpacked her trunk and arranged her clothes in the huge, almost empty wardrobe, stopping at intervals to touch and smell the heavy jumpers and coarse shirts belonging to her new husband.

When Margaret came downstairs, her sister-in-law was in the kitchen, baking, her red hands pounding and shaping the dough on the wooden table.

'Owen says I'm to show you around the place.' Hannah's voice was sullen. 'So, what do you want to see?'

'I don't want to take you away from your work, Hannah. I'll find my own way around. I love the bedroom ... the view is wonderful.'

'Huh! When you're living on the island for a while, you won't take much heed of views.'

'Do you cross to the mainland much, Hannah? I've never seen you in Ballymona.'

'And what business would I have over there? Haven't we all we want on Inishbawn? Much good it did Owen, going to the mainland.'

Margaret flushed at the implication. 'You could visit the shops. There are some lovely shops in Ballymona. It's a grand town. Maybe we'd go over on the steamer some time? I could show you around.'

Hannah did not answer. The pounding and the shaping continued, and the finished cake was pressed into the pot, to be placed on the fire to bake. When it was obvious that Hannah was not going to continue the conversation, Margaret went outside, where her mother-in-law was working in the vegetable garden. Here again Margaret was met with silence, and her offers of help were brushed off. Feeling like an unwelcome intruder, she returned to the house, and went back upstairs to their bedroom. The earlier excitement, the sense of anticipation and of belonging had now dissipated, and she was swept up in an overwhelming sense of loss. She ached for all that she had given up and left behind. She ached for her parents, for her friend Stella, for the neighbours who had so often been a source of resentment to her, with their nosiness and their gossip. She yearned for the small room high above the sounds of the street, where she could hear the locals shouting their greetings to one another. She longed for the familiarity of Ballymona, its lights, its noise, its friendliness. All that was now lost to her. She was alone. Except for Owen, who on this island knew or cared about her? The tears when they fell were not tears of release, but tears of fear and of hopelessness. Silent tears that flowed helplessly, and that she knew could change nothing. She was Owen's wife. She was an island woman. But she was a stranger here. The people on Inishbawn would never accept her. She would always be an outsider.

# CHAPTER TWO

It was market day in Ballymona. Margaret awoke to the drone of sound that always accompanied that weekly event. Other mornings she would sleep on until the bell for eight o'clock Mass would clang out its insistent call, and she would burrow beneath the bedclothes, hoping her mother would let her be until it was time for school. Her mother never missed eight o'clock Mass, and waged a campaign of guilt inducing sighs and head shakes if Margaret did not accompany her at least a few mornings a week. It was hard to leave the downy softness of the bed for the chill of the draughty church, but her mother's freeze was even harder.

Market day was different though. From six o'clock and even earlier, the rumble of the heavy carts, the bellowing of frightened animals, and the rough voices of countrymen ensured that sleep was impossible, and Margaret would lie there in the darkness, cross and resentful. She hated Market day. Soon the streets outside their shop would be ankle deep in filth, and the smell of the animals would fill the air. By midday the farmers and dealers, their pockets bulging with wads of notes, would be coming in to spend their money, to bring home the tea, sugar and shop bread, the candles and the oil, the barley sugar sticks, the Peggy's legs, for those at home. She would be expected to help, and would spend the afternoon weighing the measures and packing up the orders, and taking her turn at brushing out the straw and manure that came in on a hundred pairs of hobnailed boots.

As the afternoon wore on, the customers would be mostly those who had been sitting for hours in the pub next door. Red-faced, glassy-eyed, confused as to what they had been told to bring home, she would have to suggest what might be needed, and ignore the groping hands which invariably found their way on to her bottom or around her waist. She would have to fill up the oily shopping bags which they would produce, and tot up their accounts for them. If they pressed a six pence or a shilling into her hands when they had finished, whispering to her that she was a 'fine girl', she would quickly drop it into the missionary box on the counter, where the black baby would nod in appreciation.

Now, shadowy images pierced the darkness. Margaret's bedroom was tiny. A little attic bedroom jutting from the roof of their three-storey house. The Crowley home was the end house on the main street of Ballymona. Tim and Ellen Crowley ran the shop which had been in the Crowley family since before the turn of the twentieth century, and which now, in the mid-thirties, stocked everything edible that a rural family could want, as well as keeping a stock of nails and screws, kettles and saucepans, seed potatoes and onion sets, bales of twine, animal feed and various other bits and pieces which would from time to time be called for.

The ground floor was the shop area, spilling out the back door into the cobbled yard where the grain and the potatoes were stacked in a large storehouse. Here the sacks of brown and white flour would be scooped and measured into smaller bags, and the chests of sugar filtered into sturdy cardboard containers. The timber tea-chests, with their Indian origins stamped along the sides, were stacked from floor to ceiling, and these had to be levered open and their contents measured into brown bags of varying sizes. The massive scales by the door, its brass weights and plates illuminated by the long clear window, was where all the dry goods were weighed, and a convoy of trolleys stood by to transport the goods from the storehouse, across the cobbled yard, to the shop. A door behind the counter of the shop opened up on to a hallway and stairs, steep and uncarpeted, leading to the living quarters. Here the kitchen, where most of the living took place, was ruled over by Mary Kate, the 'girl' who did for them.

Mary Kate had been with the Crowley family since Margaret was born. She had come, raw from the mountainy countryside north of Ballymona, to be taken in hand by Ellen, who had trained her, scraping off layers of backwardness and applying a thin veneer of polish, which often vanished in moments of crisis. But Mary Kate was a great worker, and she loved Margaret ...which left Ellen free to concentrate on the business. Ellen's head was designed for business! It was well known all over town that Ellen Crowley was really the one who ran the shop. The Crowley place, which had been a small huckster's shop when Ellen had moved in there following her marriage to Tim, had expanded and prospered over the years, until now it rivalled Kavanagh's, the other all purpose store in Ballymona. Ellen Crowley was ambitious; ambitious for her slow, good-humoured husband, who had no hold on money, and who had been the solace of many of the town's credit customers until he had married. She was even more ambitious for Margaret, their only child. She would inherit the business – and it would be a business worth inheriting. If Margaret played her cards right, and with a little push from her mother, she might also stake a claim on one of the Kavanagh boys! Three fine sons, all as yet unmarried. Ellen Crowley had high hopes of Margaret snaffling one of them.

Beyond the kitchen were a scullery and a bathroom. Besides the Kavanagh's, and Dr Harris's, the Crowleys' house was the only one on the main street to have a bathroom. Ellen Crowley was not going to have her daughter brought up in a house without an indoor lavatory! The parlour was also on this floor. This was a claustrophobic room with a musty smell, despite Mary Kate's best efforts to keep it aired. At Christmas time the fire was lit there, to draw protestingly up the narrow chimney, and belch puffs of smoke back into the room, covering everything with a dusting of soot. On the next floor were the main bedrooms, and then came the attic rooms. The smaller of these was the 'maid's room'. Mary Kate slept here, surrounded by the trappings of her past – a battered suitcase and a selection of plaster statues of saints. Her bed was draped with a patchwork quilt, each patch carrying its own piece of history. Margaret slept in the other attic room, which was also her study and her place to daydream. The curtainless window faced west, and, sitting on the window-seat, Margaret could see the great spread of the sea, and, in the distance, the pearly whiteness of Inishbawn.

From the time when she had first been allowed to sleep in this room, Inishbawn had been the focus of all Margaret's dreams. The spare purity of the island, set in the frame of the ocean, seemed to her to belong to another world. It contrasted with the greyness of life in the town, with the sprawl of houses along the main street, branching out on to the limb-like narrow side streets, where the homes were poor, crowded and dirty. Surely life on Inishbawn must be on a higher plane than life in Ballymona? She wove fantasies about what it would be like to live there. How beautiful life would be, surrounded by the lapping waves, with only the cries of the wheeling gulls to break the stillness. Some day she would cross over there on the steamer which plied weekly from the harbour. She would stand on that white shoreline, and stare back at Ballymona, and think of the shallowness of her former life. Even the sun seemed to shine more brightly on Inishbawn. In the evenings the great fiery ball of it, sinking slowly behind the island, seemed to confirm to Margaret that that was where her destiny lay. Some day, her real life would begin, and it would begin on Inishbawn.

Margaret watched the cold greyness give way to pale sunshine. It would be a showery market day, making the street run with slime and filth, and raising pungent clouds of steam from the backs of the beasts, as they grouped around the streets and the square. Her battle with the muck would be a losing one, and the smell of manure and of sweat and of damp, unwashed clothing would be overpowering. She listened to the creak of the bedsprings and the muffled sounds of Mary Kate in the room next door, and soon the first of the cranking sounds indicated that the old range was being coaxed into life in the kitchen. The church bell began its doleful call, and within minutes was followed by her mother's voice from the bottom of the stairs.

'Margaret! Are you awake, Margaret? The bell is gone. Are you getting up for Mass?'

Margaret pressed her lips together, and debated whether to ignore the call. That would just bring her mother up the attic stairs though.

'Coming, Mother. Just getting up.' She sat up, and with the bedclothes still wrapped around her, pulled on her underwear, skirt and jumper, then swung her legs out and put her feet into the black laced boots. In the kitchen Mary Kate was stooped, red-faced, over the range, her hair as wild as a furze bush, her black and white floral overall tightly imprisoning her bulges.

'Divil take her, she won't catch on this morning. There'll be no cup of tea for the Master, and herself will kill me!'

Margaret knew that no answer was expected. The battle was a constant one, and by the time she and her mother returned from the church, the fire would be glowing, and the kitchen would be filled with the smell of rashers and eggs frying. She splashed her face with cold water, and stared at herself in the kitchen mirror as she patted it dry.

21

The eyes which looked back at her still carried a dull sleepiness.

'Will you pull the rack through your hair before going out, and don't shame us!'

'A rack is an instrument of torture, Mary Kate. And if you mean that I should comb my hair, I was just about to do it!'

'Well, isn't it a grand thing entirely to have the education. And isn't it a pity they didn't teach you to be in time for Mass while they were at it.'

'Don't start on me ... I'm just going.'

Margaret sighed as she picked up her prayer book and buttoned her heavy tweed coat. Sometimes she wished she wasn't leaving school that summer. The disciplined world of reading and learning appealed to her, but at sixteen, the nuns had taught her all they could, and they wouldn't keep her on indefinitely. For girls like her, daughters of shopkeepers and farmers, those extra two years were already a privilege. Most of her friends had left at fourteen, to go into service or to serve behind the counter, or even to stay at home and help rear their younger brothers and sisters. But for those who showed promise, and whose parents could afford to pay a little, the nuns were willing to allow them two extra years. Those years were wide-ranging, and were intended to make 'ladies' out of them. They got a taste of music, of fine needlework and of drawing, on top of the normal school subjects. These years were also considered to be a preparation for entering the convent as a novice, which a lot of the girls did. Margaret had given some thought to this. She pictured herself gliding along the polished corridors, her soft blue habit swishing against the seats, as she entered the chapel. She saw herself kneeling with the other nuns, her voice intoning the prayers of the Mass, her eyes demurely lowered, and her heart filled with the sanctity all around her. And then she thought of how her life would really be – always hemmed in by other women, never being alone. She visualised the petty jealousies, the irritating habits, the dullness; never having a boyfriend, a husband, a baby, a home of one's own ... She decided that that was not for her.

The parish church was cold and half empty. Margaret slid into the seat beside her friend Stella, who nudged her and indicated one of the Kavanagh boys, kneeling beside his mother across the way. Joe Kavanagh, at twenty-two, was as rotund and florid as his father. His hair was already beginning to recede, and his black-rimmed glasses gave him an air of self-importance which was echoed in his carriage. He was a good catch, and he knew it! Ellen Crowley never tired of reminding Margaret of how fortunate any woman would be to get him. The two younger brothers were miniature versions of Joe, and they too were watched and weighed up by all the mothers of eligible daughters in Ballymona. Now, looking across at Joe, Margaret thought that maybe she would be better off in the convent after all!

'Isn't it nice to see the young people making the effort?' Mrs. Kavanagh folded her arms across her chest, and nodded approvingly at Margaret and Stella, as the two groups exchanged a few words after Mass.

'Oh, sure they're grand girls. Margaret hates to miss her morning Mass. Isn't that right Margaret?' Ellen Crowley's eyes dared her daughter to contradict her. Margaret smiled and nodded. She wished her mother would not always be licking up to Mrs. Kavanagh, especially with Stella and Joe looking on. She'd lost count of the number of times that her attributes had been dangled before that woman. No wonder Joe looked smug!

'You'll be saying goodbye to the nuns soon, I suppose Margaret? Unless of course you're thinking of joining up?' Mrs.Kavanagh's black eyes glittered with curiosity.

'Only three more months now.' Margaret answered. 'And no, I don't think I'm cut out for the religious life.'

'Sure, she'll be needed in the business ... though if the good Lord called her, we wouldn't stand in her way!' her mother said piously.

'With all that education, I'm sure you'll be able to turn your hand to anything. If ever you want a job, look no further!' said Mrs Kavanagh. 'Isn't it very hard to get good staff these days, Ellen? We're for ever replacing them. Don't forget that now Margaret!' With a nod and a wave, she hurried away, leaving a fuming Margaret and a giggling Stella in her wake.

'Did you hear how she didn't ask *me* if I wanted a job!' Stella whispered to Margaret, as Ellen headed back to the shop. Stella was one of those who had left school at fourteen, and was now at home helping her mother to look after six younger children. 'Maybe she'll keep one of the sons for me instead!'

The very idea of Murphy the Blacksmith's daughter marrying into the Kavanagh emporium sent Stella into fits of laughter, and Margaret joined in, in spite of herself.

'Well, she didn't offer me a son ... just a job! And did you see the look on my mother's face when she made the offer? If she hadn't just come out from church, she'd have spat in her eye.'

Margaret and Stella walked part of the way together, until Stella turned off at a laneway which led to her house. Already the town was beginning to fill up. Tall cattle drovers in their belted coats and brown boots eyed the farmers, and weighed up the possibilities in the bellowing cattle. Donkey carts and pony traps caused hold-ups all along the main street, and red-faced women with baskets of geese and chickens picked their way through the animals to take up their pitch on the market square. Shopkeepers and pub-owners were taking down their shutters and brushing the already mounting heaps of dirt from in front of their premises. Margaret wished she could go to school, and spend the day in the tranquillity of the convent, but this was one of the market days when she was expected to stay at home and help. She would be at everyone's beck and call for the rest of the day, and would not have a minute to herself.

'Eat your breakfast quickly, and start weighing out the tea and sugar bags, Margaret.' Ellen Crowley drank the cup of tea that Mary Kate had poured for her, and angrily recounted the story of Mrs. Kavanagh to her husband.

'The cheek of that one! Does she think she's going to get my daughter to serve behind her counter? Over my dead body she will! If my daughter goes in to that place, it will be as mistress of it, and not as a servant!'

Tim Crowley winked at his daughter.

'Sure, wouldn't she have to pay a servant? She'd have her free the other way.'

'Isn't that just like you, to treat everything as a joke! The woman insulted me and my daughter, and all you can do is laugh about it.'

'Ahsha, it was only a remark. And anyway, how is she to know that you've earmarked her son for our Margaret?'

'You'd only have to see the sheeps' eyes her Joe was making across the aisle at Margaret this morning to know it! Oh, she knows it well enough. He won't do better for himself.'

Margaret let the conversation float over her head. Joe Kavanagh with his pop eyes and his red face. In ten years he'd be bald, and his stomach would be stretching out over the top of his trousers, as his father's did.

There'd be plenty of money there ... she'd want for nothing. And at least he was clean. And he didn't drink. She thought about Stella, and where her future lay. Stella's father drank. He was very violent when he went on a batter. Stella would try to keep the younger children out of his way, but her mother had that cowed, timid look of one who accepted that she was going to be beaten, and she frequently was. Sure the whole town knew that. Stella said that she'd never get married; she wasn't going to end up like her mother! But yet she flirted with every boy who looked twice at her, and was talked about around the town as being 'cheap'.

'Where's the harm in having a good time?' she'd protest when Margaret would criticise her. And her small face would glow at the thought of all her admirers. But she never seemed to connect her behaviour with any consequences.

The shop was bustling all that day. The morning's rain gave way to a hot afternoon. It was a good day for the farmers. Livestock changed hands and wads of lank notes were rolled out, fingered and counted, and slapped on to red calloused palms moistened with spit. The pub next door vibrated with the comings and goings of farmers and dealers, and as darkness shadowed the debris of the day's trading, donkeys and ponies drooped neglected on the green while their masters sweated over a succession of frothing pints and gulped chasers. Moods grew more expansive, purse strings loosened, and bursts of tuneless singing spilled on to the roadway, as the pub door opened and closed to embrace or disgorge more drinkers. The Crowley shop remained open for as long as there were customers to stagger in for cigarettes or sweets or some little delicacy to buy favour at home. Ellen Crowley, her feet now puffed from standing, and the veins arching out on her legs like ivy on a tree, fetched and carried, and kept a sharp eye on Tim as he talked and listened to countrymen now reluctant to face the road home. There would be no 'tick' in her shop, but she knew that her husband wouldn't have the heart to say no to any sob story.

At ten o'clock Margaret took off her apron, and cleared the last of the boxes around to the yard. The soft whinny of a pony tethered to a pole in the alleyway behind the pub drew her attention. He had been standing there, between the shafts of his cart, since early that morning, and his eyes, dull with acceptance, watched her as she came near. She got some hay from the yard, climbed over the low wall to the alleyway, and was feeding the hay to him when the owner came up the alley, unsteadily feeling his way along the wall, and muttering to himself. Margaret's fury at the neglect of the animal turned to fear as the man cut off her exit from the dark alley, and began to stroke her arm.

'Aren't you the good girleen? Looking after the pony for me, were you? Waiting for me to come back?'

The fumes from his breath made her stomach lurch as he pressed his face nearer to hers. He reached into his pocket and pulled out a handful of money.

'Here now. You buy yourself something nice. Aren't you the fine-looking girl? Come here to me ... come here, come here!' He caught hold of her and pulled her against him, and Margaret felt his mouth coming down on hers. She pushed him off, and he fell in a drunken heap by the wheel of the cart. Stepping over him she ran down the alley, stumbling in the darkness, and as she entered the side door of the shop, she prayed that she'd reach her bedroom without meeting her mother or father. She felt soiled and frightened, and worried in case the man had injured himself in falling. She had heard him shouting after her, so she knew that he couldn't have been badly injured. Common sense told her that in a few minutes he would pick himself up, unhitch the pony, and take himself off. And she would forget about what had happened, until next market day. There must be something about her, she thought, that attracted men like him. Something bad. This wasn't the first time. There had been many other such incidents. Always on market day.

Shivering, she wrapped the quilt around her body, and sat on the window seat to stare out across the rooftops. The slates glittered in the moonlight, and in the distance she could see the dark bulk of Inishbawn, dotted with pinpricks of lights.

# CHAPTER THREE

Margaret stood nervously outside the door to Sister Gertrude's office. It was her final day as a student in the convent school, where she had been since she was four, and in which the nuns had carefully moulded her character. Now she was sixteen, and their task was complete.

'Come in, Margaret.' Sister Gertrude looked up from her desk as Margaret entered the room. Her pale face and thin mouth seemed to merge with the chill, over polished surroundings, but her eyes were caring.

'You're leaving us today, Margaret?'

'I am, Sister.'

'You've been an excellent student. We'll be sad to lose you. Have you decided on your future?'

Her future? She would serve behind the counter. Count out money, keep the books, pack bags of sugar and tea. Fend off groping hands of old men, until eventually Joe Kavanagh or one of his brothers would 'honour' her, and she would exchange Crowley's store for the more prosperous Kavanagh one... and fulfil all her mother's ambitions.

'I suppose I'll work in my parents' shop, Sister. They need the help.'

'And of course you have no brothers or sisters.'

'No, Sister.'

'Then you must do your duty, and do their bidding, if that is what they want of you.'

Sister Gertrude sighed, studied some papers on the desk in front of her, and then went on.

'It's a great pity really. I had hoped ... you've shown such promise, and you always appeared to fit in here so well. I had hoped that perhaps you might have considered becoming one of us. Bright, intelligent girls, with some background, are always needed in the Community. Teacher-training, or perhaps even university ... but always subject to God's call of course. You have never felt that special calling, have you Margaret? Remember the Lord prompts, suggests. He doesn't force. But one should always be open to that voice.'

Margaret studied her hands, folded on her lap. She could be a teacher ... even a graduate. She could get away from the sordidness of life in Ballymona. The serenity of the Convent, where no demands would be made on her, except to pray and to study. It seemed very tempting. Her father would be proud – maybe even her mother! A daughter a nun. How Mrs. Kavanagh would envy that!

'I'll think about it Sister', she said slowly. 'I'm not sure I'd be suited to the life, but I'll certainly think about it.'

'Very good, Margaret. That's all the Lord asks – that you are open to hearing His voice. And pray, child, that your decision may be the right one. Talk it over with your parents, but ultimately the choice must be your own.'

The nun stood up, signifying the end of the interview. She took Margaret's hand in hers.

'Perhaps you won't be leaving us after all,' she smiled. 'And whatever decision you make, may God go with you.'

The long, dusty avenue from the convent was deserted when Margaret came out. All the other pupils had gone home, and she was glad to be alone. The familiar walk seemed precious to her now, heightened by feelings of loss and nostalgia. The crunch of the gravel, the heady smell of the exotic-looking azaleas, the distant drone of bees circling around the hives behind the convent – all taken for granted by her for almost twelve years. Suddenly they seemed very precious, a world apart from life in Ballymona. The convent on the hill above the town had always been apart.: the great grey building with its own secret life, and its special inhabitants, towering above the frailties and struggles of the town below. Margaret loved the sense of order, the aura of discipline and predictability, which surrounded the lives of the nuns. The polished corridors, the formal gardens, the bell-dominated days ... no wonder even the oldest of the nuns had that clear, furrowless skin, quite foreign to the women of the town!

Margaret reached the end of the avenue, and turned left into the narrow street which skirted the convent walls. It was hot and airless down here. Dogs lay panting outside the open doors of the houses which fringed the street. Smells of food, sewage and drains vied with each other. Stella Murphy lived in the last house in the street. It was no shabbier than the others, and since Stella had left school, she had made many efforts to brighten it up, whitewashing the front walls, and even putting a basin full of nasturtiums near the front door, to create a splash of colour. The door was open, and two little boys sat on the step, playing cards.

'You looking for Stella?'

'Yes, is she home?'

'She's in the scullery helping Ma.'

Stepping over their legs, Margaret entered the house. After the sunlight outside, the room was dim. A baby snuffled in the corner, and a small, dark-haired child sat in the middle of the flagged floor, chewing on a heel of bread. A dog sat beside the child, eyes fixed on the food. From the scullery came the sounds of swishing water. Stella was bent over the washtub, vigorously rubbing clothes on the washboard. She looked embarrassed when she saw Margaret, and glanced quickly through the open back door, to where her mother was pegging clothes on the line.

'What are you doing here?' Stella liked to meet Margaret at the shop, or outside the school. She rarely asked her into her house.

'I've just come down from the Convent – my last day. I thought you might come for a walk with me. I'll tell you what Gert. said.'

'I'm sure that's worth hearing! Did she give you the lecture about modesty in dress, and not to be inflaming men's desires? That's what she told me when I left.'

From the other room the baby's snuffles changed to a high pitched cry, and the child on the floor joined in.

'Will I pick her up?' Margaret hesitated in the doorway.

'No, it's alright. Ma will feed her in a minute. Look, I can't go out now, but I'll meet you after tea. I'll call over to the shop, and you can tell me everything.'

Margaret agreed with relief. Stella's home depressed her, and she was always uneasy in case the blacksmith walked in while she was there. Murphy did his drinking in the pubs in this part of the town, and sometimes his binges lasted for days on end. Stella tried to cover up, but the bruises on her mother's face were their own witness.

'Why don't you leave?' Margaret had once asked her. 'Why don't you go to England or somewhere?'

'How can I?' Stella's voice was matter of fact. 'Sure he'd kill her if I wasn't here. And who'd mind the little ones? Anyway, he's alright when he's sober. He can't help himself.'

The shop was empty when Margaret arrived home. Her mother sat on the high stool behind the counter, the tattered red ledger in front of her. Over on the far end her father was weighing out potatoes, and loading them into different -sized sacks. The bruised ones and those with the marks of the spade on them were thrown into big galvanised buckets. Ellen Crowley looked up as her daughter came in, and was struck by the sad expression on her face.

'Well, who's been biting your tail? It isn't lonesome for school you are surely, is it? That friend of yours, Stella, couldn't wait to get her heels out of it. I thought you'd be the same.'

Margaret put her schoolbooks on the counter and smiled at her mother.

'That's what I thought,' she said, 'but it's different when it actually comes to it. All the nuns were really nice to me, and Sister Gertrude called me in to her office after school.'

'Oh, and what did she have to say?' Ellen Crowley's eyes narrowed.

'She wanted to know if I'd like to join the Order.'

The clunk of the spuds landing in the bucket seemed unnaturally loud in the silence which followed. Margaret glanced across at her father. He had a look of deep concentration on his face, as he weighed, sorted and segregated.

'And what did you say? What gave her that notion anyway? Have you talked about it before with her? Does she think you have a dowry to bring in?'

'She's not looking for a dowry, Mother. She just thought that ... well, that I might be suited to the life. And she hinted that the Order would put me through training college, or even university.'

Ellen Crowley was impressed. The nuns above in the convent looking for her daughter, and willing to pay for her education into the bargain! Even her highest ambitions wouldn't have stretched that far. But then, she always knew that Margaret was special. She was a cut above all the other girls in the town. No wonder that Kavanagh boy was for ever making eyes at her. A nun in the family ... the next best thing to having a priest! How she had prayed for a son, but it was not to be. There had been only Margaret, and Margaret was everything a mother could wish for.

The shop bell tinkled, and two women came in. Ellen turned to greet them. Business was business.

'We'll talk about this at teatime', she whispered to Margaret, pushing her schoolbooks towards her and gesturing to her to go on up to the kitchen.

Mary Kate was ironing sheets at the kitchen table, puffing and glowing as she pressed the iron on to the linen.

' Well, how was your last day? Are ye glad to be shot of the place? A woman of the world now, no less. Watch out Joe Kavanagh! Kavanagh and Crowley ... or will it be Crowley and Kavanagh? You're bossy enough for it, though I'd say you'd meet your match in Sissie Kavanagh, whatever about her menfolk.' She thumped the iron down on the folds to emphasise the point.

Margaret helped herself to a glass of milk.

'Why are you always on about Joe Kavanagh for heaven's sake! I'm not remotely interested in marrying Joe Kavanagh, or anyone else either for that matter. In fact, I might even become a nun.'

'Hah, you've about as much notion of being a nun as I have!'

'Sister Gertrude asked me to think about it. She seemed to think I might be suited to the life.'

'Have a bit of sense, girl. What would you want to be locking yourself away up there for? A great barn full of women, squabbling among themselves, and parched for the want of a man! You wouldn't stick it for a week – and how would you escape then? You'd never face back into the town with the disgrace of it.'

'Oh you don't know what you're talking about, Mary Kate. How would you know anything about the religious life? You've never been inside the door of the convent.'

'Maybe not, but I've eyes in my head, and I've known you since you were a baby. You've not got the makings of a nun in you, that's for sure. Now, will you take your books out of my way, and let me get on with this pressing.'

Margaret went up to her room, threw her books on the bed, and sat on the window seat. Mary Kate was a good sounding board. She never said what people wanted to hear, just what was in her mind. And Margaret had a feeling that she was right. There was something about the religious life which appealed to her, but it wasn't the community life, and it wasn't a need to devote herself exclusively to God either. It was more the sense of order. Order and tranquillity and calm. Words with a smoothness about them. It was life without the messiness she could see all around her. She thought about her own mother's life. All the time struggling to keep up a standard – battling for a place in the hierarchy of small town life. Money was the god here. Her father had to be watched. He didn't realise the importance of being seen to look prosperous, and would let the side down if left to his own devices. For Mother, life was all uphill. Then there was Stella's mother. How could she endure living like that? The blacksmith's moods dominated their home. She was humiliated and violated, and she carried her air of cowed fear like a cross which she had been born to endure. And Stella, for all her spirit, would probably follow the pattern. She was being conditioned to expect little. When she married it would be to someone just like the blacksmith; someone who would initially heap trinkets and promises on her, and would then turn her into a domestic drudge, or worse. But Stella could never see that. The men that she flirted with, those with whom she walked out on Sunday evenings, they were the men whom sensible girls avoided. But Stella was drawn to them like a moth to the light.

It was a hot summer, a summer suspended between Margaret's life as a convent girl and the time when real living would begin. Margaret felt strange and disoriented, as if these months were the testing time for some new kind of reality. She learned all there was to know about the shop, spending her days measuring and weighing, totting up and calculating. She learned to hide her impatience with customers who dithered and then changed their minds. She also learned to fend off unwanted advances and to smile away the lewd suggestions of countrymen. Her mother coached and prompted her, and drove her harder than any paid hand could have been worked. Her father encouraged and praised her, and tried to shield her from the rougher element on market days. And after work there was Stella. Cool evening hours spent walking the dusty roads outside the town, where the honeysuckle and the fuchsia grappled for supremacy in the thick hedgerows, and their cloying perfume assailed the senses. Then they were two best friends, responsibilities momentarily suspended, sharing confidences and aspirations, and projecting the fantasy of their dream worlds into the hopelessness of their present situations. Stella's optimism in the face of her problems cheered up Margaret. After all, what had she, Margaret, to complain of? A stable home life, and being the only daughter of Crowley of the Shop made her a good marriage prospect. She would marry some day, rear a family – a son to carry his father's name, daughters to comfort her. She would grow old comfortably. What else was there? And wasn't that more than most people had?

The farther she was removed from life as a convent girl, the more preposterous the idea of becoming a nun seemed. Mary Kate was right: she was not destined for the convent. Her mother was disappointed at being deprived of such a feather in her cap, but she was also glad. The business needed Margaret, and she would shape her to become a fit inheritor. Tim Crowley could barely conceal his relief. How could he bear to see his little girl being locked away in some forbidding institution? To know that her beautiful long hair was being cut and trapped behind that tight headband? That her independent spirit was being broken and moulded to the shape of some unknown Superior's wishes? Margaret was the flowering of all his hopes and ambitions, and her place was in Ballymona, where he would watch his grandchildren grow up, and know that in them the meaning of his own existence would be justified. A convent was no place for his daughter.

With autumn arriving, the countryside surrounding Ballymona was plunged into a frenzy of activity. The landscape flamed with the gold of the ripened corn and the early russets of leaves on the turn. The sounds of the threshing machine could be heard whining across the still air, as Barty Fleming moved his cumbersome monster from farm to farm. 'Meithils' of farmworkers shared their labour as each crop became ripe for harvesting. Women from the town went to assist in the preparations of huge meals to be served to the men at the end of each harvesting day, and there was an air of excitement and togetherness that was absent for the rest of the year.

The Crowley shop was busy, as vast quantities of food were bought for the threshing festivals. Sometimes stocks ran low, and then Margaret would be sent to the Kavanagh store to replenish items. On one such trip, Joe Kavanagh hoisted the sack of meal on to Margaret's trolley, and since it was heavy to push, he offered to wheel it back to the shop for her. Margaret walked alongside him. He looked ill at ease, his florid face, like some overripe fruit, incongruous against the khaki brown of his shop coat. They talked of business, of the threshings, of the weather holding up until all the harvest was saved. Their awkwardness increased as they both became aware of the twitching curtains and curious eyes in houses along the main street. From now on, people would speculate if they were 'walking out' together. When Joe asked her if she would come with him to the hooley in Donovans that night, she found herself agreeing. It seemed inevitable. It was expected of her, and her mother showed no surprise when she told her. Donovans' party was the first of many threshing parties which Joe and Margaret attended as a pair. They would walk or cycle there together after their respective shops had closed for the evening. They would join in the music and the dancing with most of the other young people from the parish, and afterwards he would see her safely home. She would turn her cheek for his good night kiss, tensing herself as his lips sometimes slid across her mouth. And afterwards she would lie awake in her attic bedroom and watch the strange orange brilliance of the autumn sky.

'You're so lucky!' Stella would tell her.

'Am I?' she would ask, as if by hearing it again and again she could force herself to believe it.

'Of course! Isn't he mad about you? Sure anyone can see that he's mad about you. And him with that grand business and plenty of money. Half the girls in town would give anything to have Joe Kavanagh courting them. If I were you, I wouldn't let the grass grow under my feet! What's wrong with him anyway?'

'Nothing's wrong with him, Stella. He's nice really. It's just ... I... Oh, I don't know.'

Maybe all women felt like this. Maybe that's just the way it was. Weighing up the good and the bad, and if it wasn't too much out of balance, settling for that.

By the time Christmas came around, Joe and Margaret were accepted as a pair. Margaret was invited every Sunday to tea in Kavanaghs' house – a sumptuous spread overseen by the majestic Cissie and served by the timid little Sadie, who was their latest in the long line of maids. Kavanaghs' maids never lasted long. Cissie picked the timid ones, and then, day by day, quashed them until they could take no more. Her husband and her sons filled the place with their male bulk, but it was Cissie who dominated. It was she who planned the future of the business, who decided what schools her sons went to, and who told her husband what he should wear on a Sunday. And she had obviously decided that Margaret Crowley had some potential as a future member of the family. Without saying anything, Margaret went along with this. Sometimes she felt as if she was being lifted by a wave, and her survival depended on her swimming with it. Her mother smiled approvingly whenever Joe's name was mentioned. Her father teased her about her big business prospects, and Stella stopped making fun of Mrs. Kavanagh and her three lambs. Only Mary Kate demurred.

'Has that fella asked you to marry him?' she quizzed Margaret one Sunday after her return from Kavanaghs'.

'No he hasn't!' Margaret felt irritated by the question.

'And when he does, what are you going to say to him?'

'Don't be so nosey Mary Kate. It's nothing to do with you.'

'You wouldn't be so touchy but that you knew it isn't right. Joe Kavanagh doesn't mean as much to you as ... as that table there. What kind of a girl are you, heading blind into something like this? Surely be to God you're not going to spend the rest of your days with a man you don't give tuppence for?'

She was right, but Margaret did not want to think about it. If she thought about it, the foolishness of what she was doing would overwhelm her. But what else was there? She would be pleasing her parents, she would be placing the business on a firm footing, she would be giving herself the respectable status of a married woman. Was all that so terrible? And Joe ... well, Joe would be getting an efficient and hardworking wife, a wife any man would be proud to be seen with at Sunday Mass or walking out with on a Sunday afternoon. Mary Kate was talking rubbish; what did she know about anything? Margaret put her uneasiness to the back of her mind, and carried on as before.

It was a difficult winter of sudden violent storms that ripped the slates from the houses along the main street, and strewed the roads with uprooted trees. People did whatever business they had to do in quick morning spurts, and sought the refuge of their homes as soon as the light began to fade. All through January it was as if Ballymona was under siege. The gales claimed many victims, mostly crushed beneath fallen trees, or washed from buffeted fishing boats. When they ventured out to the shops, people huddled in groups discussing the latest tragedies. Ellen and Tim Crowley delivered parcels of food to housebound neighbours, and many mornings Tim harnessed the pony to bring food to some of the isolated cottiers outside the town. Margaret, at almost seventeen, was considered experienced enough to take complete charge whenever Tim or Ellen were away. She didn't see much of Joe Kavanagh during this time, and her spare hours were spent reading or day-dreaming in her bedroom. Then in February, almost overnight, a hush seemed to fall over the town. The winds died down. The temperature dropped. There was a sense of the worst being over.

Two days after her seventeenth birthday Margaret was alone in the shop when the bell tinkled and a man entered. Margaret could see immediately that he was an islandman; one of the men of Inishbawn. She had never seen him before, and was surprised that anyone from the island should come into their shop, because they rarely shopped in this part of the town. When the islanders came ashore for provisions, it was always to the harbour shops on the other side of the town, and they were viewed with suspicion on the rare occasions they ventured up the main street. But this man entered the shop with an easy familiarity. He wasn't tall, but he gave the impression of height in the way he carried himself. He had the sallow skin and dark hair that so many of the islanders had, and his eyes were the grey-blue of a winter sea. All this Margaret noticed, and afterwards it surprised her that she should have registered every detail about him with such clarity. In spite of the cold weather, he wore no top coat, just a heavy knitted jumper and grey frieze trousers.

'You were hard hit by the storms I see.'

She wasn't sure whether it was a statement or a question.

'Yes, it was terrible here. What was it like on the island?'

'No worse than usual. On Inishbawn storms are part of life; we're prepared for them.'

His voice was very low and soft, but he made no more small talk, just asked for tea, sugar and tobacco, and watched her in silence as she weighed and wrapped those items, and totted up the bill. He paid the amount due, thanked her and left.

Margaret stood at the window, staring after him. She wished she had kept him talking longer. Now, she thought of many interesting things she could have said to him, and questions which she could have asked him. Maybe he would come back again ... maybe she could ... .

'Was that one of the islandmen I saw going out there?' Her mother appeared from the storeroom, cutting in on Margaret's thoughts.

'Yes. He said the storms weren't so bad over there. He seemed surprised there was so much damage done here.'

'What brought him up to this part of the town? Couldn't he get all he wanted down at the harbour. Curiosity, I suppose!'

'He's a customer, isn't he? His money is as good as anyone else's.'

'We wouldn't get fat on the custom the likes of him would give us.'

Margaret wondered at the hostility in her mother's voice. The man had been polite and pleasant, and yet, because he was an islander, there was immediately this barrier thrown up between them. It was strange, when she thought of some of the objectionable people they had to be civil to in the shop. But then they were 'our own', and that was the difference.

That night before getting in to bed, Margaret stood at her window, oblivious of the cold, and gazed across at Inishbawn. There was no moon to light up the darkness of the sea, and the island was indistinguishable from the blackness all round, but here and there little dots of light indicated where the island dwellings were. She wondered was his house one of those.

37

# CHAPTER FOUR

Nothing had changed, and yet everything had changed. In Margaret there was now a restlessness that she could not explain. Her days behind the counter seemed unbearably dull and restrictive. She made up any excuse she could think of to avoid being alone with Joe Kavanagh, and even Stella's company she found childish and immature. She longed for some wider vision – something to give her life a fresh impetus. Maybe she should have taken up Sister Gertrude's suggestion after all. She would have got a chance to escape from the drabness of Ballymona and at least explore a different kind of world. But she knew that the convent was not what she wanted either. She didn't know what it was she did want, but she felt she would just wither away if this was all there was for her.

Then, three weeks after his first visit, the man from Inishbawn came again. This time the shop was busy. Her mother was serving a group of women at one end of the shop, whilst Margaret was piling skeins of wool on to the counter in front of a rough-faced countrywoman who couldn't make up her mind between the green and the brown. She was conscious of him as soon as the twang of the bell announced his entrance. She continued to serve her customer, but now her heart was thumping and her mouth felt so dry that she could barely talk to the woman, who finally decided on the brown wool, and asked for it to be wrapped up. He walked across to where she was serving, and stood in front of her. A silence had fallen on the other side of the shop. The townswomen were watching him, disapproval on their faces. Her mother was watching her. Margaret smiled a welcome to him.

'I was hoping you'd be here', he said. He seemed oblivious to the waves of hostility coming from the other end of the shop, and continued to talk in the low, soft tones that she remembered from his last visit. He wanted a particular type of tea, a specific brand of tobacco, flour, meal ... things which took time to fetch and weigh and pack, and under the scrutiny of those grey-blue eyes Margaret felt slow and awkward. He told her that his name was Owen McDowell; that he lived with his mother and sister on a farm on the far side of Inishbawn; that he had been thinking about her constantly since his last visit to the shop, and that he already knew her name.

'I asked in the pub next door. They told me ... very reluctantly. They said you were going to marry into the Kavanagh family. Is that so?'

'No, it's not,' Margaret answered, with a certainty she had not felt until now. 'Joe and I are just ... well, just friends. But I don't see what business it is of yours!' She was immediately aware of how abrupt that comment sounded, and she wished she could take it back.

'I'm sorry,' he said. 'That was a very personal question. I shouldn't have asked it. But it was important to me. I had to know.'

He packed the groceries into the bag by his feet, handed her his money, and with a smile and a nod, left the shop. Immediately the hum of conversation started up, and there was a visible air of relaxation amongst the customers her mother was serving. It was as if an indefinable threat had been removed from them. As soon as there was a quiet moment, her mother spoke to her.

'Wasn't that the same islandman we had in here some weeks ago?'

'Yes ... he seems very nice, Mother. I don't know what you have against him.'

'I've nothing at all against him, child. I'm sure they're decent enough people, in their own way. Far be it from me to judge. But each to his own, I always say, and they should stay where they belong!'

The matter did not end there. It quickly became known that the islandman had been enquiring about Margaret in the pub, and that put matters on a different footing entirely.

Joe Kavanagh came storming into the shop that same evening, and there was a pop-eyed indignation in his face as he asked to speak to Margaret.

'What's wrong, Joe? You look all flustered.' Ellen Crowley had a shrewd idea what it was that was bothering him, and she hoped that her daughter would deal with him tactfully. When Margaret came down to join them, she had a faraway look in her eyes and a faint smile hovering around her lips, which Ellen knew at once had not been caused by the unexpected visit of Joe Kavanagh.

'Go on up to the parlour, let ye. It's too cold to be standing around here.' Ellen ushered the two young people into the fusty formality of the little-used parlour, and prayed that her daughter would be sensible.

'There's gossip around the town about you!' Joe could have been his own father, so pompous and self-righteous did he look.

'What are you talking about? What kind of gossip?'

'That island fellow ... the one who has been frequenting your shop recently. I've been told he's been showing an interest in you.'

'Don't be so daft, Joe. He's only been in here twice. And why would he be interested in me anyway? Sure, isn't he years older than me?' She didn't know why she had added that. She wasn't even aware that she had noticed his age, but it seemed as good an argument as any other against Joe.

Joe appeared to be at a loss for words now. He shuffled his feet and examined his fingernails. Margaret watched him in silence. She wished he would go away. Was the islandman ... Owen McDowell ... really interested in her? The idea sent shivers of excitement through her. She wanted to go back up to her bedroom, to sit in her window seat, gaze across at Inishbawn, and think about Owen McDowell. The way his black hair fell across his forehead, those strange sea-coloured eyes, the way he had looked at her, his soft voice, his smile ...

'You're not listening to me Margaret! I've been telling you that you mustn't give rise to gossip. You have to watch it that you don't encourage the likes of him. You could be taken advantage of, you know. Do you understand what I'm saying?'

Suddenly she felt furious at him, at his self-righteousness, his possessiveness, even his awkwardness. She jumped up out of the overstuffed armchair and stood over him, her face hot with temper.

'Who do you think you are, Joe Kavanagh! What gives you the right to come in here and tell me what way I should behave? If people have nothing better to do than gossip about me, then I ... I feel sorry for them. And for you too!'

His pop eyes protruded even more, and she could see his tongue encircling his open mouth as though trying to form words. Finally, he shook his head in a sorrowful gesture.

'Ah, I can see that you're overwrought. It's not nice to see a lady lose her temper like that, but I'm prepared to overlook it. I know you well enough to realise that you don't mean it.'

'You don't know me at all, Joe Kavanagh! You never have, not the first thing about me. And what's more, you never will!'

'Of course I know you,' he said patiently, as though explaining something complicated to a dense child. 'Haven't we been walking out together now for months? And you know, Margaret, I haven't just been playing with your affections. No indeed! My intentions towards you have been of the serious kind. My mother will vouch for that.'

'Oh, so you had to clear it with your mother first, had you?'

'She's a very good judge of character, Margaret. And we have to remember that there's the business to consider.'

'Well, it looks like she was mistaken in this judgment, doesn't it!' Margaret was so angry now, she hardly knew what she was saying.

Joe stood up. His eyes were on a level with hers.

'Maybe she was,' he answered quietly. 'Maybe she was at that.'

She waited for him to continue. Words appeared to be forming in his mouth but he seemed unable to voice them. In the end he gave up the struggle, and fumbled his way out of the parlour and down the stairs. She heard the front door closing quietly – wasn't it just like Joe not to bang it! She didn't know whether to laugh or cry, but was conscious of a great sense of release. When her mother came in a few minutes later, she was still standing there, staring blindly at the pattern on the rug.

'Has Joe gone? I was going to ask him if he'd like a cup of tea. Is anything wrong? Is he coming back again?'

'Yes, he's gone Mother, and no, he won't be coming back. I think we've seen the last of Joe's visits here.'

'Margaret! I hope you haven't said something foolish, something you'll regret! Joe is a nice boy, and he seems very interested in you.'

'Well, I'm not interested in him, Mother. I'm tired of this pretence. Let his mother find some other girl for him.'

'What kind of foolish talk is that! His mother only wants the best for him, just as I want the best for you. The two of you would be well suited, and Joe would make you a kind husband. It's too soft you've had things, miss. That's what is wrong with you! It has all come to you too easily. Now my advice to you would be to go around to him tomorrow, and apologise for whatever you said to him. Joe will understand ... he won't hold it against you.'

'Mother, haven't you been listening? I am not seeing Joe Kavanagh again. I am not going to apologise to him. And above all, I am not going to marry him!'

'We'll see about that, my girl. Miss High and Mighty, that can afford
to throw away such a grand opportunity! We'll see what your father has
to say about it. He'll talk some sense into you.'

But, her father said nothing to her. She heard them arguing about it.
She heard her mother's angry accusations; she heard his soft rejoinders.
But he studiously skirted around the subject of Joe Kavanagh whenever
they were alone together. Mary Kate, however, was not so tactful.

'So you finally gave him the shove? Sure wasn't it time for you, and
you not caring a thrawneen for him? The poor divil can look around
now ... some fine fat farmer's daughter with a dowry to dangle before
Cissie Kavanagh's nose. That would smooth her ruffled feathers quick
enough!'

'Why are you always thinking of money, Mary Kate? Aren't there
more important things in life?'

'Bedad, I haven't found too many of them if there are! Wasn't it a
pity all the same, though, that you couldn't have fallen for Joe? Look at
the grand comfortable business you'd be moving in to? And 'twould set
your mother and father up in their old age. A nice little nest egg for
them. Ah well, sure there are plenty more fish in the sea, even if they're
not as big or as easy to hook.'

Her mother was angry with Margaret for some weeks after the
confrontation, then she took on an air of martyred resignation. She had
done everything in the world for her daughter, and now it was all being
thrown back in her face. Ungrateful child! She didn't know when she
was well off. Well, time would tell who was right. Time would tell.

It was a month before Margaret saw the man from the island again.
Having burned her boats with Joe Kavanagh, she became increasingly
obsessed with the images of Owen McDowell and Inishbawn. Night
after night she sat in the window seat of her bedroom and gazed across
the darkness, straining to see the lights of the island, and weaving
fantasies about the home of the islandman. When, one day, alone in the
shop, the shop bell twanged and he stood before her at the counter, it
was as if the time in between had never been. They spoke easily to one
another, and their friendship now moved onto a different level. Joe's
name was not mentioned between them, but the islandman seemed
aware that Kavanagh was no longer an issue. There was an

undercurrent, an excitement, between them that made Margaret feel that she was only now coming truly alive. Owen McDowell began to come to Ballymona weekly on the steamer. If the weather was kind, he sometimes rowed over in between times. He was courting her, and making his courtship a very public one, and Margaret floated on a haze of blissful happiness. She knew that the neighbours were whispering about her. She knew that curtains twitched every time she walked down to the harbour with him. She knew that she was being ostracised by the Kavanaghs and their friends, and she knew the antagonism that she was arousing in a lot of people, who believed that girls from the town should not be 'walking out' with men from the island. But she didn't care. None of that mattered. Within the family, however, it was a different situation. Her mother was almost hysterical in her opposition. She pleaded with Margaret to stop seeing him. She shouted, cried and begged; she threatened and beseeched. She even slapped her face one evening when Margaret arrived home, having walked back as far as the steamer with Owen. Her parents were there, sitting in the kitchen waiting for her, when she returned. Her mother flew at her, throwing off the restraining hand of her husband.

'How can you do this to us, Margaret?' she shouted. 'How can you destroy everything we've built up in this town? You're making a laughing stock of us and bringing shame on yourself. You're killing your father ... do you hear? You're killing him, killing him!'

'Hush Ellen, hush. Don't be upsetting yourself. There, there, calm down. Things will work out. With the help of God, things will work out.'

They stood together, her parents, in a rare display of unity ... unity against her. Her face stung from her mother's slap, her heart was thumping in fear, yet it made no difference. She loved Owen McDowell. She knew he wanted to marry her. And she had never been so happy.

'Why him?' her father asked. 'Of all the men in the town and the parish – and plenty of them would be proud to get a second look from you – why a man from the island that we know nothing about, and who can never offer you anything but a hard life on that godforsaken lump of rock? A man years older than you at that. Why on earth does it have to be him?'

'Because I love him, Father. I love him and he loves me, and if you'd only get to know him you'd see what a fine person he is. You've never given him a chance. You've just closed your minds to him.'

'Love ... what do you know about love, girleen? Love is something that grows between people when their lives together are right. It's not the flash in the pan feeling you get from a stranger. You're putting the cart before the horse. He's not right for you, child. Trust us, he's not right for you.'

'It's like mixing oil and water,' her mother butted in. 'Nowhere in my family or your father's has anyone had to resort to marrying somebody from the island. Backward and ignorant ...your grandparents would turn in their graves. Will you talk to her Tim ... for God's sake, will you talk sense into her before it's too late!'

'But Mother, if only you'd try to understand ...'

'I understand. Oh, I understand alright! Isn't it a fine feather in his cap for that ... that man, to be thinking of marrying you? Oh, he knows what he's doing alright, and little fool that you are, you can't see through him!'

'You're wrong. You're all wrong. Owen is not a bit like that. He loves me. And if he asks me to marry him – when he asks me to marry him – I'm going to accept. You can't stop me. There's nothing you can do to stop me.'

Her mother's face took on a look of cold fury. Margaret could see her body trembling, as her father's hold tightened around her, but the words she now spoke were deadly calm. Calm and chilling.

'The day you marry Owen McDowell from Inishbawn,' she said, 'is the day you cut all ties with your family. You will never come inside this door again. Never, while there's breath in my body.'

The wedding took place on a cold April morning. Margaret was eighteen, Owen McDowell was thirty-three. The little church by the harbour was almost empty. Father Sweeney's stooped form moved slowly across the altar, accompanied by a solemn-faced altarboy. The altar was stark and unadorned, and to Margaret's tearful eye even the face of Christ on the cross above the altar had a disapproving look. Owen, looking stiff and uncomfortable in suit and collar and tie, had one of the harbour men as his witness. Margaret wore a new woollen coat over a cream dress. The net on her hat shaded her pale face. Beside her, her red coat throwing a splash of colour into the gloomy church, Stella shuffled nervously. Tim and Ellen Crowley had refused to attend, but huddled at the back of the church, her black shawl pulled around her, was Mary Kate, rattling noisily through her beads. There were no members of the McDowell family present. The ceremony was short and impersonal, and the only moment of intimacy came when Owen slid the gold ring on to his new wife's finger. He pressed her hand gently as their eyes met.

# CHAPTER FIVE

The early morning sunshine wakened her. It poured through the half-closed curtains, filling the room with a silvery light. Sleepily, Margaret looked across at the dark head on the pillow beside her. She reached out and touched Owen's lips. In sleep he looked young, almost like a boy. Nothing like a man fifteen years her senior. Moving closer to him, she felt the warmth and comfort of his body. She loved him so much ... so very much. Her parents, his parents, all those who had been so damning in their condemnation of the marriage – she would prove to them how wrong they had been. She would not dwell on the fears and doubts that had overwhelmed her the day before. On the terror of being away from her home for the first time in her life. On the enormity of what she had done – cutting herself off in such bitterness from her family. Becoming part of this strange island family, who had made no attempt to disguise their hostility. It was Owen who mattered. Only Owen. And Inishbawn too. All her life had she not ached to be a part of this island? And now her home was here. Her home and her husband. Her new life was just beginning, a life where all the yearnings of her girlhood would be fulfilled.

Margaret wondered what time it was. The house was silent. No Mary Kate cranking at the range. No clip clip of early morning Mass-goers passing beneath the window. Just the boom of the waves on the shore and the occasional shriek of the gulls. She crept out of bed and looked across the white tipped ocean. Banks of dark cloud were already gathering on the horizon, but for the moment the sun glittered on the water. Margaret shivered, and, closing the curtains properly this time, she got back into bed and into the circle of Owen's arms.

When Margaret next woke, she was alone in the room. Owen's clothes were missing from the chair beside the bed, and now she could hear the clatter of buckets in the yard below, and the hungry bellow of the calves. Rolo, the old collie, barked excitedly, and Hannah's voice shouted at him to be quiet. Guiltily Margaret sprang out of bed, and pulled back the curtains on a now grey, drizzly morning. Why hadn't Owen called her? Everybody was up only her, and now her mother-in-law would think her a lazy good-for-nothing. Oh, why hadn't she woken up sooner! She could have been down in the kitchen preparing breakfast for the others. She could have had the porridge ready when Hannah returned from feeding the calves, or whatever she did at this time of the morning. And Owen ... Owen would have the milking to do and the pony to look after, and at least she could have prepared their breakfasts for them.

Margaret opened the big wardrobe, chose a heavy brown skirt and jumper to wear, and quickly laced up her sensible school shoes. They couldn't find fault with her attire; she'd be properly dressed this morning, ready for anything! She knelt down and said her morning prayers, and thought of her mother kneeling in the cold church in Ballymona, Cissie Kavanagh kneeling across the aisle from her. Maybe Joe and his brothers too. She wondered did people go to morning Mass here ... probably not, with the church being on the other side of the island. Cissie Kavanagh would never again look her mother in the eye, after the disgraceful way her Joe had been treated. Oh well, as Mary Kate had said, a nice dowry from some farmer's daughter would soon fix that.

Having made the bed and tidied the room, Margaret hurried down the stairs. Her mother-in-law was bent over the fire in the kitchen, feeding it with sods of black, damp-looking turf, which sent thick smoke puffing up the chimney. The cloth was still on the table, but there was only one place set. The clock on the wall over the settle said ten minutes to ten.

'I'm sorry I slept so late ... I was up, and then I fell back to sleep again. I didn't hear Owen going out ...'

'It's no matter. I'll wet some fresh tea for you. The kettle is boiled, and there's some stirabout in the pot.'

Margaret sat down. She felt uncomfortable having Julia, her mother-in-law, serving her, and wrong-footed at her late rising. She swallowed the porridge quickly, with gulps of hot strong tea.

'In future, I'll be up much earlier, and you can take a rest in the mornings. I'll make breakfast for everyone.'

The old woman's eyes, so like Owen's, but without their softness, narrowed.

'I've never been one for stopping on in bed of a morning, and I won't be starting now,' she said sourly. She began to sweep the hearth with quick, jerky movements, and then took the broom around the kitchen floor. Margaret brought the dishes into the scullery, and scraped the scraps into the bucket, as she had seen Owen do the day before. There was no running water, just a cauldron of warm water standing on the flagstones, and two enamel bowls in which to wash and rinse the ware. There was no bathroom either, but outside the back door a shed contained an old-fashioned water closet.

When Margaret returned to the kitchen, the old woman was kneading soda bread at the table. The fire was blazing warmly, the kettle singing on the hob.

'Where's Owen?' Margaret asked, as she stood around wondering what she should do.

'He's out on the land with Thomas. Gone this past hour'.

'And Hannah? Has she gone with them?'

'She has not. She's seeing to the calves. She'll be in shortly.'

'You'll have to show me what to do ... I want to be a help to you.'

The bony hands stopped pounding, and the eyes studied her, looking for something to criticise, but she could find nothing. She removed her apron, and handed it to Margaret, wiping the flour from her hands as she did so.

'Here then,' she said. 'You do the baking. A plain soda and a brown. And Owen likes the currant bread, so you could do one of those too, seeing that you have the time. I'll get on with doing the mash for the poultry'. She pulled her shawl across her shoulders, and went out the back door.

Margaret stood looking at the half-prepared bread. She had never baked before. Mary Kate had always done that, turning out loaves that would melt in your mouth, and making it look the simplest thing in the world. Margaret had often watched her, pinching bits of the dough while she chatted to her after school. She was confident she could do it now, no bother. She finished off the brown that her mother-in-law had been preparing, cut a cross on the top and placed it in the bastible. Then she started on the white soda. Carefully she measured out the flour, the soda, the salt, the sugar. She poured in the milk, mixed it, and then tried to knead it. She had put in too much milk. It was too wet. Now she couldn't shape it. She added more flour, but the sticky mess just would not come together for her. Twenty minutes later she was still there, red-faced and almost crying with frustration, pieces of dough clinging to her clothes, her hair and the table. The door opened behind her, and Hannah stood there, rubber boots just visible beneath her man's coat, rain clinging to her head scarf.

'Are you having trouble? Or is this some special kind of cake?'

There was no humour in the question, just grim sarcasm.

'I put in too much milk. It's a white soda, but it won't bind for me. I haven't done much baking at home.'

'I can see that.'

'I worked mostly in the shop, you see. Mary Kate did the housework, and she liked to do all the baking herself.'

'Well, there's no maid here. If we can't do it ourselves, then we do without.'

Hannah removed her coat and scarf, and changed into her indoor shoes, all the time watching Margaret from the corner of her eye. Margaret continued to struggle with the dough, until eventually she got it into some kind of shape. She put in into the tin, a grey, unappetising-looking mess. She didn't dare attempt the currant bread, and was relieved when Hannah said that she would watch the baking of the bread, since she knew the strength of the fire. Margaret went back up to her room, making some excuse about changing out of her dough spattered jumper.

Once in the security of the room she let the banked-up tears spill. She looked at her reflection in the mirror. At her red, angry face, at the flecks of flour on her cheeks, at the dough-speckled hair. She had made a complete fool of herself. She had shown herself for the useless wife that she was. What must they think of her, marrying Owen without knowing the first thing about how to run a house? Oh, if only she had paid more attention to Mary Kate. Why hadn't her mother seen to it that she knew how to do those simple things? Why hadn't somebody told her? She felt a wave of loneliness for the familiar messy kitchen, with Mary Kate cursing at the temperamental oven, and herself sitting at the edge of the table, reading or talking. Right now her father would be busy in the shop, her mother would be chatting to customers, listening to their troubles and exchanging advice. She wondered were they thinking about her. She had hurt them terribly. But they were in the wrong. They should have accepted her choice ... wasn't she old enough to know what she was doing? They didn't want to know anything about Owen or Inishbawn, so how could they know whether she was doing the right thing?

Margaret cleaned up her face and sat by the window looking out at the rain. Now the sea and the land had blended into one blanket of grey. There was no dazzling whiteness in the rocks, no chink of blue in the uncompromising darkness of the sky. Inishbawn did not now look like the magical island on which she had focused all her dreams. It looked as dreary and as soulless as Ballymona had ever seemed. She was still sitting there, motionless, when Owen came in.

'I had to go out early this morning. I didn't want to wake you. You looked like a little girl all snuggled up in the big bed.' He put his arms around her and drew her close to him, and at his nearness and gentleness her tears began to fall again.

'What is it, Margaret? What's the matter, my love? Has Hannah been saying mean things to you? Take no notice of her. She'll get used to you in time.'

'It's not just Hannah, Owen. She hasn't said anything to me. It's everything ... it's me! I don't think I'm going to be a good wife to you Owen.' She told him the saga of the bread, and the disaster it had been, and of how Hannah had had to take over. But he only laughed.

'You're not going to let an old bit of baking bother you, are you? Sure you'll learn to do that in no time. A girl with your education, and you as sharp as a razor in the shop? Well, well, well. What a small thing for my wife to be worrying over.'

'That's just it, Owen. I don't feel like your wife when you're not around. I feel like a visitor here – your mother doing the housework, and Hannah doing the poultry and the calves, and you out on the land. What's there for me to do? What am I supposed to *do* in Derryglas? They don't need, or want, me around!'

'Don't you talk like that! I don't ever want to hear you saying such things. You're my wife. You're the mistress of Derryglas, and it's up to you to make that clear to the other women. They've been used to running things their way, Margaret. It will take time for them to get used to you. But my mother isn't getting any younger, and believe me she'll be glad of your help. And if Hannah ever gets married ... well, won't she be even more glad?'

He wiped her face clumsily with his hand.

'Let there be no more crying now. We'll go on down and have a bit of dinner. The mother has it all ready. Alright love?' He kissed the tip of her nose.

Margaret nodded, and followed him down the stairs to the kitchen, where Julia was serving up a basin of fluffy potatoes and a hunk of bacon. Two plates of bread accompanied the meal. One of soft, crumbly brown, one of white, close-textured and hard. Margaret saw her mother-in-law and Hannah eat slice after slice of the brown, while Owen chewed his way bravely through four pieces of the white.

The cold wet weeks dragged by. Margaret found the climate on the island harsh and unrelenting. The wind was like a fury that tore through the small, poorly sheltered fields, and pelted Derryglas with sheets of spray ripped from the sea. The rain seemed constant. It ranged from the grey clinging mist that seeped through the heaviest protection, to the sudden downpours that flooded the roads and left the low-lying fields looking like lakes. It was much colder than on the mainland, and soon after her arrival Margaret developed a cough which turned to bronchitis, and which left her weak and out of sorts. Her illness was yet another proof that she was poorly equipped to be an islander's wife. Being confined to her room for over a week, with Hannah up and down the stairs bringing her broth and soup, did not do much for her self-esteem. And Hannah made it quite obvious that she resented the extra work.

As her strength returned, Margaret gradually began to find her place in the household. She took over some of the cooking and the household jobs, and as a wary warmth crept across the island, Owen and Thomas took time to show her the running of the farm. She learned how to hitch up the pony to the 'Sunday' trap, and Thomas would let her take the reins on the runs down to the village. The pony could have made his way there blindfolded, so it wasn't long before Margaret felt she could cope on her own. She liked these weekly trips. She could get away from the surliness of the two women, and it gave her an exhilarating sense of freedom to be out in the emptiness of a land where houses were well-scattered and where few people were to be seen.

In the village, the tiny shop beside the public house supplied the island people with whatever was needed in the span between their visits to the mainland. Clusters of women always filled the shop, black shawls pulled tightly around weathered faces. A silence greeted Margaret when she entered. Here she was also regarded with suspicion. It was not hostile, but there was an uneasiness in these women when faced with the woman from the mainland who had been transplanted among them. They waited to see how she expected to be treated, and she reacted by backing off. She was terrified of those huddled silent groups, and spent as little time as she could in the shop.

'A stuck-up young wan' was the verdict, when she had gone out of earshot, and shawled heads nodded in agreement.

The ordeal of the shop behind her, Margaret always stopped the trap outside the church on the way back up the hill. She liked to sit quietly in the darkness of the building, and absorb the tranquillity of the stone built structure which had given comfort to generations of islanders. Her mother would be surprised if she knew how much time Margaret spent in that church. The forced early morning visits to Mass in Ballymona now seemed so long ago.

Although Margaret wrote to her parents regularly, they never wrote back. There was a twice-weekly delivery of mail from the mainland, and each time it was due she watched eagerly for the figure on the black bicycle. But though the postman brought some official looking envelopes to Derryglas, he never brought the blue envelopes with the flowing handwriting which would signify a communication from her mother. Margaret felt rejected and sad, but she continued to write, telling her parents all about life on the island. About the grand solid house in which Owen lived, about the prosperous farm, and the high standing in which he was held by the other islanders, about her mother-in-law, and Hannah, who were teaching her the island ways. She tried not to communicate her loneliness to her parents. She had made her bed, and if they were right to have warned her of what a difficult bed it would be, she wasn't going to tell them so. When Owen took the boat to the mainland, she remained on the island.

# CHAPTER SIX

S   ummer crept on to the island. It seemed like the long winter was
    loath to depart, and only reluctantly relinquished its grip when
    June was well established. The valley fields around Derryglas
took on a shimmer of green, and the grey stone walls became
chequered with minute flowers that sprang into life in the crevices
between the rocks. The roar of the Atlantic breakers now sank to a
murmur, and Margaret gradually began to rid herself of the sadness
which had enveloped her since her arrival on Inishbawn. For the first
time, she felt she was on the island which had fired her dreams from
afar. Every afternoon when she had completed whatever chores she
had set herself, she hitched up the pony to the trap and explored her
surroundings. The contrasts on the island intrigued her : the poverty
and harshness on one side, where the cottiers eked out a meagre living
from the rocky soil, and the rich lushness of the valley, where Derryglas
and its well-kept fields sat almost smugly above the shingle beach. All
the cottages housed large families, and as the sound of the pony's
hooves rang out on the roads, clusters of children would gather outside
to watch Margaret go by. She soon discovered that the women of
Inishbawn never rode without their menfolk. They walked or cycled. So
she was the object of intense curiosity.

One afternoon at the end of June Margaret cleared up after the
dinner, and was just about to go down to the field to catch the pony
when her mother-in-law followed her out. By this time she seemed to
have accepted Margaret's presence around the place. She made little
effort to talk to her, but by stepping aside from some of the running of
the household, she had indicated that there was at least a place for
Margaret in Derryglas. Hannah still resented her presence, expressing
that resentment in her surly attitude towards her sister-in-law, but after a
few sharp words from Owen she now kept her critical comments to

herself.

'You shouldn't be taking that trap out alone', the old woman said.

'But why not? I'm well used to the pony now, and he's very gentle.'

'You'd be better on your own feet ... all that bumping. It's only foolishness. And people will talk.'

'I don't understand. Why would they talk? What am I doing wrong that they should talk?'

The old woman never took her eyes off her face. After a small silence, during which time she seemed to be weighing up whether or not to speak, she said curtly, 'When women are that way, they have to be careful.'

'That way? What way? What do you mean?' Even as she said it, realisation was sweeping over her. That would explain her queasiness in the mornings, the tightness in her waist bands, even the strange longings she was getting for foods she had never eaten.

Oh, how could she have been so blind? How could she have ignored all those changes, in spite of the bits of information she had picked up from Stella? Stella, who knew all about these things, whose mother was forever getting pregnant. All the whispered conversations, the veiled hints – why had she never put two and two together? She had put the symptoms down to her adjustment to island life, and her new home, and to being so lonely and miserable. It had never crossed her mind that she could be ... could be ... Margaret had difficulty even shaping the word in her mind. But her mother-in-law had known. Her mother-in-law, and probably Hannah too.

Margaret felt the heat in her face spreading down her neck, prickling beneath her arms and behind her knees. A rare softness came into the old woman's eyes. She smiled at Margaret.

'You'll not take the pony out anymore now, will you? Walking is better for you, and Owen wouldn't want you to take any risks now, would he?'

'No, I suppose you're right. I ... I'll just walk down as far as the strand. I won't be long.'

She found Owen in the long field, thinning turnips. His back was bent over the drills, the sacking apron tied around him giving him a strange humped appearance.

'Owen! Owen!'

He straightened up, and looked puzzled at the hurrying figure approaching him.

'What's wrong?'

Margaret drew alongside him, suddenly feeling shy.

'Nothing's wrong. Everything is fine. I just wanted to see you.'

'Bedad, aren't I the lucky man, that my wife should come all the way down here just to have a look at me? Now that you're here, what about doing a bit of thinning with me?'

'Well, I would, but then again maybe I shouldn't ...' She let the implication hang in the air. 'Your mother wouldn't let me take out the pony. She thought the bumping about might be bad for me.'

Owen looked at her, but she wouldn't meet his eyes. His expression of disbelief gradually changed to one of wonder. He touched her cheek as if to check that she was real, and then he closed his arms around her, pressing her gently against the roughness of his clothes.

Everything changed after that. Now Margaret had become a figure of importance in Derryglas. She was carrying Owen's child, the child who would be the future of Derryglas, who would take the island family into the next generation. Hannah's contempt for her vanished, and her attitude now became one of guarded acceptance. Old Mrs. McDowell began to treat her with a new respect, and went out of her way to make life comfortable for her. She was anxious that she didn't get overtired, that she didn't work too long, that she should eat well. And Owen himself could not conceal his pride at the thought of becoming a father. Margaret would find him staring at her at odd moments during the day, and his face would break into a broad smile as he met her gaze.

'Why do you keep looking at me, Owen,' she asked him one day in exasperation. 'Haven't you seen a pregnant woman before?'

'Not when it's my child she's carrying. A son for Derryglas.' He took her hands in his. 'Now I have something to work for Margaret ... a future. And I'll see to it that my son, our son, will be proud of his inheritance. Proud to be an islander. There'll be no need for him to leave, not for England or America or anywhere else. Derryglas and Inishbawn will give him everything his heart could want.'

It was a long speech for Owen, a man not given to revealing his feelings. Margaret felt touched, but frightened also, because of his intensity.

'What if it's a daughter, Owen? It might be a girl.'

'It will be a son.' He put his hand against her stomach. 'It will be a son. The daughters will follow, but this one will be a son.' And Margaret knew that he was right.

That summer was hot. As if to make up for the lateness of its arrival, the sun filled the island days through July and August. Heat drowsed in windless hollows and sizzled on rocky heights. Margaret felt contented. She no longer needed to assert herself. With her pregnancy she had gained acceptance, and now she relished the care and attention with which she was being surrounded. Hannah showed her how to knit the soft wool into tiny baby garments, and she spent hours creating the layette for her baby. Owen, on one of his trips to the mainland brought back some oak timber, and spent the long evenings carving an elegant crib for the child, which the old woman lined in fine-spun material. In August Margaret wrote to tell her parents of her pregnancy, but they did not reply. She cried about that. She had hoped that this news might have ended the rift, but the only indication she had that they had received her letter was a note from Mary Kate. In her almost illegible hand, Mary Kate urged her to 'come back home to have the child. They'll be glad but won't style you by saying so.' But Margaret was too proud to do that, her mother's words of banishment still haunting her.

She wrote also to Stella, and had an immediate reply. Stella would come to Inishbawn when Margaret's time was near. She would be better than any midwife, knowing as she did 'all about those things'. Her own love life was non-existent at the moment, but she had hopes of a certain fellow who had come to work in Sullivan's public house. He was very-good looking and all the girls were eyeing him, but she fancied that he was giving her a special look, and she was waiting for the right chance to build on that! Margaret, reading the letter, was transported back to the past. When they were schoolgirls together Stella had been the 'knowing' one, who was always one step ahead, and who had regarded Margaret as 'innocent'. Now Margaret felt she had lived a lifetime since she had come to the island, and had left Stella behind, like the things of her childhood. She wouldn't tell Stella, when it came near to the time to give birth. She wouldn't want Stella with her. Stella would be all wrong on the island. She would create a new barrier, just when she was gaining acceptance, and would shock the island people with her flighty ways and the knowing looks she would give to every man. No, it was better to keep Stella where she belonged, as part of the past.

With autumn came the busiest time for the islanders. Shoals of fry were in, and the shortening evenings were a frenzy of hauling in catches and salting them for the winter. Margaret longed to go out on the boat with Owen and Thomas, but they wouldn't let her. In her present state it was unthinkable, and besides it was unlucky to have a woman with them on the fishing trips. There was something about those autumn evenings that drew Margaret down to the shore, where she would stand in the gathering twilight and watch the little boats bobbing on the calm water, creating shadowed silhouettes against the moon, rising like a giant orange above the rim of the sea. She felt very much a part of Inishbawn in those moments.

With the harvest to be saved while the weather held, all the women put their weight behind the men. Neighbours came together to form *'meithils'*. The long swishing sounds of the scythes cutting swathes through the corn competed with the murmur of the sea. The women and children stacked the swathes into stooks, the children running excitedly around the stubbly fields. Margaret worked slowly on the fringes. In the not too distant future, her son would be part of that excited group, and she would join the other women in exasperated scoldings. When it was time to rest, Margaret brought Owen his can of tea and his currant bread – at which she was now an expert - and together they would sit down on the bundle of coats. All around them family groups talked and laughed. Sometimes Margaret could not understand their quick dialect, but she didn't feel excluded. Their easy conversation was an indication of their acceptance.

During those sessions in the cornfields she became friendly with Thomas's youngest daughter, Sinead, who had married a fisherman from the island, and who was now carrying their first child. It surprised Margaret that Sinead should walk the two or three miles from her cottage to help with the harvest, but the young woman only laughed when she mentioned it.

'I'd go mad with loneliness in the house. I'm used to being part of a crowd. Eight we had in our family, and all the others in America now.'

'You never thought of going yourself?'

'Oh I thought of it alright, but then I met Cormac Doyle! Anyway, my father needs someone around to keep an eye on him, especially since my mother died!'

Margaret nodded. No wonder Thomas thought so much of his youngest daughter. It must have been sad to rear a big family and then see them leave the island one by one. Margaret liked Sinead. She was the nearest thing to a friend since Stella, and Margaret hoped that their children too would be friends.

The mellow autumn lingered on. The shortening days gave a sense of urgency to the work which had to be done, but now with the harvest saved and the potatoes pitted and covered with straw, it was time for the festivities. The island people entered into the spirit of the harvest festival with an almost pagan exuberance. Sometimes the dancing and the music went on all night, and Margaret wondered at this other side of the islanders' character. It was as if this ritual was a guard against the silence and isolation of the long winter. For almost a week there was little else talked of; even Hannah shook off her usual dour demeanour to become one of those seeking the gaiety of the various vantage-points where the musicians gathered.

But then in mid-October the first bite of winter made itself felt. Overnight the weather hardened into frost. There were filigree patterns of ice on the bedroom window, and a white crust covered the water in the basin. In the early mornings the island was transformed, with a ghostly mist hanging low and pressing down on the stiff, frosted grass. The mournful sound of cattle waiting to be fed echoed across the island with a strange clarity.

It was difficult getting any work done on these mornings. Margaret's fingers turned blue as she mixed the poultry feed, and washing which she hung on the bushes stiffened even as she lifted it. Winter nights closed in early, the darkness pressing down on Derryglas long before the evening milking was done. Margaret could now understand the frenzy of the harvest festivities. The long isolation of winter was fast becoming a reality. People were reluctant to venture outside their own territory. Her friendship with Sinead was now limited to Sunday Mass, after which the women would gather outside the church while their menfolk smoked and talked and the children skated and slithered on the icy roadways.

Two weeks before Christmas, Owen made plans to cross on the steamer to Ballymona, to buy the provisions for the festive season.

'We could be stormbound later on. I'll go this Wednesday to make sure we have everything that's needed. Why don't you come with me, Margaret? It's likely to be your only chance before the baby is born. Wouldn't you like to see your parents before Christmas? It might be a way to heal things?'

Margaret was silent. This time the year before she was caught up in the pre-Christmas bustle in the shop: filling box-loads of groceries for customers, stacking shelves with exotic fruit, biscuits and cakes, especially ordered for this time of year. Mary Kate run off her feet mixing, baking and cleaning. Her mother decorating the windows with red crepe paper and sprigs of holly, which her father would have gathered in the woods outside the town. As a little girl, Margaret had always gone with him on those trips. They knew the best spots to go to for the red-berried holly, and while he cut it and she tied it into bundles, he would tell her stories about his own childhood. It was a time of special closeness, and now thinking about it, she felt a lump in her throat. How could she go back to Ballymona to be snubbed? They had told her that if she married Owen, they didn't want to see her again. They hadn't even answered her letters! She thought about it, but no, she couldn't bear to face their rejection once more.

'No, you go, Owen,' she said. 'You go. Call up the town to the shop, and see how they all are. Bring me back whatever news there is. Maybe you could find out if ... if they want to see me? Maybe they'll ask you then to bring me over?'

Owen looked down with pity at the childish face above the swollen body. He felt deep anger at what they had done to her. But touching her face, he just said, 'I'll get some of the stuff in your shop, and see how things are. Maybe they'll have softened. Maybe they will ask me to bring you across ... what with Christmas and the baby and everything.'

'Yes, maybe they will.' But in her heart Margaret knew that it was a vain hope.

Thomas took the trap down to the harbour to meet the steamer. Margaret waited, restlessly filling the time with an assortment of small tasks. Surely when they saw Owen, when they heard about her ... about the baby. When they saw her favourite biscuits on the order list? The biscuits which they had always got in especially for her, ever since she was a child. Surely they'd relent. Yes, they would want to hear all about her from Owen. Her father would laugh when Owen would tell him how well she was adapting to being an islander's wife. Her mother would be surprised to hear about the knitting and the sewing she was doing. And Mary Kate ... Mary Kate would bless herself and exclaim 'Holy God!' when she learned that she was now an expert at baking, not just brown bread, but currant soda bread as well. Yes,Christmas was the time for making up. They had just needed these past months to get used to the idea and to make their authority felt. But now, she felt sure, they would be ready to accept her marriage and her new life.

The day dragged by slowly, until finally it was time for the steamer to return. Margaret paced restlessly around the house. She wished Owen would hurry back. How could it be taking him so long to come from the harbour? Even allowing for the fact that he would be dropping Thomas off at his own house, surely it could not take him all that time? What was keeping him? Throwing her shawl over her head Margaret went out into the darkness, her ears straining for the sound of the pony's hooves. Soon she heard the familiar clip clop, and in the distance she could make out the faint beams from the two lamps. She hurried to meet the approaching trap, the cold wind nipping at her face and dragging her hair in bunches from beneath the shawl. Owen pulled up the pony, surprised to see the bedraggled figure of his wife blocking the road.

'Margaret, what are you doing out here in the dark? You'll catch your death. Is anything wrong?'

He jumped down and helped her up on to the seat beside him. The pony, anxious to get back to his stable and his feed, pawed restlessly on the road, while Owen settled the rug around his wife's legs.

'Did you get everything? Did you see them? You were so long coming back, I got restless and came to meet you.'

Owen guessed that she didn't want to be in the house when she heard about his trip to the mainland. She didn't want Hannah and his mother sitting there, all ears, while he told her about the shop and her parents. He kissed her cold nose and rubbed her hands in his, before giving the pony the signal to move on.

'Well? Come on, tell me. I want to hear everything. How was Ballymona?'

'Cold.'

'Owen! Tell me. Don't tease! Did you go to the shop? Who was there?'

'Yes, I went there, and I got all the things that you had on your list, including your special biscuits. And I was talking to your mother, but I didn't see your father, though I could hear him out in the storeroom.'

'And what did she say about me, about the baby? Will they come to Inishbawn, or do they want me to come over to them?'

Owen remembered the hard, closed face of the woman behind the counter, the pale eyes that revealed nothing of her feelings. The abrupt answers as he tried to appeal to her ... to plead with her.

'I'm sorry, my love. I'm really sorry. I tried ... but I don't think they're ready yet. Maybe after our son is born. Then they'll be proud ...'

He saw the light go from her eyes, her shoulders slump.

'When you'll have the boy to look after, Margaret, then it won't seem so important. And anyway they'll feel different when he arrives. They won't turn their backs on their first grandson!'

Margaret didn't answer. She questioned him no more about Ballymona. When they reached the house, he unharnessed the pony and took him down to the stable. Margaret unpacked the boxes, storing all the Christmas things on the scullery shelves. Then, ignoring the questioning looks of Hannah and Julia, she went up the stairs to their bedroom.

Christmas was a quiet time. It was very different from Christmas on the mainland, where the shop drew Margaret and her family deep into the community. Serving behind the counter, Margaret had known what all the neighbours were hoping for their Christmas, who was expecting visitors, who was worried about a 'dry' husband falling into old ways, what Santa would be bringing to whom. There was an air of anticipation around the town, with its decorated shop windows and its influx of rural shoppers. But in Inishbawn it seemed that the festivities of the harvest dances had exhausted people's need for further excitement. Christmas was more a time of retreat. There were no returned emigrants, no visitors, no sense of bustle. Work had to be done, just as at any other time of the year, with a vigilant eye on the weather. With winter gales being anticipated, outbuildings had to be secured, animal fodder stacked up, and the fishing for cod and ling carried on while the seas weren't too rough.

For the Christmas dinner Owen's mother had selected a fine goose from their own flock. Owen himself had killed the goose, which was then plucked and prepared by Hannah. Margaret had always been used to turkey at Christmas, and the fatty flesh of the goose made her feel nauseous. She could only pick at the dinner, but her pregnancy excused her from any criticism. The rest of the day was like any ordinary day. Coming back from midnight Mass in the village church on Christmas eve, Margaret had been awestruck by the sight of the lighted candles in every window. Right across the island faint, wavering lights struggling against the surrounding blackness, like souls reaching out to eternity, she thought. It was the most beautiful sight she had ever seen. Nothing on the mainland could compare with it.

A stillness hung in the air, as if the island was holding its breath. Margaret felt that Inishbawn, like herself, was waiting. She was now into her eighth month of pregnancy, a time of heightened awareness, of acute sensitivity, and for her the waiting was almost over. Only one month to go. All the preparations were completed. The cradle stood in the corner of their bedroom, waiting to be occupied. Nurse O'Grady, the local midwife, had been notified. She lived on the other side of the island, and would attend the birth when the time came. Margaret felt the child stir and kick. He would be a healthy boy, strong like Owen. She wondered if he would have the dark colouring of the islanders, or would he be more like her people. Probably a bit of both ... a link between Ballymona and Derryglas.

At the end of January Sinead's baby was born. Thomas took Margaret in the trap to visit her and her new son. The cottage seemed crowded with this newcomer, a fine boy, a miniature Cormac. Sinead had no trouble giving birth, and the baby was a placid child. Seeing Thomas with his first island grandchild, seeing his pride in this boy who would grow up on Inishbawn, Margaret understood why Sinead could not leave the island like her brothers and sisters had done.

# CHAPTER SEVEN

L ike a deep breath being expelled, the hush of the past weeks ended, and the first stirrings of the approaching gale whispered through the sedge grass and sent shivers through the bare trees. As Margaret took the bucket down to the milking stall for the evening milking, she saw the dark clouds pushing the sun from the horizon and gathering in thick banks. In the stall the cows were restless, sensing the storm. Hannah was there before her, her face pressed against the body of the cow she was milking. She looked up when Margaret entered.

'Leave the milking,' she said. 'The cows are giddy. I'll do them.'

'It's alright, I'll just do the little black one. We'll be finished before the rain starts.'

Hannah made no reply, and returned to her milking. Margaret pulled out the milking stool and placed the bucket beneath the black cow. Soon the high-pitched patter of the milk in the bucket filled out to become a deep swish. The hypnotic sound lulled Margaret into an almost trance-like state. The smell of the warm milk, the straw, the breath of the cow, the semi-darkness of the stall ... all contributing to an unguarded relaxation. She was barely conscious of the world outside. Then suddenly there was a loud bang. A gust of wind had lifted the top of the half-door, causing it to slap back against the jamb. The black cow, with a startled bellow, kicked over the bucket of milk. Margaret grabbed to try to save the steaming liquid. The stool overturned, and she found herself on the flat of her back. She felt no pain, just a shocked light-headedness. Hannah screamed and rushed over to her.

'Are you alright Margaret? Oh God, are you alright?'

'I think so ...' Margaret lifted her head, but felt so dizzy that she had to close her eyes and lie back again.

'Get Owen, Hannah. Please! I can't get up. Get Owen to help.'

'Oh God ... the baby. Did you do any damage to the baby? Will he be alright?'

Margaret tried to speak, but her words were lost in the frantic bellowing of the cows and the whine of the wind through the open door. She felt a dull ache in her back, and her head was now pounding.

'Stay where you are,' Hannah shouted above the wind. 'I'll find somebody. Don't move.'

Margaret couldn't move even if she had wanted to. She felt like some monstrous sea creature, beached on the shore following a storm. The stall was now quite dark, and the normally placid cows were stamping, lowing and twisting about in the milk spattered straw. Soon she heard Hannah returning, accompanied by Owen and Thomas, and with her mother-in-law bringing up the rere with the oil lamp.

'What business had you milking, and you the way you are.' Owen's voice was angry in his concern.

'I told her not to. I warned her that the cows were giddy.' Hannah rushed in defensively. 'But she wouldn't listen to me.'

Thomas bent over her. 'Steady now. We'll get you back to the house in no time. You'll be fine'.

The two men got her to her feet, and gently helped her back across the yard and into the house, setting her down on the settle by the fire.

'A cup of strong tea is what she needs.' The old woman busied herself preparing the tea, while Hannah stood awkwardly in the middle of the floor.

'I told her not to ... I warned her!' she repeated. 'She wouldn't heed me!'

Oh, leave it, will you? There's nobody blaming you!' Owen eventually snapped at her.

Margaret felt guilty at all this fuss. 'I'm alright, really. I'll just take the cup of tea and then I'll go on up to bed. I'll be grand in the morning. I'm sorry about the milk, Owen. The whole bucketful went. I couldn't get it in time.'

'Ah, what matter about the milk. But you're a foolish girl. You wouldn't be said by me, would you? Out milking on a night like this, when you should be resting yourself.'

'I know, Owen. I'm sorry. I won't do a hand's turn now until ... until after the birth.'

'Do you want Thomas to call to Nurse O'Grady on his way home? You might need attention.'

'Do you not hear the storm, Owen? Why bring her out in this weather when I'll be fine by tomorrow. She'd only tell me the same thing anyway: go to bed and rest.'

'Well, if you're sure ...' Owen looked dubious.

'I'm sure. Honestly Owen. You go on home Thomas. Get back before the storm worsens.'

Margaret finished her tea, and Owen helped her up the stairs to the big bedroom. He stood at the window while she took off her clothes and slipped on the flannelette nightgown, then he tucked the quilt around her, smoothing her hair back from her forehead.

'I'll sleep in the spare room, so as not to disturb you. Relax there now. I'll tell Hannah to look in on you shortly. And don't you stir in the morning ... she'll bring you a bit of breakfast. Will you be alright now?'

Margaret noticed the deep furrows on her husband's face. Anxiety made him look old. It was the first time in their marriage that she had been made aware of the difference in their ages. Now he reminded her of her father, and of how he would fuss over her when she was sick as a child, patting the sheets and puffing up the pillows, and standing awkwardly by her bedside. Her father had never been able to cope with sickness in the family. He just seemed to crumble, and it was left to her mother to attend to the practicalities. Now Owen had that same look in his eyes. She smiled at him and squeezed his hand.

'Don't worry, Owen. Go on down. I'll be asleep in no time.'

When Owen had left, she lay back and closed her eyes. The ache in her back was still there, a dull, low ache that made relaxation impossible. She tried propping a pillow behind her waist, but it made no difference. Her head was throbbing, and she felt cold all over. Outside she could hear the wind, now risen to a shrieking fury, snatching and tearing around the house. Every now and then the rain slashed against the window, and she could smell the salt in the air. Down on the strand the waves crashed on to the shoreline, sucking up the shingle and spewing it back in the mouth of each breaker. She wondered if any of the fishermen were out. Thank God Owen was home.

All night long the storm raged. The pounding in her head now seemed but an echo of the sounds outside. The pain and the wind were as one, rising and falling with relentless intensity. She heard herself crying out. The voice sounded like a disembodied scream bouncing off the walls of the dark room. Then there were voices. There was a lamp flickering on the washstand, and shadows grotesquely large surrounding her. Faces loomed in, frightened faces, grey in the lamplight. Now the pain enveloped her, until there was nothing else but pain. She cried out again, and it was her mother she cried for. She was going to die. Oh God let her die ... let her die before the next wave of pain. She became aware of the voices again. Someone shouting. 'Get Nurse O'Grady ... tell her to come quickly. There's no time to lose.' Then Hannah's high-pitched crying and whining ... 'I told her not to go near the cows. I warned her. Oh, Owen ... it wasn't my fault. Oh, do something, do something, before it's too late.'

'Hold your tongue, woman!' Owen's voice, angry. Then his face bending over her. His hands gripping hers.

'Margaret, Margaret, my poor love. I'm going for Nurse O'Grady. I'll have her with you in no time. It's going to be alright. Nurse O'Grady will come and everything will be alright.'

The old woman and Hannah hovered around her, sponging her forehead, moistening her lips. She wished they would go away and leave her. She wanted to yell at them, to hit out at them. She wanted Owen. She wanted her mother.

The pale dawn light now crept into the room, smothering the yellow flicker of the lamp. Morning brought no respite in the fury of the storm, and Margaret could hear the rattle of the window panes above the roar of the sea. She drifted in and out of consciousness, and at one stage became aware of the arrival of Nurse O'Grady. Wet hair plastered around a red, weathered face. Kind eyes, cold hands. A soothing voice.

'It won't be long now, a gra. You must help. You must push. Now ... now... push! Good girl. You're doing fine. Now ... push!'

Her body was being ripped apart. Her screams echoed around the room. She pushed, again and again, but it was no use ... there was no respite from the pain.

'Is it too late, nurse? Is it too late?' Her mother-in-law's voice.

'I'm doing all I can. It's a breach, and she's getting weak. I'm not sure if the baby, if it can ...'

Margaret was carried up on another mountain of pain. She bore down, and gave herself totally to the agony. And then it was over. The child was expelled.

Above her own screams of pain she was aware of the hoarse

weeping of the old woman, of her prayers and of her incantations as she dropped to her knees beside the bed. It was all over. There was no more to be done.

# CHAPTER EIGHT

I t was the first anniversary of Margaret's marriage to Owen, and the memory of that awful February night, and of what followed, still consumed her. She thought of nothing else, playing it over and over again in her mind. The memory of the voices and the whisperings surrounding her bed. Of Nurse O'Grady's cold hands. Of the savage howling of the wind, and Hannah's shrill weeping rising above it. And of Owen's mother, praying and lamenting her dead grandson.

Now, lying on the bed on this April morning, Margaret, as she had done on so many other mornings, remembered how the voices and the prayers rose and fell around her exhausted consciousness.

'Do something, nurse. Do something ... it's Owen's son. Oh God, do something!'

'The child is dead, Julia. What can I do ... he's dead. There's nothing I can do for him. But the mother ... she's losing a lot of blood. She'll have to be brought to the mainland, to the hospital. It's her best chance.'

'Oh Jesus have mercy. May God and His blessed Mother protect us from this darkness. The child ... the child! Gone without the grace of baptism. Oh, have mercy on us all this night. Have mercy on us.'

Her voice went on and on. And then Margaret was aware of Owen beside her, and the old woman still moaning about shame and limbo and baptism..

'Be quiet! What are you ranting on about, woman?' Owen's voice, low and insistent. 'Hannah, will you take her out. Take her out of here ... she doesn't know what she's saying. Nurse, will Margaret be alright? Will she be alright?'

A scrambling in the background, a door banging, and then Owen's face pressed against hers. A face rough with stubble, wet with tears.

'Oh, Margaret, don't go. Don't leave me. My poor love, what have I done to you? What have I done? I should never have brought you here.'

'Move back from her now Owen. You're not doing any good there. Move back! I'll do what I can, but she should be in the hospital. She's bad ... she should have a doctor.'

Owen had lifted his face from hers.

''Twould be suicide to try to cross to the mainland in this weather. We'd never be able to make the crossing. Even the steamer won't put out in this storm. You'll have to look after her, nurse. You'll have to do the best you can. We'll not be able to make it to Ballymona.'

'You're right ... but it's looking bad, Owen. Very bad.'

Nurse O'Grady had hovered about her, bathing her, sponging her, administering to her. At one stage Margaret, turning on her side, saw the shape of her son, bundled up in sheets, lying in the crib, the solid oak crib that Owen had carved for him so lovingly. She had wanted to ask the nurse to let her see him, to let her hold him, but she was so weak ... the words wouldn't form for her. And then the nurse had given her something to drink, holding up her head, and pressing the liquid between her parched lips, and she had drifted into a restless sleep.

When she had woken up, Margaret had found herself alone. Bright sunlight filled the room, and she was very cold. She listened. There was no wind. The soft murmur of the sea belied its recent fury. Outside, the cackling of the hens made a familiar morning chorus. She had turned her head slowly. The crib was empty.

Now Margaret dragged herself up from the bed and moved across to the window-seat. Her body felt like that of an old, old woman. She heard Owen enter the bedroom, sensed him standing behind her.

'Margaret, will you come down to the strand with me? Walk by the sea like we used to do? The fresh air might do you good.' He touched her shoulder. She stiffened. He removed his hand and went on. 'Maybe you'd like me to take you across to the mainland? Yes, that's what we could do. Maybe go on the steamer. Buy you some new clothes? We could even spend the night in the Harbour Hotel. How about that for style, Margaret?'

Owen's voice had an appeal in it. Appeal tinged with exasperation. He felt so helpless. What was he going to do with her? God, it was two months now, and she had hardly spoken to him. If only she'd talk about it, or cry, or something. But no, she had just withdrawn into herself, built an icy wall between herself and everyone else. At night she lay beside him, untouching. If he tried to hold her or comfort her, she recoiled and turned away. Most of her days were spent in their bedroom, lying on the bed or sitting on the windowseat, staring out at the sea with unseeing eyes. When she did come down to the kitchen she huddled over the fire, ignoring Hannah and the old woman, and their tentative attempts at sympathy or pity. She ate the food that was put in front of her. She didn't ask for it, nor did she eat when it wasn't put there for her. Her face was thin and pale, her once beautiful hair lank and dull, her body shapeless.

'Margaret, are you listening to me?' Owen touched her shoulder again, and felt her shiver of distaste as he did so. For the umpteenth time he wondered what it was she was staring at, sitting at that window for hours on end.

'You would like to go to the mainland, wouldn't you? And Margaret, maybe we'll call up to see your mother and father. And Mary Kate! You might even feel like staying with them for a week or two?'

They had written to her ... her parents. When he had told them that she had lost the baby, they had written to her, tried to make amends. She had glanced over the letters, then thrown them on the fire.

He waited now for a response, but she continued staring out at the ocean. He took her hand, and rubbed its numbness with his fingers. She tried to pull away, but then seemed to feel that it wasn't worth the effort. Owen knelt on one knee beside her. What was he going to do with her he wondered. What could he say to reach her? Maybe his mother was right. Maybe she did need to be sent away for some kind of treatment. Other women lost babies, didn't they? But other women didn't carry on like she was. No, they got on with the business of living.

'Well, will you come across to Ballymona with me? Will you, love?'

She turned from the window, and looked at him. Owen was reminded of the look in the eyes of a young seal which he had once caught in his nets.

'Where is he?' she asked. 'Where did you put him?'

'Put who? What are you saying?'

'Where did you put my baby?'

Owen shifted from his uncomfortable position and continued rubbing her hand.

'It was taken care of, Margaret. Don't you be fretting about that now.'

'Where did you put him? Is he in the graveyard by the church? Is it marked by a cross? Is it, Owen? Is it?'

'We did what we had to, Margaret. Can't you put it behind you love? There'll be other babies. Fine strong babies.'

'You haven't answered me. Where is my son? Is he in the graveyard by the church?'

Margaret thought of the tiny, motionless bundle in the crib ... the old woman's wild incantations ... and then the empty crib, cold and bare – images she had tried to blank out, but which kept coming back. Flickering emotions clawing at the deadness inside her. What had they done with her baby? What had they done with his little body?

Owen stood up abruptly.

'He was born dead, Margaret. He was dead before anyone could make a Christian out of him. So how could he be buried in the churchyard? You know yourself the priest wouldn't have that.'

'Then where is he? Where is he? I have to know where he is.'

She got down from the window seat, slowly, awkwardly, and took hold of the sleeve of his jumper. He could feel her grip through the heavy oiled wool.

'Please, Owen, tell me what you did with him. I have to know ... please.'

Owen, looking into her eyes and seeing there all the pain and the sorrow of her life, felt his heart turn with pity for her. He had tried to put the events of that night, and his own part in them, behind him. An islandman could not survive if he was soft or sentimental. Nature was harsh, and nowhere more so than in places like Inishbawn, and that night in February he had done what was expected of him. He had taken the body of the child – he wasn't going to think of it as his son – well-wrapped and swaddled by Nurse O'Grady. He had placed it in a plain wooden box, and had nailed down the lid on the box. In the greyness of the pre-dawn on that cold February morning, he had ridden to the killeen, the place set apart for the burial of unbaptised children, a mile or so from the church. The laments of his mother still rang in his ears as he had dug the tiny grave. He had then shovelled the earth over the makeshift coffin, pressing it down firmly with the spade. Soon the grass would grow over it, creeping like a thin green blanket across its bareness, merging it with all the other little mounds in this sorry place. Anonymous bumps and curves in an unblessed plot.

Why couldn't she leave it? Owen thought. A dead, unbaptised child was something families wanted to forget about. Island people did not talk about such things. They would know about it well enough around Inishbawn. Nurse O'Grady would see to that. But it would be a whispered, woman to woman knowledge. An island woman would not question her man. She would know that he had done what he had to, and that after a certain amount of time new babies would be made, babies brought to full term and baptised into the church. But Margaret was not an island woman.

Pressing her shapeless, resistant body against his own, Owen told her where he had taken the corpse, and what he had done with it. She listened, dry-eyed. Outside the watery sunshine played light and shadows on the sea. The loud braying of a donkey was answered by a barking dog. Somewhere on Inishbawn, Margaret thought, her son was lying in an unblessed, pagan grave, while all around her were people trying to pretend that he had never existed.

'When I am strong enough, you will take me there, Owen.'

'Oh Margaret, my love ... what's the sense in you going there? Why would you want to do that? People will only talk about you.'

'You'll take me there in the pony and trap, and show me where you put him. I have to see where you put him.'

'If I show you, will you put it all behind you? Will you try to forget about it, make a fresh start?'

He stroked her dull hair and put his cheek against hers, but she pulled away, to stand once more at the window.

'Tomorrow,' she said. 'Tomorrow you'll take me to the killeen, and show me where you buried my son.'

PART TWO


NESSA

# CHAPTER ONE

There were six children for first Holy Communion that year. A small number, Auntie Hannah had said, adding that when she had made hers there were at least twenty, most of whom had grown up to take the emigrant ship to America. All the best and the brightest were in America, Nessa decided, and would never again set foot on Inishbawn. It wasn't like going to live on the mainland, like the O'Sullivans had done, leaving their old grandfather to see to the cottage. No, it was going away for ever and ever.

'For ever and ever amen.' Father Deasy's voice echoed her thoughts, and Nessa made an effort to draw her attention back to the Mass. Today of all days, she must stop day-dreaming. Grandma had told her that this was the most important day in her life, when Jesus would come to her in a very special way. Her teacher, Miss Slattery, had warned her that she would be committing a mortal sin if she touched the Host with her finger or with her teeth, and Auntie Hannah had told her to keep her eyes closed tight when she knelt at the altar. Nessa's mouth went dry at the thought of all the things she must remember. She glanced across the seat at the other children. She could see two of the huge Connors tribe, looking slightly cleaner than usual, with their hair slicked down with oil, and wearing matching trousers and jumpers which Auntie Hannah said came from the big sister who worked in the doctor's house on the mainland. Next to them was Martin O'Breen, jigging restlessly on his seat and looking around him, mouth open. Nessa wondered would he swallow the Host without touching it. If he dropped it, Miss Slattery would be so angry; she had been threatening him for weeks, but poor Martin didn't seem to care. Auntie Hannah said he was half-witted like his father. The twins, Killian and Bridget Doyle were next. Though they were younger than the rest of the class, Father Deasy had said they were sensible enough to join the first Communion group. Nessa liked

Killian. He was the best rider and the fastest runner on the island, and Miss Slattery said he was sharper at his books than his big brother Brendan. Bridget had a nice dress on her, white with a lace collar, and she wore a big white bow in her hair.

Nessa looked down at her own dress. Her Grandma had made it for her, and Auntie Hannah had stitched on the tiny rosebuds all around the skirt. Dada had said she was like a princess, and when Mama had curled her hair and brushed it back from her face, he said she looked like an angel. Nessa wondered now did angels have hair. She looked up at the picture above the altar – all the angels there seemed to be fat and bald.

A cough from Miss Slattery brought her wandering attention back once more to the Mass. The priest was giving Communion to the two altar boys, and now it was time for the six new communicants to line up at the altar rails. Nessa's heart boomed loudly as she knelt in front of Father Deasy. She squeezed her eyes tightly shut and put out her tongue to receive the Host. She waited to feel the wave of holiness and joy which Father Deasy had told them to expect, but all she felt was the churning of fear in her stomach as her throat tightened up and swallowing became an effort.

After the Mass there were photographs to be taken, and family and neighbours made a big fuss of the first communicants. Then Miss Slattery led the way down to the school, where a special breakfast was made for the six children and their brothers and sisters. Sinead Doyle, the twins' mother, was there with a tray of sandwiches. Mrs. Connors, children clinging to her skirts, was laying out mugs and plates on the makeshift table, and Martin O'Breen's mother, talking and laughing loudly, was cutting thick slices of soda bread and piling them on to the plates. Nessa looked around hopefully. She hadn't really expected to see her mother there with the other helpers, but she had hoped that someone from the family would be at the school. The night before, when Mama had been curling her hair, Nessa had said that Miss Slattery had invited all the families to help with the breakfast.

'So, will you be there, Mama? Will you come to the breakfast?'

'I'll be at the Mass child. That's what's important.'

Nessa didn't pursue it. Mama never mixed much with the neighbours. From as far back as Nessa could remember, Mama would sit alone in her bedroom, or would disappear for hours on her bicycle.

Nessa would help her Auntie Hannah around the house, or sometimes would follow her Dada about the farm or go on the cart with Thomas to visit Killian and Bridget, his grandchildren. But she had learned not to intrude on Mama's time.

Now, in the small schoolroom, surrounded by the island women and by the boys and girls who had always been part of her life, Nessa felt content. The ordeal of doing everything right in the church was over, and she did indeed feel that maybe this was the happiest day of her life. Killian sat beside her at the table, Bridget on the other side. Across from her Mrs. Doyle talked to her and admired her dress, and asked if her Mama had made it for her. Nessa knew that her Mama and Mrs. Doyle had been friends a long time ago, but now Mrs. Doyle seldom came to Derryglas, and Mama never went visiting.

When the breakfast was over, the children played in the schoolyard, while the women cleaned and swept out the schoolroom. Then they scattered to their various homes, some to the poor cottages around the village, others, like Nessa and the Doyles, to be taken by cart or trap to the other side of the island. Mrs. Doyle had the Sunday trap waiting, the high stepping pony restless between the shafts. Killian, Bridget and Nessa piled in, and Killian was allowed to take the reins. It was exciting sitting up so high, with the pony pulling up the hilly road. The warmth of each other's bodies cushioned the children from the blasts of cold wind coming in from the ocean. Bridget talked non-stop, telling her mother every detail of Miss Slattery's warnings to them and what Father Deasy had said to them. Killian was silent, intent on the responsibility of guiding the pony. Nessa thought he handled the trap even better than his big brother Brendan could have done. There was nothing Killian couldn't do. Nessa was going to marry Killian when they grew up. She had no doubt about that. She and Killian would marry. They would live in Derryglas, where Killian and Dada would work the farm together. Grandma and Auntie Hannah would be able to take a rest, and she and Killian would have lots of children who would love Inishbawn just as much as she did, and who would never have to go to America or even to the mainland to work.

'There you are now, Nessa. Off you go, and give my regards to your Gran and Hannah – and your Mam and Dad of course.'

The pony pulled up at the gates leading to Derryglas, and Sinead Doyle helped Nessa down, carefully folding back her white dress to avoid getting any axle oil on it.

'Thanks, Mrs. Doyle. See you tomorrow in school, Bridget and Killian!'

Nessa stood at the gate and watched the pony and trap until it disappeared on the bend of the road, then skipped up the path to the house.

'Did the Doyles bring you home girleen?' Her Grandma was stooped over the fire, poking the turf to bring the kettle to the boil.

'Yes Grandma. Mrs. Doyle was asking for you. Where's Mama?'

'Ah ...she's gone off on the bicycle.'

'She didn't come to help with the breakfast. All the other mothers were there. Why does Mama not want to talk to the other women, Grandma?'

'Don't you be asking so many questions now. Go up and change that lovely frock before the smoke gets on it, and then you can go down with the mash to the hen-house. Hannah is searching for that auld black hen's nest. She's the divil itself for laying out. Your eyes are young and sharp – *you* see if you can find it.'

Nessa ran up the stairs to her room. When she had turned eight Dada had cleared out the little attic to make a bedroom for her. He had moved her iron bed out of Hannah's room, and put a new piece of linoleum on the floor, and had given her a fine chest of drawers into which she could put her clothes. It was cosy up there, and if she stood on a chair Nessa could see the sea. At night, burrowed beneath the quilt, she could listen to the swish of the waves on the shingle and the sad cries of the birds. Down below her she knew that Mama was sitting, still and silent, watching until darkness swallowed up the ocean. Dada would be in the kitchen, his boots off, his feet in their thick grey stockings stretched out to the fire, and the weekly newspaper being read, line by line, sometimes aloud, to his mother and sister. Nessa liked to know that everything was as it was supposed to be before she fell asleep at night.

Now, her dress folded neatly and placed with her white shoes and socks in the deep drawer, Nessa put on her old skirt and jumper and the black wellington boots that were her normal footwear. Then she raced downstairs and out into the yard, to find her aunt.

'Well, what was the breakfast like? Was that mad O'Breen one there?'

'She was, and she brought a grand soda cake too. And Killian's mother brought sandwiches. And Mrs. Connors made the tea. Why didn't you come Hannah? Mama went away straight after the Mass, and I was the only one without someone at the breakfast.'

'Haven't I enough to do here, without standing in for your mother? Amn't I worn out trying to do everything. We can't all live like ladies! Anyway,' Hannah's voice softened as she looked at the child, 'didn't you have the Doyles? And at least your mother was at the Mass. At least she did that much! Now will you see if you can find where that black hen is laying. Put the eggs in the scullery if you find them, and you can have a couple of nice boiled eggs for your tea.'

Nessa wandered off, searching under the old machinery and into cobweb-draped corners, and poking a long stick into the tangle of briars at the bottom of the yard. Mice scurried, startled, from their hidden nests, and the two farm cats waited on the barn roof. Nessa eventually found the black hen, nesting behind a screen of thistles and nettles. Pulling the sleeves of her jumper over her hands, Nessa shushed the hen from her hiding place, and removed four warm eggs, which she carried back, rolled in the rib of her jumper, to the house. Then she blocked up the entrance to the nest. That done, she dawdled down the laneway and out on to the field. In the distance she could see smoke rising from the chimney of Doyle's farmhouse. Killian would be out with his father by now. Bridget would probably be helping her mother. Nessa wondered what it would be like to have brothers and sisters. Sometimes it was lonely on her own, but mostly she liked it. She made up her own games. When Killian was with her, they climbed the trees, made swings from pieces of rope, fished in the shallow streams and built hide-outs in the dim barn. Sometimes Bridget joined them, but it wasn't the same with Bridget there. Bridget got bored easily. She called Nessa a tomboy, and said their games were daft, and Nessa was always glad when she decided to go home. Bridget liked being at home helping her mother. Brendan was his father's favourite; he spent all his time out on the boat with Cormac, or helping him on the land. Everyone said that Killian was the one with the brains.

'He's a born scholar,' Miss Slattery had told his parents, and Cormac had shaken his head and said 'And where do you think all that book-learning will get him in Inishbawn? It will be America for him as soon as he's old enough! He has plenty of family out there anyway, and there's nothing for him here, that's for sure.'

Nessa wandered across the fields, keeping a sharp eye out for birds' nests in the hedgerows. She knew the nesting places of most of the small birds, but understood that she should not touch the nests, in case the birds took fright. From the top field Nessa had a clear view of the road, empty except for a couple of donkeys grazing along its verge. She had walked a long way from Derryglas, which was now down in the valley behind her. Evening was beginning to draw in, and black clouds on the horizon heralded rain. Nessa shivered as the wind found the gaps in her woollen jumper. Suddenly she wished she hadn't come so far. She wished she was back in the farmhouse. Her Grandma would be lighting the lamps, Auntie Hannah would be preparing a meal for Dada, and buttering thick slices of soda bread for her. Nessa began to run. Faster, faster, down the hilly field, past curious looking cattle, until she was almost on to the road. Going back that way would be quicker. Nessa clambered over the loose stone wall, and jumped on to the verge, briars tearing at her legs and drawing blood on the bare skin between her skirt and the top of her boot. She was just picking herself up from the grass when the bicycle came around the corner.

'Mama! Mama!' she called out.

'What are you doing out here child, and the darkness coming?' Her mother got down off the high black bicycle. Dust clung to her buttoned boots, and to the hem of her skirt. Her eyes were red in her pale face. Nessa felt afraid, the sense of unease which always surrounded Mama's return from these cycling trips being magnified in this half-light. She began to cry.

'You weren't at the breakfast, Mama. Everyone was there except you. I was looking for you, and I kept walking and walking, and then it started to get dark and I ran and ran. And then I saw your bicycle. Where were you, Mama?'

'Aren't you the silly girl! Stop your crying now. Big girls who've made their first Communion don't cry!'

Mama didn't bend to kiss her or hold her. Instead, she lifted her up on to the back carrier of her bicycle.

'Hold on tight, and keep your feet out from the wheels.'

Nessa clung on to her mother's coat, pressing her face to its rough tweed, as the bike gathered speed on the downhill run to Derryglas. She liked this closeness to Mama. Maybe now that she was a big girl ... maybe now Mama would take her with her on her cycles. Then everything would be perfect. She tried to ask Mama if she could come with her the next time, but Mama didn't hear her. The wind snatched her voice and it was lost in the battle between it and the roar of the sea. Nessa closed her eyes and kept them closed fast until she felt the bumpity bump of the wheels on the cobbled yard.

Three angry faces met Nessa and her mother when they entered the house.

'Where in God's name have you been with that child?' Owen's voice was sharp. He was addressing his wife, but Margaret made no answer. Hannah grabbed hold of Nessa.

'You poor child! You're frozen with the cold. Where were you? Where did she take you to? You didn't take the child to that ... that place, did you?' She glared at her sister-in-law, venom in her eyes.

The old woman turned to Owen, shouting at him :

'I could see this day coming. Didn't I tell you, Owen, that you'd rue the day you brought that one in here? This child will be lost to you just as surely as the other one was. She's not fit to have a child. She's not right in the head.'

'Will you whisht, woman. You're frightening the little girl. She's here now and she's alright. Go and wet a pot of tea, I'm sure they could do with it.'

Nessa's heart thumped as she looked from one to the other. Her mother made no answer to their accusations, but slowly and deliberately removed her coat and hung it up behind the kitchen door. Then she walked out of the room and up the stairs. A soft click indicated the closing of the bedroom door.

'Did you see that?' Hannah turned on her brother. 'Not an answer from her, and we heart-scalded here worrying about the child.'

'She's not right in the head,' the old woman repeated. 'She should be put away. I said it long ago. Put away ... the only thing for her.'

'Will you wet the tea, Mother, and leave off!' Owen turned to the frightened Nessa.

'Take off your boots girleen, and sit up for your tea, and don't be taking any notice of those two women. Did you have a lovely time after your Communion? I declare you looked like a little angel, ready to float away in your white dress.'

Nessa sat up to the table, but now she didn't feel like those boiled eggs after all. Her throat was tight and she had a pain in her stomach.

She wondered about Mama all alone in the bedroom. What did Grandma mean about locking her away, and not being right in the head? That's what they said about Martin O'Breen, and about his father. But Mama wasn't a bit like that. Surely Dada wouldn't lock her away.'

'Why aren't you eating your eggs, Nessa?' Hannah sat down beside her and poured out the tea. 'Eat up now, or you won't be big and strong. Will I take the caps off for you?'

Neatly she sliced the tops off the two eggs, and cut the soda bread into fingers for dipping.

'Now, what could be nicer than that?' Hannah smiled at her, and touched her cheek. Hannah's sour manner always softened where Nessa was concerned. Sometimes it seemed to Nessa that Hannah was the only one in the house who really saw her. Mama had her own life, Dada was busy with the farm, and Grandma was so old that her prayers and her beads were all that mattered to her. But Nessa knew that Hannah loved her, and how she wished that Hannah and Mama could like each other.

Nessa dipped her bread into the egg, and chewed a bite of the soft mixture. The others sat in to the table and ate in silence. Nessa hoped her mother would come down and join them, but Mama did not reappear.

When it was bedtime for Nessa, and Hannah came to tuck her up and kiss her good night, the little girl was glad that the 'happiest' day of her life had ended.

Later, in the darkness of the bedroom, Margaret lay stiffly beside her husband.

'You shouldn't have taken her there, Margaret,' Owen said. 'It wasn't right. You're making a show of yourself spending half your life up there, but you've no right involving the child.'

He waited. When Margaret didn't answer, he took her hand in his.

'She's a grand little girl. Bright and smart and loving. And you're missing out on her childhood. Can't you pull yourself together? Can't you put the other one behind you, Margaret? Forget him? We could make a fresh start, if only you'd forget the past.'

Margaret felt the tears welling up in her eyes. How could she forget her little son? His tiny body taken away before she had held him or suckled him. Taken away in the dark of night and hidden in that bleak field, without the consolation of a Christian burial. How could she forget him? His soul in some limbo, in a vague place where they could never be together? Every day she brought flowers and placed them on the little mound. Every day a tiny bouquet of daisies or marigolds or snowdrops. And she would sit with him and talk to him and sing to him. But how could she be sure that he could hear her? Where was he? She had prayed over that mound. Surely God would hear her prayers? But the priest had told her that her son was in limbo. How could she live with the knowledge that they could never be together?

Margaret turned her face into the pillow, feeling Owen's arm around her as she did so. Owen could never understand. He loved her, but he could never, ever understand. She had given him Nessa – their beautiful, gentle daughter. But her son needed her more. He had nobody only her, and she would never abandon him.

# CHAPTER TWO

I t was going to be a very special birthday. A birthday with two numbers had to be special. Nessa felt an instant sense of satisfaction when she awoke and remembered that she was now ten, and Killian and Bridget were still only nine. The room was shrouded in half-light, and Nessa snuggled down into her quilt. It was Saturday, so she wouldn't have to get up for school, and the day stretched ahead, open to endless possibilities. She could hear the clatter of buckets and churns, and the lowing of the cattle waiting to be milked. It was too early to get up; too early and too cold. She dozed off.

'Happy birthday, Nessa!'

Mama,Grandma and Hannah were sitting at the kitchen table, tea steaming in front of them.

'Get that porridge inside you now', Hannah said as she gave her a birthday hug. Her mother leaned over to kiss her.

Nessa looked at the two parcels on the table, one bulky, the other neatly wrapped and tied with a ribbon.

'Are they for me?'

'Who else? Aren't you the birthday girl?' Hannah smiled at her.

Nessa opened the big parcel first.

'Oh Grandma, what a lovely colour. How did you knit it without me knowing? I would have seen that gorgeous red wool – it's the colour of holly berries.'

'Twas done while you were at school, and it had me nearly blinded getting it finished in time. It will be nice and bright for you to wear on Christmas morning, and warm too!'

'I love it, Grandma. Now what's this?' Nessa turned to the smaller parcel.

'Hannah, it's so pretty!' Nessa picked up the locket and chain, and held it against her. The locket was shaped like a heart, and had a cavity in it for keeping a picture or a photograph.

'I got it for you on the mainland,' Hannah said, pleased at Nessa's delight. 'It's silver, so don't you lose it now.'

'I won't Hannah. I'll be very careful with it.' It was the first piece of jewellery Nessa had owned, and it made her feel very grown up.

'Isn't it beautiful, Mama? And the jumper – isn't that the nicest jumper I've ever had?'

'It is indeed, love. Your grandma is very good to you, and the locket is a dote. You must get a nice picture to put in it'. Her mother fastened the locket into place.

'Don't you want to know what Dada and I have got for you?' she said, as she patted her daughter's hair into place.

'Oh yes! What is it? Is it something special?' This was turning out to be an even better birthday than she had hoped for.

'When you've finished your breakfast you can see it. It's in the porch.'

'I know what it is! I know what it is! Oh, I just hope it's what I think it is.'

Nessa gulped down her porridge and tea, and rushed out to the porch. Her father appeared at the doorway just then, a smile on his face as he saw her excitement.

'Happy birthday, Nessa! And no broken bones, mind.'

'Oh Dada, Mama ... it's what I've always wanted. Is it really mine? Just for me?'

'Just for you,' her father nodded. 'Twould be a bit on the small side for myself or Thomas, and your mother has her own!'

Nessa reverently stroked the gleaming black bicycle. It was a sturdy Raleigh, with a wicker basket and a bell on the front, and a spring carrier on the back. She got up on it and slowly circled the yard, feeling the power of her feet on the pedals. Round and round, gathering speed, hearing the hum of rubber on cobbles. She had learned to ride on Mama's bicycle, but on this one she could sit on the saddle and still reach the pedals.

'Can I cycle to school on it, Mama?' she shouted, still circling the yard.

'Yes, if you're careful.'

'And can I go to the village, and bring messages home for Grandma in the basket? And cycle to Mass by myself? And visit Killian and

Bridget?'

'Yes, yes and yes, but not all on the same day!'

Hannah and Nessa's grandmother had come out to the porch to watch, and Nessa was conscious suddenly of her whole family united in a rare way, in loving and admiring her. Then her mother turned and went into the house, and her father waved at her and went around the side to the dairy.

'Put your coat on child, if you're staying out there,' her grandmother shouted at her before she and Hannah returned to the kitchen.

Nessa was alone with her beautiful new possession. This was certainly the best birthday she had ever had. Now she wouldn't have to wait for Thomas to take her in the cart to places that were too far to walk to. Now she could go anywhere she pleased. The whole island would be hers, and when the summer holidays came she and Killian could explore the other side of Inishbawn and see those caves in the white cliffs which had always fascinated them. They could go fishing and take picnics and search for rare shells amongst the rocks. Maybe her mother would now let her come with her on her trips. Mama wouldn't have to be lonely ever again. The two of them could cycle together. Even as she thought of this, Nessa knew that her mother would not want her with her. She never talked about her cycle trips, not even to Nessa's father. She hadn't even answered back when they had all shouted at her on the evening of Nessa's first Communion. Nessa wondered, not for the first time, why everyone had been so angry that day two years ago. Why was everyone so secretive? But now she was ten, and she had her own bicycle, and Dada had told her that she could go anywhere she pleased on it, just as long as she was careful.

That afternoon Killian was helping Thomas to repair some fencing in the top field of their small farm when he heard shouts from the roadway. He ran to the boundary wall just as Nessa appeared, peddling furiously uphill, her red hair streaming out behind her, her cheeks flushed from the exertion.

'Killian. Killian. Look at me! See what I've got. It was my birthday present.'

Killian's eyes opened wide. 'Oh, it's beautiful, Nessa. Happy birthday. Now we can cycle everywhere together, if my old crock can keep up with your Raleigh.'

Nessa jumped off the bike.

'Do you want to take a spin Killian? Go on. You have a go.'

Killian tried out the bike, then said 'I've got a present for you too, Nessa. Lady's pups are weaned and ready to go to their new homes, and I've been keeping the black and white one for you. Come over to the house; he's all ready, and you can put his box in the basket of your bike and give him a spin home.'

Nessa knelt beside Lady and cradled her pup, which she had already named Toby.

'Don't be sad, Lady. I'll take great care of your son, and I'll bring him to visit you when he's older.'

Lady licked her hand and then licked her black and white offspring.

'She looks so sad,' Nessa said.

'She won't miss him,' Killian reassured her. 'Not while the other two are with her. She'll hardly notice he's gone.'

'I hope you're right. It's so cruel to take away her baby.'

'No, it's not. I'll be keeping Bran, so she'll always have one – just like your mother had you, when *your* brother died.'

Nessa's heart missed a beat. 'What brother? I've no brother.'

'You haven't because he's dead, but you would have if he'd been alive! My mother said he'd be Brendan's age by now if he'd lived, and they'd have been great friends and gone everywhere together.'

Nessa's grip on Toby tightened.

'What *happened* to him? They never told me about him.'

'They didn't tell me either,' Killian said in a matter-of-fact way, 'but I heard my mother and father talking about it. It was after our first Communion; remember your mother didn't come to the school with the other mothers?'

'Yes.'

'Well, that's why! My mother says she's still mourning her lost baby; she's never got over him.'

'What happened to him?'

'I don't know.' Killian got to his feet and put an armful of fresh straw into Lady's bed. 'Something to do a kick from a cow, or a pony stepping on your mother or something. I don't know. Anyway he was dead when he came out. Nurse O'Grady was with your mother and she told everyone that 'twas a boy, and there was no point in baptising him 'cause he was dead.'

Nessa felt the tears prickling her eyes. She was not going to cry in front of Killian. She was not going to cry on her birthday, with little Toby cuddled in her arms and the beautiful Raleigh waiting to take her home to Derryglas. But why had nobody told her? Why did nobody say that she had a brother? Poor Mama. No wonder she looked sad. So far away from her own home on the mainland, and then her baby dying. Poor Mama. But maybe Killian was wrong. Maybe when he overheard the conversation, they had been talking about someone else.

'I've never seen his grave,' Nessa said. 'Wouldn't he be in the McDowell plot beside the Church? I've never seen his name on the headstone.'

'Course he's not in that grave. Didn't I tell you he wasn't baptised? Everybody knows that they can't put unbaptised people in the church graveyard! They go to limbo. Don't you remember learning that in the Catechism?'

Everything began to slot into place. Mama's sadness, her trips on the bicycle. It all began to make sense. She had had a baby brother. Poor Mama. That was the reason why Hannah and Grandma didn't like her. It was because she spent all her time visiting the dead baby instead of working hard on the farm like the other island women.

Nessa buried her face in Toby's soft fur, and felt his body tremble against her cheek. He was a funny looking pup, with one side of his face white and the other black, and one ear that stuck up while the other was folded down. Killian's father had said he was the runt of the litter, but Nessa had loved him best from the time she had first seen him. And now he was hers, and she would never be lonely again. Toby would come everywhere with her.

'I'll take Toby home now.' Nessa didn't want to talk any more with Killian. She just wanted to be home in Derryglas, to think about what she had just learned, and to know that all the family were there, safe. She wrapped the pup up in an old coat that Killian gave her, and put his box into the basket of her new bicycle. At first Toby thought it was a game, and he stood with his paws on the edge of the basket, yelping, but once Nessa began to cycle, the motion immediately calmed him and he curled up on the coat and went to sleep.

Hannah fixed up a bed in the kitchen for Toby to sleep in that night.

'It's just for this first night, mind, because it's your birthday. Tomorrow he goes out to the hayshed. He'll be fine and warm out

# Phil Young

there, and maybe he'll frighten off the rats.'

The plaintive sound of the pup crying woke Nessa. The house was in darkness. Nessa crept down the stairs. In the kitchen the embers of the peat still glowed, giving a soft muted light and throwing huge shadows along the walls. Toby watched her approach, tail wagging, eyes shining. She picked him up and felt the warmth of his body against her own cold one. Then, cuddling him to her, she crept back up the stairs and slid with the pup into bed.

# CHAPTER THREE

Nessa and Killian lay, half hidden by the high grass, on the edge of the cliffs overlooking the sea. Between them Toby lay panting, unsettling dreams causing his nose to twitch and his eyelids to shiver. The grass was warm beneath them, humming with hidden life. Beyond the swell of the sea they could see the mainland, the windows in the harbour town of Ballymona glinting in the sunlight. The fishing boats below them shrank and expanded with the rise and fall of the waves, and the channelled path of the ferry boat seemed to cut a pattern like a ribbon stretching out ahead of them. Though it was only May, there was a sleepy warmth in the air. It was Saturday morning; no school for two full days, and Nessa sighed with contentment.

'Will you come across on the boat with me later on?'' Killian's question cut into her drifting thoughts.

'Can't. Hannah wants me to whitewash the walls with her.'

'I'll help you with that after school on Monday if you come across with me today.'

'No. She wants to get it done today while the weather is dry. Anyway, why do you want to go over to Ballymona?'

'My father wants me to pick up some stuff for him. We could walk around the town, look at the shops. And it's a good day for the boat. You can do your old whitewashing any time.'

'No I can't. Hannah'll be sour if I don't help her. Anyway I hate going over there. You know that. I was over there last month with Dada, and that was enough for me. It was too crowded and noisy.'

Nessa's trips to the mainland were few and far between. When Hannah was making a rare trip to Ballymona Nessa sometimes had to go with her, to help her bring the shopping back on the ferry, and now and again her father liked her to come with him on market day. But to Nessa these trips were something to be suffered. Her mother never went to the mainland, and Nessa was aware that there was bad blood between her and the family she had left behind. Mama never discussed her past, any more than she discussed the baby buried in the killeen, but from comments of Hannah and her grandmother, Nessa knew that Mama's parents hadn't wanted her to marry an islandman, and when she had defied them, they would have nothing more to do with her. If people on the mainland were like that, Nessa didn't want to bother with them. They could keep their old shops and their lights and their noise. Inishbawn had everything she would ever want, and she intended to spend the rest of her life there.

'Well I'm going over anyway.' Killian got up, wiping the loose grass off his jumper. 'They're opening a cinema in Ballymona. Did you know that?'

'Who cares? Who wants to look at some silly old pictures. I'd much rather be reading and making up my own pictures.'

'Well, I want to see it. Most of the other lads want to see it too. It's you who's the stick in the mud. You never want to go anywhere!'

Looking at him through half closed eyes, Nessa noticed for the first time how tall Killian had suddenly got. He had always been shorter than her. He stood now on the headland, looking out to sea. Nessa, still lying on the grass, studied him. He had changed. Not only was he tall, but he had also got broader, with wide shoulders stretching the loose wool of his jumper. His wrists dangled below his sleeve cuffs. He had got very restless lately. No longer content with the quiet pattern of their days on Inishbawn, he was now for ever looking for excuses to take the boat or the ferry to the mainland. She knew he had made new friends there, sons of the fishermen who lived by the harbour. Sometimes if the sea was rough he would stay with them overnight, and return to Inishbawn full of the excitement of well lit streets and lively companions. But she hadn't wanted to know anything of his adventures. It was like when she was a little girl and she would press her hands over her ears when Hannah and Grandma had quarrelled with her father about her mother. She did not want to hear it. It wasn't happening. Now she wanted Killian to stay the same, and to find all he needed here in Inishbawn, just like she did. But Killian was twelve, and was already half a man.

Nessa had come to terms with the changes in her own body. The transition from childhood to adolescence had been smooth – no stormy swings in her temperament. For Killian however it was different.

One day he was her best friend, fun loving, confident and amusing. At other times he would be silent and sullen, and critical of what he called her boring ways. Those times usually followed a trip to the mainland, which increasingly seemed to rouse feelings of dissatisfaction and longing in him. Like Nessa, Killian was approaching the end of his schooldays in the island school. He was determined to make something different of his life. Brendan would be the one to inherit the farm, but Killian was free to make his own future. Already his mother had written to relations in America, who were all doing very well for themselves. It was understood that when the time came they would send Killian his passage money, and set him up in something over there. His plan was to make lots of money and then return to Inishbawn a rich man.

'You're blocking off the sun from me. Sit down, can't you?'

Nessa pulled herself up into a sitting position. She could see the frown darkening Killian's face as he turned to her.

'You're not coming with me then. Are you?'

'I told you. I can't, Killian.'

'Right then, please yourself.'

He picked up his bike from the grass and jumped on.

'Will I see you at Mass tomorrow?' Nessa asked. 'We could go swimming afterwards if the day is nice?'

'Maybe,' he shouted over his shoulder, the wind carrying his voice out to sea. Then the bike disappeared over the ridge of a hillock and out of her sight. Toby pushed his nose against her face, and she stroked him, glad of his company. She seemed to be surrounded by people who needed careful handling, who were always looking for an excuse to fight.

Nessa was uneasy with the changes she saw in Killian. She hoped he wasn't going to spoil the summer with his moods. Summers on Inishbawn had always been wonderful, with swimming, fishing, boating and helping with the harvest. She tried to block out the conversation she had had with Miss O'Driscoll, her teacher, yesterday. She had been trying to shut it out all morning, but now, in her despondency at Killian's half-quarrel with her, she let it surface to the front of her mind.

Miss O'Driscoll had been teaching in the island school for only a year, and had injected a tremendous vitality into the job. For a start, she was young, fresh from the training college in Dublin. Also she was an islander herself, and was fired with a crusading spirit to educate the rapidly shrinking young population and prepare them for the modern world. At thirteen, Nessa was one of her senior pupils, and she liked the calm easy-going redhead. She had asked Nessa to stay on after school to help her with some preparatory work for the junior class, and in the informal atmosphere of the empty schoolhouse she had questioned her about her future plans.

'You'll be finishing here in July, Nessa?'

'I suppose so, Miss. I could stay on until I'm fourteen though. A couple of the girls did that last year.'

'A total waste of time,' Miss O'Driscoll frowned. 'There's nothing else for you to learn here. You should be going on to secondary school. Can your parents afford to send you to a boarding school on the mainland?'

Her direct question had jolted Nessa.

'I suppose they could ... but I never thought about it.'

'Do you mean to say you haven't discussed it with them?'

Nessa, picturing her mother's vague expression whenever she tried to talk to her, and her father's preoccupation with the farm and with keeping the peace between the women in his house, had shaken her head.

'They never went to a secondary school, so why would they want me to go?'

'Because it would be a terrible waste if you don't. You're very bright Nessa – you could hold your own with the best of them in any school in Ireland. And if you don't get an education, what kind of a future will you have? Staying here in Inishbawn until you're old enough to marry? You deserve more than that. With a bit of education you could find a job in the civil service up in Dublin, or in the bank, or maybe get into training college. You have to set goals for yourself, Nessa.'

'But I like being here in Inishbawn, Miss. I'd hate to work in the civil service in Dublin.'

'Ah, you think that now, but in five or six years time you'll see that life has passed you by, and it'll be too late then. And if you love living in Inishbawn that much, have you thought that there might be an opening in the school here for a trained teacher?' Miss O'Driscoll smiled.

'Sure there are hardly enough pupils for *one* teacher, Miss.'

'True ... but this one teacher doesn't intend spending all her life here. I may want to broaden my horizons you know!'

It was certainly worth thinking about. Learning was no problem to

Nessa. She knew she could pass all her exams, and as she loved reading and studying it would be no imposition on her. She had never thought that she could be a trained teacher though, and right here on the island at that. She had wanted to be a farmer, like her father. But he never took her seriously. He was happy to let her handle the little jobs – seeing to the hens and the calves and that. That's what island women did, as well as being experts in knitting, weaving and spinning. But the actual running of the farm was for sons, and since he had no son, she knew that her father was pinning his hopes on a future son-in-law. It wasn't fair. Just because she was a girl, it meant that she was ruled out for any serious, important work. If she couldn't be a farmer, though, then Miss O'Driscoll's idea of becoming a teacher was something worth thinking about. Especially if it meant that she could remain on Inishbawn and teach the island children.

Nessa, looking out across the sea, imagined what it would be like to arrive home to Inishbawn from training college to an enthusiastic welcome from all the families who wanted her to teach their children. She saw herself imparting knowledge in the little stone schoolhouse where she herself had her early education, where her Dada had received his, and her Auntie Hannah too. She would be an important part of island life, living in Derryglas and cycling to the schoolhouse every morning. Part of her monthly salary would be used to improve conditions for the poorer children, so that they would soon refer to her as the saintly Miss Nessa. The priest would look up to her and consult her about parochial and educational matters. The school inspector would report back to the Department that her teaching methods were way ahead of their time, and that the futures of the island children were secure in her hands ....

Toby's impatient whine cut in on Nessa's thoughts. She stood up, stretching. If Dada could only see what a wonderful teacher she would make, he would have no hesitation trusting her with the farm. Maybe she could do both. Teach and farm. As long as it meant that she could spend her life on Inishbawn, she didn't mind.

Nessa's despondency evaporated. She picked up her bicycle. 'Come on Toby', she shouted. 'Time for dinner, and then we'll tackle that whitewashing.' With Toby galloping along behind her, Nessa headed back to Derryglas.

# CHAPTER FOUR

Owen and Margaret sat stiffly in the little used parlour. Across from them, sipping tea from a fine china cup, sat Miss O'Driscoll. She had made a point of seeing Nessa's parents at Mass that morning, and had asked them if they could meet her in the afternoon to discuss Nessa's future. It had to be a formally arranged meeting, as it was impossible to talk in the crowded churchyard, and if she had simply cycled out to Derryglas she would have had to explain herself to old Mrs. McDowell or to Hannah. Miss O'Driscoll was aware of the friction in the McDowell household – that Margaret McDowell had been a bit 'strange' since losing her baby, and that her in-laws had little time for this woman who was such a poor wife to the much sought after Owen McDowell. It would have been easier for Maire O'Driscoll to let them sort out Nessa's future in their own way, but she knew what that would mean, and Nessa was far too intelligent to be left wasting her time in Inishbawn, waiting for the right husband to come along.

'So you see, Mr. McDowell,' she addressed her remarks mostly to Owen, 'you see how wrong it would be not to let Nessa get a chance of further education. She's so bright, and she could do so much more with her life if she had the extra education.'

Owen looked puzzled. He glanced across at his wife, but she was gazing out of the window at the fast-flying clouds scudding across the pale sky.

'Have you something in mind, Miss O'Driscoll? We appreciate your interest in Nessa, and I know she's a bright girl, but, well, there's plenty for her to do around here until such time as she meets someone she wants to settle down with.'

'Mr. McDowell!' Maire O'Driscoll's earnest face looked pained. 'The world is changing. Girls don't just sit round and wait for Mr. Right anymore – if they ever did. The intelligent ones, like Nessa, want to stretch their horizons. And when they do marry, they have so much more to offer – both to their husbands and to their children!'

Owen laughed. 'Well well, you're making a good case Miss. But you know yourself that to get secondary schooling Nessa would have to leave the island and board on the mainland. Or go to some boarding school. I don't know that she'd like that. Nessa loves Inishbawn. She loves her freedom'.

'Well, I could recommend some excellent schools, where she'd be really well looked after. The fees of course are quite high …'

'We'd manage,' Owen said. 'It isn't the cost that would worry me. It's more Nessa herself. I don't think she would take to a life of rules and regulations.'

'She'd get used to it. I did myself. I'm not saying it was easy, or that I didn't have some miserable times, especially at first, but I settled in. And I firmly believe that it was well worth the sacrifice.'

Owen shook his head. 'She would hate it. I know she would.'

'She doesn't have to go to a boarding school to get educated.' Margaret's voice cut in on what had been, up to this, a two sided conversation between Owen and the teacher. Now they both turned to look at her. There was an animation in her face which Owen had not seen for a long time, and an unusual brightness in her eyes.

'Isn't there a grand secondary school now in Ballymona? Run by the nuns. The same nuns that taught me when I was a girl?'

'That's all very fine, Margaret,' Owen said gently, 'but you're not proposing that the child travels back and fore between here and the mainland every day, are you? Think of the winter seas.'

'Of course not. But don't you see – she's got her grandparents living in Ballymona! My old bedroom must still be empty. She could stay there, go to St. Imelda's, and come back to Inishbawn at weekends … some weekends anyway. It would be the perfect solution.'

Margaret's cheeks were flushed, her eyes shining. Marie O'Driscoll looked at her curiously. The pale, silent woman, whom she was accustomed to seeing almost blending into the background, suddenly looked pretty and young.

'But that would be ideal, Mrs. McDowell,' the teacher said, catching her enthusiasm. 'I had no idea that she had living relatives in Ballymona. And St. Imelda's has a fine reputation.'

Owen stood up abruptly. 'Steady on now. We can't get this all cut and dried without talking to Nessa, and without ... well, sorting out some other details.'

He looked anxiously at his wife, and then turned to the teacher.

'We'll thrash it all out, Miss. We'll have a good talk about it, and we'll let you know what we decide. And we're much obliged to you for your interest in Nessa. She's lucky to have such a grand teacher, no mistake about it. And she thinks the world of you.'

Miss O'Driscoll took this, and the now standing figures of the two McDowells, to be her dismissal, and, thanking them for their hospitality, she left.

Owen took hold of Margaret's hot hand.

'What ails you, Margaret! What did you want saying that for? Sure you know your parents wouldn't have Nessa to live with them? They've never sent her so much as a card at Christmas. They have never even seen the child!'

Margaret clutched at his sleeve.

'I'll write to them. I'll write to my father and explain everything. And I'll write to Sister Gertrude. She wanted me to join the Order – she thought that highly of me. I'll tell her how impressed Miss O'Driscoll is with Nessa, and that there's nothing for her here in Inishbawn. She has to get away. I don't know why I didn't think of it myself. Inishbawn is no place for her. She has no future here.'

Owen's face darkened. 'Inishbawn is her home Margaret. And Derryglas will be hers some day. Who else would it go to?'

'She won't want this place. Why would she want to live here, in this God-forsaken spot, when she could have the whole wide world out there? This place that's still in the Dark Ages. That's only for the dead ...'

Her voice broke into sobs, and tears sprang from her eyes to run down her flushed cheeks. Owen took her in his arms and wiped away the wetness.

'Hush, hush, love'. He pressed his face against hers. 'It hasn't all been bad, has it? There were some good times surely? It wasn't what you were used to, I know that. But I never wanted you to be unhappy. There, there. My poor Margaret. My poor love.'

He stroked her face and her hair, and she felt the strength of his caring, and was overwhelmed by emotions which had been choking her for so many years.

'I don't want her here, Owen. The people here ... they don't want me.

They've never accepted me. And she'll be the same. Always an outsider.'

'She's not an outsider, Margaret,' Owen said gently. 'She has the island in her blood. It's part of her. And she loves it.'

'But I loved it too, Owen. I wanted to be part of it. But they wouldn't let me. They wouldn't accept me. And my poor baby ... my poor baby ...'

'Ah, I know. It's a terrible thing for a woman to lose a child. A terrible thing.'

'But why wouldn't they baptise him, Owen? Now I can never know ... never be sure.'

'But where's your faith, woman? God is good. He's not going to punish an innocent little baby just because of some rules, is he now? The child is in heaven, and it doesn't matter a thrawneen whether they buried him in the churchyard or in the killeen. Isn't it the one God, and aren't they only rules? I know my son is in heaven, and there's no one will tell me otherwise.'

'I wish I could believe you, Owen. I wish ... I wish ...' She pulled herself away from him and stood at the window. 'It's so lonely up there,' she said softly. 'So lonely, and only me to visit him. I have to be near him. He has to know that I'll never abandon him. But Nessa ... Nessa must get away from here.'

The crying stopped, and now she turned to her husband. She was calm and in control.

'Nessa must get her chance. Miss O'Driscoll is right. An education will give her a chance of a better life. My father will understand, and wasn't my mother always a great believer in education? They'll have her to stay. Yes, I'm sure of it. They'll be glad to have her stay with them.'

Having convinced herself that Nessa would be welcomed by her grandparents, Margaret straight away set about finding pen and paper to write the appropriate letters. Owen left the room unnoticed, deeply troubled at the prospect of yet another snub for his wife, and humiliation for his daughter.

Nessa spent the afternoon fishing off the rocks with Killian, and returned to Derryglas before teatime to help with the milking and get her other chores done. The May sunshine had spattered a sprinkling of freckles across her nose and cheeks and her hair glowed against the skyline as she pedalled into the yard. Watching her arrive, Owen thought with a pang that his daughter was no longer a child. A beautiful young woman had taken over at some stage, without him being conscious of the change. She jumped off the bike, all legs, movement and energy; throwing the now battered bike against the wall, she hurried into the house.

'Where's everyone?'

Without waiting for an answer Nessa cut a chunk of soda bread, plastered it thickly with butter, and sat on the edge of the table. Hannah, stirring the bucket of poultry mash by the scullery door, looked up crossly.

'Did you throw your bicycle against the wall again? One of these days your grandmother will fall over it and break her leg. Haven't you been told often enough to put it in the shed?'

'I'll do it in a minute. I was starving. I just had to have a slice of bread or I'd have collapsed. Anyway, where is everyone?'

'Your mother is where she always is, and your father is beyond with the cows. Your grandmother is about somewhere ... if she hasn't fallen over your bike. And of course the "visitor" has left this while.'

'Visitor? What visitor?'

'Oh, so you weren't in on it either, were you? Your teacher, that's who. Coming here to talk to your mother and father, and they all shutting themselves up in the parlour if you please.'

'Miss O'Driscoll was here?' Mixed emotions of apprehension and pleasure flitted across Nessa's face. 'I'll bet she was discussing what to do with me when I finish with the school in July.'

'Isn't there plenty for you to do here? I could do with some help. One "lady" about the place is enough.'

'Miss O'Driscoll wants me to go for further education, and maybe train as a teacher. I could be the next teacher here on Inishbawn!'

'Huh – what rubbish you talk!'

'No, it's not rubbish. Miss O'Driscoll said so. I'll go up and ask Mama – see what she wanted. It must have been important for her to come all the way out here on a Sunday afternoon.'

Nessa ran up the stairs and knocked on her parents' bedroom door. Her mother was sitting by the window, writing. She looked flushed and excited, and greeted Nessa with unusual warmth.

'Your teacher has been here – to talk about your future. She's pleased with your schoolwork and feels you should have the chance of going on to secondary school.'

'So I'd have to go to the mainland?'

'Of course. She suggested a boarding school, but your father was against that. He was afraid you'd be unhappy shut up in an enclosed place.'

Nessa's only knowledge of boarding schools had come from her reading of English girls' school stories. Tuck shops, netball, hikes in the country, midnight feasts – it didn't sound too bad.

'No I wouldn't mind it. I'm sure I'd get used to it ... and wouldn't I be home for holidays?'

'It would be lonely for you. You don't know what it's like to be among strangers, away from your home.'

Her mother's gaze drifted to the window. She stared out for a moment, and then turned back to Nessa.

'Miss O'Driscoll is right though. You do need to be exposed to the world outside this island. You can't grow up like a little savage; you should have a proper education! I've written to your grandfather. I've also written to Sister Gertrude of St. Imeldas in Ballymona. If she agrees to keep a place for you, then I'm sure your grandparents will let you stay with them'

Nessa's face fell. 'But ... didn't they throw you out when you married Dada? They wanted nothing to do with us. I couldn't stay with them. I don't even know them!'

'Don't be so dramatic, Nessa. They didn't "throw me out" as you put it. They just ... weren't happy with my choice of husband. They're old-fashioned. The islanders seemed a ... well, Inishbawn was a foreign country to them.'

'And you think they're going to invite me to stay now?' Nessa felt sick. It seemed that she had always, from early childhood, been conscious of the friction between the two families, and of the wrong which had been done to her mother. Her maternal grandparents had no place in her own life. Having to stay with them in Ballymona while she went to St. Imeldas would be the worst thing that could ever happen to her.

Her mother reached out, and touched her gently.

'They're your flesh and blood, Nessa. They're old and they're alone. It was my fault. I should have persisted. I should have written more ... and visited. They would have come round eventually. But I was stubborn, and I was hurt because they wouldn't accept your father. And then I had

... I had my trouble ..'

Her voice faded almost to a whisper. It was almost as if she was talking to herself. She turned back to the window and gazed out at the gathering darkness. The room was very silent, and Nessa sensed that her mother had once more withdrawn into her own private world. Quietly, she left the room.

Sister Gertrude's reply was the first to arrive. She wrote that she remembered Margaret very well, as she had been one of her most promising pupils. She had been disappointed when she had learned that Margaret had married so young and had gone to live on Inishbawn. But the ways of the Lord are mysterious and wonderful, and here now was a second chance being offered in the form of her daughter. The letter went on to say that there had been many changes in St. Imelda's in the last decade or so. Numbers had increased dramatically, girls were now being educated up to the age of eighteen, scholarship examinations were being sat for university and for top civil service jobs. They were now offering many opportunities for bright girls, without compromising the traditional religious ethos of the school. She assured Margaret that she would be happy to keep a place for Nessa in September, subject to her sitting an entrance examination in June, and undergoing an interview. The delicate matter of fees was touched on briefly in the letter. Sister Gertrude then suggested the twenty-fifth of June as a date for Nessa's examination and interview, and she added that she looked forward with great pleasure to seeing Margaret once more.

The reply from the Crowleys was much slower in arriving. The weeks went by. Sacks full of mail were dispatched from the mailboat twice weekly. These were collected at the harbour by Joe McCarthy of the post office, to be sorted and delivered by his son Jack, the island's postman. Nessa watched anxiously for Jack's familiar figure on the black bicycle, but any mail he brought was for her father, brown-enveloped and official-looking. Business and farming letters. Margaret said nothing. Owen said nothing. Hannah, however, lost no opportunity to urge Nessa to forget the whole silly idea.

'They're not going to get involved with you after all this time. Why should they? And aren't you better off here anyway? What is all that schooling going to get you, only the emigrant ship to America or to London! Have sense and stay here in Inishbawn.'

Hannah was terrified at the thought of losing Nessa to the 'other side'. She loved her niece with a singular and possessive love. If only the sister-in-law would take herself back to where she had came from, and leave Nessa in Inishbawn, Hannah would have asked for nothing more. It was what she prayed for! To have Nessa, Owen and herself tending to Derryglas and stocking it and building it up to be the finest farm on the island. The old woman wouldn't live for ever. Then it could be just the three of them. Owen should get that one locked away; he should have done it years ago. And then they could forget all this nonsense of sending Nessa to be educated in Ballymona.

On the 20th of June the letter arrived. A fat, white envelope addressed to Margaret in her father's rounded, childlike handwriting. Margaret took it from Nessa, who had rushed out to the yard when she saw Jack the postman coming. She turned it over and over, felt it and scrutinised it.

'Open it, Mama! Open it and tell me what they said.'

But Margaret put the letter into the pocket of her jacket.

'I'll read it later,' she said, averting her eyes from the stares of her mother-in-law and sister-in-law. She wasn't going to read it in front of their hostile gazes, or let them see her reaction – whatever it might be. She continued scouring the saucepans, and only when they were spotless, dried and stacked away did she make her way upstairs to her bedroom, leaving those downstairs in suspense.

Margaret closed the bedroom door quietly, and sat in the window seat. The sun was high in the sky, throwing silvery glitters on the calm sea. The room was hot, sapping Margaret's strength. She looked once more at the writing on the envelope, and then slowly and deliberately she broke the seal and removed the thick velour paper.

The letter began formally. It was as if her father was holding back from expressing any emotion, however oblique. He began the letter with 'My dear Margaret', and then went on:

Your mother and I were surprised at your request. We feel that, at our age, we couldn't take on the responsibility of looking after your young daughter.

Besides, it would be hard for her to settle down with us. However, your mother has asked me to say that if you would like to bring the child to visit us, then maybe we could work something out.

The letter was signed T. and E. Crowley, and its cold stiffness brought tears to Margaret's eyes. She hadn't expected a loving forgiveness, but this letter could have been written by a stranger. It was her father's handwriting, but contained nothing of his amiable personality. There had always been more bitterness in her mother's character, and Margaret suspected that the terms had been dictated by her. Well, she thought, it was no more than she deserved. She had defied them, had broken their rules. Now it was too late. There was this huge gulf between them, which could never be bridged. She didn't belong in Ballymona any more than she belonged in Inishbawn. The strongest bind she had now was that which bound her to her infant son.

But Nessa had her life ahead of her, and this was an opportunity to get her off the island. Margaret wiped away her tears, and sitting down at the dressing table, wrote informing her parents that she would bring Nessa to visit them on June 25th.

# CHAPTER FIVE

They travelled by ferry, which now left the island on a daily basis from the new landing pier. It was high summer and day-trips from the mainland to Inishbawn were popular with holiday-makers and families, who would picnic and swim on the island before returning to Ballymona on the evening ferry. Owen had offered to take Nessa and her mother across in the small boat, but Margaret had said,

'No. She'll be wearing her best clothes. She'll travel in a civilised manner.'

Now they sat, stiff and silent, on the wooden benches of the ferry. Beside them elderly island women clutched baskets of eggs and butter and creels of hand knit garments, ready for the market. Spare, weather-beaten men sat at the back of the boat smoking and talking. Margaret wore her best black coat and a hat with a narrow brim – an outfit that would shortly, as the sun rose in the sky, be far too warm. But it would be cold travelling back that evening, and moreover, the black coat would help her blend in with the women from the mainland. She would not go back, shawl-clad, looking like an island woman.

Nessa sat beside her, itchy with nervous anticipation. Her hair was pulled back from her face into a short plait, and tied with a ribbon which matched the brown of her knitted jumper and tweed skirt. Her buckled shoes shone from the furious polishing of the night before, and were topped by soft woollen stockings knitted by Hannah. Her grandmother had made a crochet purse for her, and her father had filled it with shillings which he had been collecting for her.

'Buy yourself something nice in the market, love. You don't often get a chance of a day out.'

It didn't seem like a day out to Nessa. An interview with Sister Gertrude, an examination, and most gruelling of all, an inspection by the grandparents whom she had never met. She glanced across at her mother. Her face was pale and tense. Nessa wondered what the reactions of her grandparents would be to the daughter they hadn't seen since her marriage. Would they find her odd and strange? As people on the island did? Or would they still be angry with her and be reluctant to have anything to do with her? Worse still, maybe they would want her to leave Inishbawn and come back to live in Ballymona. Nessa felt a shiver of fear. She wished that this day out was over, and that she could be safely back home again.

The ferry chugged in to the landing stage. The passengers filed out silently, to merge with the noisy hustling of the fishermen landing their catches on the quay and the fishwives haggling over prices. Nessa held her mother's arm as they walked up past the harbour shops, just opening their shutters to the morning light. People looked curiously at the two of them, obviously from the island, yet not quite island in dress or appearance. Her mother stared straight ahead, briskly putting distance between themselves and this harbour area. This area where, in another life, she had rushed down to meet Owen's boat, excitement making the blood pound in her head. Where they had huddled in darkened doorways, clinging in silent longing before Owen's return to Inishbawn, leaving her with an aching emptiness.

This was familiar territory for Nessa. Whenever she came to the mainland, with Hannah or with her father, it was here by the harbour that they did their shopping. People here understood the needs of the islanders and catered for them in a way that would not be found in the town proper, where the islanders were regarded with suspicion. It was here, in the Harbour Hotel, that Owen would go for his drink, Nessa sitting beside him on the bench sipping her fizzy lemonade, the bubbles tingling in her nose. It was here too that Hannah and herself would go for a bit of dinner, their parcels lumpy at their feet. One shilling and sixpence each for a plateful of bacon, cabbage and potatoes, and a cup of tea with some Marie biscuits – food that was familiar and yet excitingly different because it was served by a waitress in a white apron and with a white frilly cap hiding her hair.

Now Margaret and Nessa passed the Harbour Hotel and headed up into the town. The chill of the morning still clung in the air, a reluctant sun skulking behind the clouds. The bellowing of the beasts from the Market Square carried down to them on the slight wind, a wind which also carried the whiff of pigs and pig manure from the trucks that were

gathering around the town. Activity mounted as they approached Main
Street. Here the shops were preparing for business. Men in khaki coats
or sack aprons brushed the footpaths outside their doorways. Women
polished shop windows. A youth arranged fruit in the window of the
vegetable store. Up over the Chemist's shop a striped blind was being
unfurled by the elderly chemist, the sinews on his thin white arms
bulging with the effort. Nessa longed to stop and gaze at the display of
perfumes and creams in this window, but her mother hurried on, not
slowing to acknowledge the raised caps or the curious glances. When
they came to Kavanaghs' Emporium, Margaret gasped at the display of
affluence in the lavish exterior and the deeply recessed windows.
Kavanaghs had expanded to take in what used to be two private houses
on one side and P.J. MacCarthys' Grocers on the other. Now it spread
over almost a full block, beautifully laid out with mens, ladies and
childrenswear on one side, and grocery and hardware on the other side.
The Kavanagh brothers had certainly prospered! While Margaret and
Nessa hesitated, taking in the wonders of this display, a portly man
wearing a long white apron over dark trousers came to the door. His
bald head rose moonlike above the purple folds of his face, and his
protruding eyes fixed on the two women who were looking so awestruck at his shop.

'Good morning, ladies!' His voice had become deeper with the years,
but it still had the nasal tones that Margaret remembered.

'Good morning, Joe.'

He looked closer, then his jaw sagged.

'Is it Margaret? Margaret Crowley? Well, glory be to God! Well, well ...
I didn't recognise you ... Margaret Crowley!'

'Margaret McDowell now, Joe. And this is my daughter Nessa.'

Nessa extended her hand to this stout gentleman, whose forehead
was now breaking out in beads of sweat.

'She has a great look of yourself Margaret ... when you were a young
one. A great look.'

He took Nessa's hand in his and shook it vigorously.

'Your mother was a real beauty, so she was, Nessa. There wasn't a
finer looking woman in the parish!'

Nessa smiled and glanced at her mother's faded face. Two spots of
red had spread across her cheeks. Maybe she had looked pretty once.

'Are you paying a visit to the old couple? It was only last Sunday at

Mass I was talking to himself, but he didn't let on a word about you coming. And your mother is looking well ; she'll be delighted to see the granddaughter. Would you come inside, the two of you? A cup of strong tea to warm you up after the boat?'

Joe Kavanagh babbled on, not waiting for a reply, telling her how pleased his wife would be to meet them. She was one of the O'Gormans from Lisgorman Farm. 'You remember them? A big family of girls?' He had married Gretta, the second girl.

Margaret cut him short. 'They'll be expecting me at home, Joe. Maybe I'll get a chance to talk to you again, and to meet Gretta. But right now we have to hurry. We have a lot to do.'

'You'll be staying the night ...?'

'No. No ... we're getting the ferry back this evening. But maybe we'll get a chance to see you before then. Goodbye, Joe. Give my regards to all the family.'

Margaret took Nessa's arm and firmly steered her away. Nessa would have liked to have gone into the Emporium to see what other delights were displayed inside. She wondered what Gretta was like, and who else made up the Kavanagh family . But her mother hurried her on up the street until they came to the much more modest Crowley's Store. Gold lettering on a plain green background, one large window displaying faded advertisements for Fry's Cocoa, Lyons' Tea, Willwood's Sweets, Jacob's Biscuits. Rows of glass jars filled with coloured sweets. Open boxes showing wools and threads, stockings, underwear, aprons. The shop door was open. The shop was empty and there was no one behind the counter. Margaret pressed the bell and a girl of about fifteen appeared. She looked blankly at Margaret and Nessa.

'Yes? Can I get you something?'

'Are they home ... Mr. and Mrs. Crowley?'

Margaret felt a pang, seeing this young girl standing behind the counter where she had stood at that same age. Business seemed slow ; if this child could handle everything there couldn't be much going on. No doubt Kavanaghs' Emporium had absorbed all the business in Ballymona. What place would smaller shops have when Kavanaghs stocked everything?

'Are they home?' she repeated, as the girl seemed puzzled as to what to do with these unexpected visitors.

'Oh, they are. They're above stairs in the kitchen. Do you want to go on up to them? Or will I tell them you're here?'

'No, that's alright. I'll go straight up.'

Nessa followed her mother through the door at the back of the shop, and up the stairs. After the shabbiness of the shop, the room they now entered was large, bright and warm. Feeling as if she were watching a scene in a dream, Nessa stood in the doorway as her mother went ahead of her into the room. A red and white cloth covered the long table, set for breakfast. Two people – her grandparents – were sitting at the table. The man was stooped, with a wrinkled face and white hair. The woman, good looking, with hair that must once have been auburn but was now faded and streaked with grey. She stopped in the act of pouring tea from the earthenware teapot. Her eyes turned towards the door. Nessa watched fascinated as she lowered the teapot. The silence seemed to go on for ever, and then from the far side of the room came a shriek.

'Margaret, child. Is it you? Is it yourself, come home to us?'

Mary Kate opened her arms and Margaret crossed the room to be enfolded into the layers of mismatched clothing, and hugged and slapped and stroked.

'Oh Mary Kate ... you haven't changed a bit. You're just as I remember you. Oh, Mary Kate, how I've missed you!'

Margaret disentangled herself from the old woman's embrace, and turned to her parents. Her father got up from the table and approached her shyly.

'It's been a long time ... too long. I'm ashamed we let it go so long.'

He pressed her hands in his, and turned to his wife. Ellen Crowley still sat as if transfixed. She made no move to get up and join the little tableau at the other side of the table. Nessa, watching in silent fascination, wondered what her grandmother's reaction would be. Margaret, her hand still in her father's, looked at her mother, unsure of herself.

'Mother ... how have you been? You look well.' Her voice trailed off as the older woman still sat, staring at her. It seemed forever before she spoke, and when she did, it was with a firm effort to control the emotion in her voice.

'Has it been all you wanted, Margaret?' she said. 'Has life as an islander's wife been what you'd hoped for?'

Looking at her daughter's face, etched with lines, she already knew the answer, and her heart twisted in pain for the girl, full of freshness and hope, who had left Ballymona. The years between rolled away, the bitterness of defiance and anger with them, and what she now felt for this woman who had chosen such a difficult path was pity. Pity, and a protective love which she had buried so long ago. Tim Crowley drew Margaret forward just as Ellen rose from the chair, and the three of them merged in silent union, Margaret's face buried in her mother's shoulder.

Nessa stood awkwardly by the doorway, an outsider observing this strangely intimate scene. She felt distant from it, as if she were studying a picture in a book, where the characters were people she had been reading about, playing out a role expected of them. The dreamlike sequence was suddenly interrupted by a second shriek from Mary Kate.

'Margaret! What are you thinking of – leaving that poor child standing in the doorway like a stranger. Come in love. Come over here until we take a look at you.'

Mary Kate pulled Nessa into the room. From the corner of her eye Nessa saw the group at the table unfolding, and her mother, blotchy-faced and red eyed, turned towards her.

'Nessa,' she said, 'this is my ...our family. Your grandparents, and of course Mary Kate.'

Nessa shook hands gravely with her grandfather, and touched cheeks with her grandmother. She felt no intimacy with them, and she sensed their shyness of her. The sensation of standing outside of herself and observing their reactions was strong, and she wondered at her lack of emotion.

'She's like you, Margaret,' her grandfather said. 'She has your colouring - and the same beautiful smile you always had.'

'She has a look of her father too,' her grandmother added. 'Around the eyes she's like him.' The statement hung in the air as if waiting for someone to expand on it, and it was Mary Kate who broke the tension.

'It doesn't matter a bit who the child looks like! Isn't she herself, and she seems to me to be in need of a nice hot cup of tea. Am I right, girl?'

Nessa smiled, feeling an easiness with her that she couldn't feel with her grandparents. Mary Kate pulled out a chair for her and poured her a cup of tea from the pot. She buttered two slices of brown bread and told Nessa to 'eat up now!'

Nessa sat down, and discovered that she was hungry, and that the fingers which encircled the cup were white and cold. It seemed such a long time ago since they had left Derryglas to catch the ferry. As she ate and drank in silence, she listened to the talk going on between the others, who seemed to have forgotten her presence.

'You've a grand new landing pier on Inishbawn they tell me?' Tim struggled to keep the conversation on a less emotional level.

'Yes,' Margaret replied. 'It's much easier now for the ferry. You should come across yourself during the summer. It's no journey these days.'

'Ah sure, we're past that now. We're too old to be making the sea journey.'

'I should have come back to Ballymona .... to see you. I should have come long before now. I meant to. I wanted to ... I'm sorry I left it until now.'

'It wasn't your fault. It was ours. We were in the wrong. We were very wrong. Especially after... after the ... Ellen, tell her. We haven't had a minute's ease since you left, with the worry of you and the wondering about you.'

'You shouldn't have gone against us Margaret.' Ellen cut in on her husband's talk, and all at once the barrier was down and emotions and accusations spilled like rain from a swollen sky.

'You did a terrible thing to us. Marrying him in spite of us, and sneaking off to the island, and the whole of Ballymona talking about you and laughing at us behind our backs! Marrying the likes of him, and we having such great hopes for you.'

'Whisht Ellen,' Tim Crowley lowered his voice as he glanced across at Nessa. 'Sure there was no one laughing at us. And I'm sure Owen is a good man ... isn't he the child's father? What's done is done.'

'Weren't there plenty of men on the mainland who'd have given their right arm to marry Margaret? Plenty ... without her doing what she did!'

'But I loved ... love ... him, Mother. And Owen has always been kind to me.' Margaret's voice was barely a whisper, and Nessa had to strain to hear her.

'You loved the idea of love. And you picked him because he was different. Weren't you always like that ... dreaming about things you couldn't have, and yearning for the far off hills? That old island always held a fascination for you, and of course nothing would do you but to marry on to it. No half measures for you!'

Ellen's voice had taken on a hard and bitter tone now, and Nessa knew that if she raised her eyes from her food she would see anger on her grandmother's face and bleak misery on her mother's. She continued eating.

'It wasn't like that, Mother ...'

'Well, what was it like then? Tell me, what was it like? Was it the wonderful life you'd hoped for? Or was it what I'd warned you of? Hard work and cold winters and a backward people who were not yours and who would never understand or accept you?'

'That's enough Ellen,' Tim said. 'She's been bottling it up for years,' he explained to Margaret. 'Her heart was broken when you left – she never got over it. Tell me, Margaret, is it a very hard life? Are you happy?'

Nessa held her breath awaiting her mother's reply, and released it slowly as she heard Margaret's soft voice.

'It was my choice, Father. It was what I wanted for myself. Of course I'm happy.'

Nessa thought of the lone bicycle rides, the hours spent by herself in the bedroom, the tension between her mother and Hannah, and she wondered. But the reply appeared to be the one which was needed, for from there the tension lifted and the conversation took on a more general tone. Margaret answered questions about Inishbawn, mostly from her father. She enquired about neighbours, school friends, people with whom she had dealt in the shop in the old days. She asked about the young girl who was now serving behind the counter, and felt a faint tremor of interest when she learned that she was the niece of Murphy the Blacksmith, and a first cousin of her old school friend Stella. She was about to ask about Stella, what she had done with her life, but it all suddenly seemed like too much trouble. Ballymona and its inhabitants no longer impinged on her life, and it would take too much emotional effort to try to interest herself in their comings and goings. A great burden had been lifted from her in having, even partially, breached the rift between herself and her parents. She had been shocked to see how old and faded they had grown - what if one or both had died without breaking the silence between them? Her mother was still withholding herself, still wielding the power of the wronged over her, but they were talking, and that was something. Her father had accepted her as if she had never gone away, and kept glancing at her under his eyebrows.

Nobody asked her about her first baby. It didn't matter. What mattered now was to give Nessa a future, an education that would open doors for her. She would not have her trapped on Inishbawn, waiting to marry some fisherman or farmer, and then sinking into the narrow role of an island wife. She looked across the table at Nessa, now talking freely to Mary Kate. So long ago she used to sit there herself, drinking her cocoa after school, filling in Mary Kate on all the details of her day, impressing her with the things she had learned, boasting to her of her achievements. She had told Mary Kate things she would never have told her mother, and now she could see Nessa opening up to her in the same way. There was something so unjudgemental and so eager about Mary Kate's interest.

The talk stumbled on, hesitant at times, free at others, interrupted now and then by the shop bell, and conducted over a second and a third pot of tea. It was the angelus bell, dolefully announcing midday, that reminded the group that the morning had gone.

'Glory be to God, is that the bell, and not a stroke done around the place.' Mary Kate got up and began to clear away the table. Tim, his face flushed from the fire, went down the stairs to the shop, and Ellen turned to Nessa.

'What time are you taking your test up at the convent, Nessa?'

'Two o'clock ... and I've to meet Sister Gertrude first.'

'Then you'd better get yourself ready, child. You can use your mother's old room, and Margaret, you show her where the bathroom is. If you're accepted in the school, then you had better stay here. Your mother's room is empty, so you may as well use it.'

It wasn't the most gracious of offers, but it was an offer. Nessa, her heart heavy at the thought of sharing this woman's home, smiled her thanks, and followed her mother up the stairs to the attic room, which had not been used for such a long time. To Margaret's eyes it hadn't changed at all. The narrow bed still sagged in the middle like a hammock. The same rug, with its thin worn centre, still took the cold feel from the lino, and the window seat – her window seat, where she had spent so much of her childhood reading and day-dreaming and gazing longingly at the dazzling whiteness of the cliffs on Inishbawn – still bore the traces of blue ink blobs, and the scuff marks from her shoes.

'This was your room?' Nessa looked around with interest, flicking her fingers across the spines of the books on the bookshelf, and examining the ornaments on the dressingtable.

'Yes.' It was smaller than Margaret remembered, with its sloping ceiling and cluttered space. It was smaller than Nessa's room in Derryglas.

'I like it ... it's cosy. And I can see Inishbawn from here.'

Margaret showed her where the bathroom was, and told her to wash her hands and tidy her hair in preparation for the inspection by Sister Gertrude. She well remembered the sharp eye of the head nun, who with one glance could detect any flaws in personal hygiene.


At one forty-five Margaret and Nessa went through the empty shop, and out on to the street. The heat on the crowded Main Street was now overwhelming, and Nessa was immediately conscious of being overdressed and 'different' in her heavy clothes. They drew curious looks from locals, and Nessa noticed flickers of recognition in the eyes of many of the women as they rested on her mother. Margaret, however, strode straight on, looking neither left nor right. As they passed Kavanaghs' Emporium to take the hilly road up to the convent, Margaret couldn't but be aware of the bustling stream of customers making their way in and out of the black and gold doorway. It was no wonder Crowley's shop was empty on market day. With the flame of her mother's driving force burnt out, her father had not the wherewithal to keep the business going. He had never been a good businessman. The Murphy girl did not look too bright, or too interested in the job, but she was probably adequate for what custom there was.

A young nun opened the front door of the convent to them, gliding ahead of them down the corridor to the parlour at the very end. Here they awaited Sister Gertrude's arrival. Nessa sat on the high-backed chair and looked around her. She had never before been in such an intimidating room. The huge mahogany table in the centre was so polished that she could see the reflections of the two pictures hanging on the brown walls. One was of the agonised Christ, face contorted in pain, blood clinging to his head and neck. The other was a portrait of a stern-faced bishop, whose eyes seemed to meet Nessa's in an accusing glare. Ornately carved chairs surrounded the table, in the centre of which was a large Bible. A powerful smell of wax polish hung in the air. In spite of her thick clothing, Nessa felt the cold chill of the room.

The silence was broken by the click of the door handle. Margaret was startled to see how little the nun had changed. Not a line, not a wrinkle, not an ounce of weight more that she had had all those years ago.

'Margaret, how nice to see you! I do so like meeting up with my past pupils. And this is your daughter?'

The shrewd eyes were turned on Nessa, as Margaret introduced her and answered the nun's questions. Nessa felt that Sister Gertrude was looking right through her mind, reading all the doubts and fears there. She wanted to make a good impression, but she felt awkward and tongue-tied. Then Sister Gertrude smiled, and all at once Nessa felt that she was on her side.

The interview went well. Sister Gertrude remembered Margaret as being a bright pupil with tremendous potential which had originally been stifled by the narrow outlook of her parents, and later by an adolescent infatuation which had rushed her into an unsuitable marriage. The girl she saw before her now had a clear-eyed innocence about her. She answered her questions with a steady consideration which Sister Gertrude often associated with children brought up surrounded by adults. She was intelligent and serious, and the nun had no doubt but that she would make an apt pupil. How she would get on with her fellow pupils, however, was another matter. It remained to be seen whether she would have difficulty in adapting to the ways of the mainland children.

'You wouldn't be boarding with us, Nessa?' the nun asked. 'We do have a small boarding section now, you know.'

'No, Sister. My grandparents want me to stay with them – in my mother's old room.'

'That will be very nice for you ... although,' Sister Gertrude hesitated, then turned to Margaret. 'She might adjust more easily if she were living with our boarders. We draw them from a diverse background, as you know. Most of them start out not knowing anyone, so they quickly find their level and make new friends.'

'Nessa will have no difficulty making friends, Sister. She's a very easy-going child.'

Sister Gertrude said no more on the subject, though she had reservations. A girl who looked so different and dressed so quaintly would not have a smooth passage in any school. Children, in her experience, were uncannily quick to spot anyone who did not conform, and could make life miserable for the over-sensitive. Still, this girl had an inner tranquillity and self-containment about her. The nun hoped that she could rise above it.

'I think you can take it that we will accept you in September, Nessa,' Sister Gertrude said. 'All that remains now is for you to do our little entrance test. It's very simple – no more than a formality really. It should take you about one hour, and I will correct it myself, so that you shall have your answer before returning home.'

Sister Gertrude stood up and turned to Margaret.

'If you would like to come back in a couple of hours, Margaret? I'm sure you can find some shopping or whatever to do. In the meantime, I'll show Nessa to one of the classrooms where she can sit her exam.' She shook hands with Margaret, expressing her pleasure at having renewed their acquaintance, and hoping that she would visit the convent more often in the future.

Margaret wished Nessa good luck, and pressed her hand encouragingly before leaving.

'I'll be back for you at half past four,' she said.

Nessa felt a flutter of panic as she watched her mother's retreating back. Then she was alone with the head nun, being led back up the gleaming corridor, through a door with a jangling bell, down another equally polished corridor, and then through a double door and into a large classroom. This was at least three times as large as the classroom in Inishbawn school, and was laid out with rows of single desks, with a high desk on a platform at the front of the room. There were maps and charts all along the walls, and a blackboard on an easel on either side of the platform. Sister Gertrude went to the platform and removed some test papers from the desk.

'Now, Nessa. Sit anywhere you wish, and you may take the test papers in whatever order you like. You will find paper and writing material in the desks, and I shall expect you to have completed the questions at about half-past three.' She indicated the clock behind the platform, and then took up her own position at the high desk, upon which she placed what looked to Nessa to be an open prayer book. Nessa sat at one of the desks, found the paper and pens, and began her test.

The sun shone through the window, creating an airless atmosphere in the still room. Nessa wrote steadily, her face flushed, her clothes sticking to her. The test was easy. She could have finished it in half the time, but she lingered over the last questions, glancing periodically at the clock to see its hands creeping towards half- past three. The heat was intense. It was almost making her feel faint. She was conscious of her breath coming and going in shallow gasps, and wondered what would happen if she fainted. She had once seen a girl faint at Mass – falling with a thud in an undignified slump right in front of the altar, distracting the priest's attention at the moment of Consecration. She prayed that it didn't happen to her now in front of Sister Gertrude. The nuns would not want someone like that in their school – falling about the place every time it got warm.

Nessa wrote her answer to the final question, and with a low click the clock reached the half hour. Sister Gertrude stood up.

'Have you finished, Nessa?'

'Yes, Sister.'

'Good girl. You may leave your papers here and I shall look them over. Would you like to wait in the grounds? You look very warm. Take a little walk around the gardens and get a breath of fresh air.'

She opened the glass doors of the classroom, and Nessa walked out into the sculpted green of the lawn. She walked quickly along the path until she felt out of sight of the school, then stopped and took deep gulps of air until the dizzy, lightheaded feeling had passed. It was so good to feel the wind on her face – a warm, scented wind, heavy with the perfume of the roses that lined the pathway. Nothing like the rough, bracing winds that sang across Inishbawn even in the height of summer, but so good after the airless classroom. Everything here in the convent garden had a structured perfection that spoke of hours of dedication. Beyond the lawns, straight lines of early vegetables were bordered by fruit bushes heavy with unripe fruit. In the distance she could see the stooped figure of a gardener methodically clearing and weeding around the potato beds. At the end of the path a timber seat had been placed beneath an overhanging laburnum tree, and on this seat sat a very old nun, her beads clutched in her fingers and the monotone of her rosary audible to Nessa long before she reached her. Nessa walked around her, and silently up across the grass, without disturbing her prayers. The grass lawn brought her around the side of the convent to where it met the gravel driveway by the front entrance, just as her mother came up the driveway.

Margaret's heart sank when she saw the red face and damp hair of her daughter. What in God's name had possessed her to let her wear that heavy woollen jumper and thick skirt on a June day in Ballymona? She had forgotten the difference in the temperature between the mainland and the island. It was always cool on Inishbawn, even on the best summer days, with the Atlantic winds blowing across its exposed surface.

'How was the test? Was it hard? You should have taken that jumper off. You look roasted.' She touched her daughter's hot face.

'I *am* roasted.' Nessa tried to blow the damp hair off her forehead. 'I didn't know if I should take it off – I was afraid she'd say something to me. The test was simple.'

'Let's see what Sister Gertrude has to say then, and afterwards we'll just have time to call in to the shop for a cup of tea before heading down to the harbour.'

Nessa led the way back to the classroom. Through the open door they could see Sister Gertrude sorting papers on the desk.

'Ah, you're back, Margaret. No doubt Nessa has been telling you that she had no problem with the test.' She smiled at Nessa. 'I can see that she is going to make an excellent student. Just like her mother.'

'Then you'll take her in September, Sister?'

'We'll be happy to. You'll receive a formal letter of acceptance in the post, setting out details of fees, uniform, book list and so on. If there is anything else you wish to know, please don't hesitate to get in touch with either myself or Sister Katherine. She will be in charge of the first years.'

They spoke some more about the town, the island and the number of students now attending the secondary school, and then Sister Gertrude shook hands with Nessa and her mother and wished them a safe journey back to the island.

'Sure didn't I know she'd fly through it. Why wouldn't she?' Tim Crowley was weighing out flour in the empty shop when Nessa and her mother returned there, and his eyes lit up on hearing that Nessa had been accepted. Upstairs, Mary Kate hugged first Margaret and then Nessa on hearing the news. Ellen was more subdued.

'I'm sure you'll find it lonely here, child. We're not used to having young people around, and we're too old to change our ways. However, we'll see how we get on.

'She'll work hard and not give you any cause for worry,' Margaret assured her.

'And she'll be spending the weekends on the island – at least until the worst of the winter draws in.'

Tim came up to the kitchen to join them in a cup of tea.

'It's slack down below there. Breda can manage for a while,' he said in answer to the unspoken question in Margaret's eyes. 'It isn't like it used to be in the old days! Would the two of you not stay overnight? What's your hurry to get back?'

'Oh no, we couldn't do that,' Margaret shook her head. 'Owen will be meeting the ferry.'

'You could send word, couldn't you? What's one night, when we haven't seen you for such a time?'

'No, we have to get back.' Margaret was suddenly overwhelmed by an urgent need to return to Inishbawn. It was almost like a panic inside her. Her mind felt as if it was about to crumble at the mere thought of having to re-establish a relationship with her past, or re-connect the links that had been severed so long ago. It was too late now for all that.

'We have to get back,' she repeated, ignoring the disappointment in her father's eyes. Her mother turned away at her loud insistence, her features set in a closed hardness. She wasn't going to be hurt all over again.

'There are things to be seen to,' Margaret shot a warning look at Nessa, 'and Nessa will be expected back. She has her chores to do.'

'Well, if you must …We'll not be holding you.' Her father's tone was consciously light hearted. 'But you'll come back, won't you? The two of you will come to visit us before September?'

'Yes, I'm sure we will. And I'm so glad to have seen you both, and grateful to you for agreeing to take Nessa. I don't know what we'd have done if she couldn't have stayed with you. Owen would hate her making the sea journey on a daily basis – even if that were practical – and he didn't want her to be a boarder.'

'There's nothing to be grateful for,' her father cut in. 'It's the least we could do. Isn't that so, Ellen?'

'Yes, yes, of course.' Ellen touched her granddaughter briefly on the shoulder, and Nessa got the feeling that even this small intimacy was something which was distasteful to her grandmother.

Margaret hurried Nessa out of the shop and back down to the harbour. The ferry was due to leave in fifteen minutes. As they rounded the corner at the bottom of the street Margaret looked back. Her father and mother stood outside the shop door. Two small stooped figures, watching motionlessly. She waved, then continued on without slackening her pace. In less than an hour she would be back on Inishbawn.

# CHAPTER SIX

The steady drumming of the rain on the roof soothed Nessa into a state of reflective half-consciousness. The strain of almost two weeks of examinations had left her drained. It was the final day of the Leaving Certificate, and she had squeezed the last morsel of energy from her tired brain to tackle the history paper. She liked history. She hoped she had done enough to pass, but right now she was beyond caring. The culmination of five years at St. Imelda's, and if she didn't do well in her Leaving Certificate it would have all been in vain. How could five years have sped by so quickly, when at times each day had seemed to have been never ending? She stretched her body, aching from tension, and felt her toes pushing against the end of the little bed.

The first night Nessa had slept in this bed, she remembered, there had been a cold space between her feet and the end of the bed. She had changed a lot in those five years. Now she was taller than her mother ... almost as tall as her father. She had his slight build – an islander's build – with no spare flesh. She had her father's eyes too, calm, steady, with eyebrows and eyelashes so dark, they seemed incongruous with her creamy colouring and auburn hair. When she looked at herself in a mirror, trying to fix her face into a pose like she'd seen the good-looking girls in her class do, she was always aware that she was different - an odd mixture of McDowell and Crowley. She had always felt different too, and was *made* to feel different by her classmates and by her teachers. For five years she had done her best to come to terms with that. Nessa had tried hard to merge with the other girls, and it wasn't until her last year that she had finally accepted that she would never be one of them. Now her life as a schoolgirl was nearly over. Her years of travelling between Inishbawn and Ballymona were over too. The next Saturday she would return to the island, the long summer stretching ahead of her, to await her results and think about her future. A shudder of pleasure and anticipation ran through her at the thought of two unbroken months on Inishbawn.

Life with her grandparents, living above the store, had been a strange experience for Nessa. She had been so excited when the letter from Sister Gertrude had arrived at the end of July that first year, setting out formal acceptance and giving information about fees and uniform. She knew of no other girl on Inishbawn who had been a pupil at St. Imeldas, and she plagued her mother with questions about what the nuns were like and what the girls did after school, and what all the unfamiliar subjects like French, would be like.

'A fat lot of use that'll be to you,' Hannah said crossly. 'I don't see your mother needing much French when she's skiting off around the country on her bike!'

Margaret glared at her sister-in-law. Stupid, ignorant women, she thought. Both of them ... Hannah and her mother-in-law. What did they know? When Nessa had completed her education, she would see them for what they were. She would know then what her mother had suffered, and would thank her for giving her the opportunity to escape. Getting Nessa away from Inishbawn now seemed to Margaret to be a matter of urgency.

As soon as she could after the letter from Sister Gertrude had arrived, Nessa had cycled across the island to the Doyles, waving the white envelope like a flag in front of Killian and Bridget.

'It's all arranged. I'm going to St. Imeldas!'

'Oh, you are lucky,' Bridget's eyes opened wide in wonder. 'God, I'd love to be living in Ballymona. All those shops and the cinema and everything.'

'Well I wouldn't,' Killian retorted. 'I'd hate to be cramped into some rotten school all day long, and having to stay over there.'

'But I'll be coming home at the weekends,' Nessa said.

'That's what you think ... wait until the winter storms start. You'll be lucky if you can get home for Christmas.'

'You're just jealous! He's jealous, isn't he Bridget?'

Bridget laughed. 'Course he's jealous. Wouldn't he give his right arm to be taken on in a posh boarding school.'

'Just shut up, the two of you. Leave me alone.' Killian turned away sourly.

Killian's attitude to Nessa had changed as soon as he had heard that she was going to Ballymona. From then on he withdrew from her, throwing up a barrier between Nessa and himself. Suddenly he had no time to be with her. His days were full, and his evenings were spent on the hurley field with the other lads. He had always been a good sportsman, but now she rarely saw him without the hurley in his hand, or surrounded by boisterous friends, who told her to go away, when she tried to get Killian's attention. Nessa couldn't understand what she had done wrong. Had she said something? Or was he really jealous? It took the gloss off the summer for her and she eventually decided that she would have to confront him and have it out with him. She cycled over to the Doyles early one morning. She knew that it was Killian's week for the early milking, and that she would find him alone in the milking stall. He was sitting on the milking stool, his face pressed against the flank of the big black and white friesian. He looked up when Nessa entered.

'What are you doing here?'

'Nothing. I was awake early, and thought I'd go for a spin. Do you want me to help you? I could milk Flora – she knows me.'

'Suit yourself. There's a second bucket there.'

Nessa sat beside the gentle Flora, who turned curiously to reassure herself before allowing herself to be milked. Killian and Nessa worked in companionable silence, the soft morning light gradually creeping into the dim corners of the stall, the shufflings and rumblings of the cows sounding muted against the thick straw.

'I'll be off to the mainland next week.'

'I know.'

'Will you come to see me in the shop, when you're across in Ballymona?'

'What for?'

'Just ... just for a talk and a laugh. I'll have loads to tell you. All about my new friends and the school and everything.'

He didn't answer. She felt irritated by his silence and tried to goad him into some reaction.

'Course, I mightn't have much time to spare. I'll have all those new subjects to study, and I'll be very busy.'

'Yes. You'll be all stuck up and snobby, with your uniform and everything. Well, you needn't bother trying to find time for your old friends. I have plenty of other things to do.'

'So that's it. You are jealous!' Nessa stood up and glared at him across Flora's broad back. 'You think just because I'm going to St. Imelda's that I'm somehow going to be different? That's just stupid. I want to go to secondary school and there isn't one on Inishbawn, is there? So what am I supposed to do?'

'Who cares? Anyway, once you go over there you won't want to come back.'

His face was gathered into a scowl. He got off the stool and carefully covered the milk bucket with muslin, before pouring it into the churn.

'But I will, Killian. I will come back! I'll always want to live on Inishbawn. I'm going to train to be a teacher, so that some day I'll be able to teach here. We can still be friends. Nothing will change.'

Killian looked doubtful. 'You won't want to come back here. It will be too quiet after the town, and anyway who says you'll get a job teaching on the island? What about Miss O'Driscoll?'

'It was she who put the notion in my head, so there! She thinks I'd be able to take over from her eventually. And I won't find Inishbawn too quiet. You know how I love the island. You're the one who's always looking for an excuse to go to Ballymona, not me!'

'Yes. well, we'll see.' He smiled, looking more like the old Killian. 'Maybe I will come over to visit you. We could go to the cinema or something.'

Nessa finished with Flora and took the milk out to the churn. It was bright in the yard, with the early morning sunshine rolling back the bundled clouds. Everyplace looked clean and fresh. Nessa sealed the churn, and shouted to Killian that she was going home for her breakfast. She cycled home feeling much more lighthearted.

The first chills of autumn were just beginning to nip on that September morning when Nessa and Margaret set off for the mainland. Owen had already carried across her heavy case, and now Nessa clutched a little brown bag containing her schoolbooks and a few bits and pieces. Her new uniform – navy skirt and jumper, white blouse and black stockings – had been carefully placed on the bottom of the case, having first been inspected by Hannah and proclaimed 'grand ... plenty of room to grow.' Nessa wore her best coat, a good strong tweed, over a cotton blouse and skirt, and she pulled it across her as a shiver of anticipation went through her, watching the mainland draw nearer. Five years she would spend here. It stretched ahead of her, holding out promise of new friendships and new experiences. She was sad at leaving Inishbawn ; her grandmother had held her hand, lingering over their goodbye as if she would never see her again. Hannah had cried and warned her to 'mind yourself over there!' Her father had hugged her and told her she'd be fine – top of the class in no time – and had then added 'You're to come back to us if you don't like it over there, do you hear me now? There's nobody forcing you to stay.'

Toby had followed the trap all the way to the harbour, bounding along beside them, then taking short-cuts across the rocky fields and appearing in front of them, his black tail pluming out behind him. He had tried to jump on to the ferry, but was shooed off by the boatman, to be left sitting forlorn on the quayside.

'Goodbye, Toby,' Nessa shouted. 'I'll be back soon.'

Leaving Toby seemed to encompass all her feelings of sadness, and she was suddenly overwhelmed by a flow of tears. The engines of the ferry sprang into life and the boat moved off from the pier, Inishbawn gradually becoming just a speck on the horizon.

Nessa settled well into the rhythm of life above the shop in Ballymona. Her room was her retreat. It was where she studied, where she read, where she shut herself off from the noise of the street, and where she indulged her loneliness, sitting on the window seat drinking in the sight of the stark whiteness of the cliffs on distant Inishbawn. At first she had taken the ferry home each weekend, but, as Killian had predicted, the winter storms soon meant that there was never a guarantee of getting back in time for school on the Monday mornings, so weekly became monthly or sometimes longer. Even in the spring and summer, she found herself staying on the mainland. There was a lot of study to be done, there were various Saturday activities in St. Imelda's in which she was expected to participate. It seemed there was always something preventing her return. She tried to toughen herself, but inside was a well of aching loneliness that felt like a physical pain.

She got on well with her grandfather. He was easy-going and sentimental, spending hours telling her stories of Margaret as a little girl, Margaret as a baby, Margaret as a young woman walking out with the Kavanagh boy. Her grandmother was more guarded. It seemed to

Nessa that every time her grandmother looked at her, she saw Owen. She saw the man from Inishbawn who had shattered her dreams for her only child. Although she was always kind to Nessa, it was the sort of kindness one would extend to a stranger. She could not bring herself to like her, and that was never quite disguised. Nessa learned to live with it, and the attention which Mary Kate showered on her went some way to compensate. Mary Kate bossed her and scolded her and listened to her, just as she used to do with Margaret. At times she even called her by her mother's name, and Nessa suspected that she was a bit confused about her identity. She was getting on in years, but she still took charge of the cleaning and the cooking, and still made sure that 'himself and herself' were well looked after.

Sometimes Nessa helped out in the shop. She loved the sense of importance she got from fetching things for customers and running up the price on the brass cash register. There was so little business being done in the shop, however, that her help was rarely needed.

Nessa's first day in St. Imelda's set the pattern for her five years there. At nine o'clock on that Monday morning she entered the assembly hall – a heaving mass of shouting, jostling schoolgirls. It seemed to be one sea of faces, with a noise level louder than anything she had experienced before. She searched, hoping to find some familiar face, or even someone like herself, not attached to a crowd, but there was no one. Eyes met hers, then flicked away quickly. She stood awkwardly by the door, feeling conspicuous yet invisible. The weight of her schoolbag made her arm ache, but she was reluctant to put it down on the ground, to be kicked or stepped on by this noisy crowd. There were cries of greeting : 'Hi, Mary – you cut your hair!' 'Josephine, what did you do over the holidays?' 'Oh Patty, I love your shoes!' Everyone seemed to be taking up where they had left off some months previously, renewing old friendships, catching up on news, swapping information. Nessa realized with a sinking feeling that most of them had come on to secondary school from the convent national school, and those who had not, were coming in pockets from outlying rural national schools.

Suddenly a hush fell over the room, voices dwindling to a low buzz. Through the door came a tall thin nun, who walked briskly to the top of the hall, mounted the rostrum and stood there until there was total silence.

'For those of you who are newcomers, my name is Sister Katherine, and I am in charge of the first years. Will those of you who are first years please file *in silence* to room 1A at the bottom of the corridor, and take your seats.'

There was a scrambling rush, during which Nessa, still standing by the door, was almost knocked over. Then about thirty girls dislodged themselves and marched quickly down the hallway to the classroom. Nessa tightened her grip on her bag and followed them. By the time she got to room 1A, all the seats had been taken up. She searched desperately for a vacant place, feeling her face burning with embarrassment as the other girls watched her and whispered behind their hands. Then to her relief a tall girl with black hair and round glasses called out, 'There's an empty desk over there.'

Nessa was making her way to the desk as Sister Katherine entered the room. The nun's lips pressed together as she saw Nessa stumbling towards the empty desk.

'You – that girl there. Why aren't you in your place?'

'I'm ... I couldn't find it, Sister. I'm just going to it now.'

Nessa's face grew even hotter, as she felt all the eyes in the room turn to her.

'We're not rushing you I hope? Do take your time!' The nun waited until the laughter had subsided, then went on, still addressing Nessa.

'In this school it is customary for the girls to be in their places before their teacher arrives. Do you understand?'

'Yes Sister.'

'Now would you like to stand up and introduce yourself to the rest of the class, seeing that you have wasted so much of our time?'

'I'm Nessa McDowell.'

'I take it you haven't been to St. Imelda's before? You were not one of our junior pupils?'

'No, Sister. I went to school on Inishbawn.'

'Ah, that explains it. You're the girl from the island. Well, we must make allowances I suppose.'

She turned to the class, who watched silently, alert for the signal to laugh.

'I'm sure they have their own way of doing things on the island, girls. We must make allowances for Nessa, mustn't we? Won't you all show her how to fit in and become one of us?'

'Yes, Sister,' the girls chorused, delighted with the entertaining start to the day.

'Very well then. You may sit down now, Nessa, and in future be good enough to follow the example of the other girls.'

Nessa sat down, her face now burning more in anger than in embarrassment. She knew that in a subtle way she was being mocked for the benefit of Sister Katherine's popularity with the class, and her intense dislike of Sister Katherine remained with her throughout her school years.

Nessa's place in the school hierarchy was established at that moment also. The name Nessa McDowell became, in the minds of her fellow scholars, synonymous with the ignorant outsider from Inishbawn, who had come from such an uncivilised background that she didn't know how to behave in a classroom situation. This image was compounded by the fact that she looked different, with her over-long skirt, her hand-made jumper and her unruly, auburn hair. This she quickly tried to alter, by turning up the hem of her skirt, and by plaiting her hair severely away from her face. She had to work hard to win acceptance, and she deeply resented this battle for approval. Emer Sullivan, the dark-haired girl who had pointed out the seat to her, became her only friend. She too was an outsider, being a scholarship girl, and she too was the butt of Sister Katherine's jokes. It didn't bother her though. 'Take no notice of her,' Emer would say to Nessa. 'She's only two steps removed from the bog, and she's desperate to cover her tracks'.

Nessa learned that a studied indifference was the best way to deal with the nun.

# CHAPTER SEVEN

'The house will be empty without you.' Her grandfather shook his head and pushed away the half-eaten breakfast.

'I'll come over to visit you, and maybe you'd come to Inishbawn some time?' Even as she said it Nessa knew that her grandparents would never make that trip to the island.

'We're too old to be making sea journeys now.'

'Well, I'll call up to you whenever I'm on the mainland. I'm really grateful that you had me to stay here while I was at St. Imelda's,' Nessa went on, feeling guilty saying it, knowing how relieved she was that this was her last day in that gloomy house. It hadn't been so bad while Mary Kate was alive, but last winter she had died, and with her went the only spark of joy and humour. Business had got steadily worse – the Murphy girl was no longer needed – and Nessa knew that it would only be a matter of time before Tim and Ellen would close the shop for good and move to one of the small bungalows that were being built beside the church. They had done what they could for their grand-daughter, and had to some extent healed the rift with Margaret, but Nessa knew that Ellen at least would be glad to see the back of her, and not have a daily reminder of Owen McDowell.

Nessa was to catch the twelve o'clock ferry. She could barely contain her excitement at the thought of returning to Inishbawn. Her trunk was packed and ready, and after breakfast she cleaned and polished the little attic bedroom. When the local hackney car arrived at the house for her, her grandfather loaded up her baggage and hugged her awkwardly.

'Give our love to your mother. She did a good job on you. And mind yourself, child.'

Ellen pressed her dry lips to her grand-daughter's cheek.

'Let us know how you did in your exams, won't you? And good luck with your future. I'm sure we'll see you before you make any decisions.'

She held her briefly, and Nessa felt unexpected tears welling up in her eyes. She had come there hardly knowing of their existence, and now she was going from them again, having made little impact on their lives. It was all too late.

Nessa sat restlessly on the ferry, eyes waiting for the first glimpse of the pier in Inishbawn. The rain had stopped and the white cliffs rose up against the dull sky. Each chug of the engine brought her nearer to home, and this homecoming was like no other. Her five years of testing had strengthened her in her certainty that Inishbawn was where she wanted to spend her life. She would teach there, eventually marry Killian, and their children would carry on the island tradition into the future.

Nessa shook herself out of her daydream as she saw her father waiting by the pier. She waved, and he raised his hand in acknowledgment. Her mother wasn't with him, but then, had Nessa expected her to be?

Five years had seen many changes in Derryglas. Her grandmother McDowell had died two winters ago, and each time Nessa returned she expected to see the black-shawled figure fingering her rosary beads by the fire, and was sad when she remembered that she was no longer with them. Hannah had looked after her mother with the dedication expected of an only daughter, and had nursed her in her final illness.

Toby loped across the yard to greet them as the pony and trap approached the house.

'Toby, Toby!' Nessa jumped down and hugged the excited dog.

'Welcome home,' Hannah held out her arms to embrace her niece. 'What's that pasty face? You've been stuck too much in those old books. Were the exams hard?'

'Desperate. But they're over now, and I don't want to talk about them or St. Imelda's. I'm just glad to be home. Where Mama?'

Hannah's lips pursed. 'Where else but off on that bike? I tell you girl, she's getting worse, but he,' she nodded in Owen's direction, 'won't listen to me. Years ago he should have done something about her. She's the talk of the island, but he pretends it's not happening.'

'Will you leave over, Hannah? The child is barely inside the door and you're starting on her.'

'She asked me, didn't she? Look at her Owen. She's not a child; she's a woman. And hasn't she a right to know what's going on?'

Hannah turned back to Nessa.

'Your father was always as stubborn as a mule. He could never see what's right in front of his nose until he tripped over it. But, come on in and have a bit of dinner. I kept it hot for you. Owen will unload your stuff while you're eating, and you can tell me all about Ballymona.'

For Nessa, the joy of her homecoming was now touched with a cold finger of fear. Her mother's behaviour over the years had become more and more strange. Each time Nessa had returned to Derryglas, she had felt the distance between them growing wider. Having made the huge effort of getting her daughter accepted in the secondary school, and putting her into the care of her own parents, Margaret seemed to have switched off from her daughter's life. She took little or no interest in her schooling or in her life in Ballymona, and had withdrawn more and more into herself. When Nessa returned for holidays, she would smile and touch her and say 'how tall you've grown,' or 'how pretty you are,' and would sometimes ask her about Sister Gertrude and St. Imelda's, but in such a vague and distant fashion that Nessa knew that she didn't really want an answer.

The old woman's death had barely impinged on Margaret's consciousness. She ignored Hannah completely. With Owen, she was kind and polite but had moved so far beyond his reach that they were like strangers. Her days were spent either in her room, staring out across the ever-changing ocean, or cycling and walking in the more remote parts of the island. Her obsession with the burial place of her baby son had long since merged into a broader obsession to be free of any human contact, or the need to relate to anyone around her.

'She's crazy. Anyone can see that.' Nessa heard Hannah shouting at her brother one night. 'You should have her across in the madhouse with the rest of them.'

But Owen wouldn't hear of it. 'She stays here. This is her home, and this is where she stays!'

When she took to wandering around at night Owen would search for her, bringing her back, sometimes wet and dishevelled. He would gently dry her hair and put her to bed, and the next morning would go about his chores hollow-eyed, and would walk away from Hannah when she yelled at him that they were all being driven to an early grave.

On that first night of Nessa's homecoming, she lay awake listening

**130**

for her mother's return, and when she heard the clunk of the bike against the outside wall and the squeak of the back door, her tense body sagged with relief. Then she closed her eyes and slept.

Nessa slid quickly into the routine of her old jobs, helping Hannah with the house, the vegetable garden, the hens. She noticed a certain shabbiness about the farm, a neglect that she had never been aware of when she was younger.

'Sure it's all getting too much for your father!' Hannah, starved of an audience for so long, poured out her grievances. 'He spends half his day waiting on her ladyship, and half the night searching the roads for her. It's more than any mortal could be expected to put up with! And she won't let me near her.'

'Maybe he should bring her to a doctor on the mainland. Do you think that would help?' Nessa felt torn between loyalty to her mother and sympathy for Hannah.

'Long ago he should have done it. But what could they do for her now? They'd put her in the Mental, and that's what he's afraid of. Better off she'd be there too if you ask me. But he has a mortal terror of her being locked up.'

'Well I'm home now, and I can look after her. I don't want her sent away either.'

Hannah's voice softened. 'Sure of course you don't! What young one would want her mother sent to that place? But you have your life in front of you. You'll want to get married and bring a man in to Derryglas to help your father. And would anyone be daft enough to come in with her around? They wouldn't come within an ass's roar of the place.' She slid a sideways look at her niece, and added,

'That Killian Doyle will have to be getting out of the home place. His brother Brendan will be working that ...'

'I know what you're getting at, Hannah. Killian is barely eighteen. He's going to go to America and make loads of money, and then maybe buy his own farm.'

'Is that a fact now! There's talk that he has different plans.'

'What do you mean? What kind of talk?'

'You can ask him yourself.' Hannah wouldn't be drawn any more on the subject, but, a coy look coming over her face, she went on to talk about herself.

'I'm thinking of settling down myself, Nessa.'

'You? You're thinking about getting married?' Nessa was shocked. How could her middle-aged frumpy aunt be thinking of marriage?

'There's many women older than me take the plunge,' Hannah said defensively. 'Amn't I still strong and healthy, and hasn't Paudie Barrett been pestering me for years? His mother is gone now, and his two sisters married in the States, so there's a fine place there, just waiting for a woman.'

'Have you said yes to him?'

'Yerra, what yes does he want? I've told him to get the place ready and then we'll have a word with the priest. The banns will be read before the autumn. It'll be a quiet time for Owen, so he won't need me so much. Anyway you're home now.'

'God, Hannah, I'd never have thought of you leaving Derryglas and getting married. Are you in love with Paudie?' How could she be, Nessa wondered? Paudie Barrett, with his stack of grey hair and his long, horselike face.

'Long ago I gave up any notions of love. He's a decent man and he's got a tidy bit of land and a house that needs a woman. And I want a place of my own. So it suits us both. If you marry what you know, then you won't be in for any shocks, and his people have been on Inishbawn for as long as the McDowells.'

Nessa made no reply. She didn't want to think of Derryglas without Hannah. Hannah was now its stability. She was the normality in an atmosphere of fear and anxiety. And if she did leave, how on earth would Nessa's father manage? Derryglas was already showing signs of neglect. She, Nessa, would have to rethink her own plans. How could she just go off to teacher training college and leave her father to cope with the farm and Margaret and everything else? It would be out of the question. He couldn't possibly cope alone.

Hannah's voice cut in on her thoughts.

'Don't you be jumping ahead of yourself now, girl. You're looking all worried there, but things will work out, you'll see. And, sure, I have to take my chance. You see that don't you? I want a place of my own, and Paudie has been waiting a long time.'

'Of course ... you're right, Hannah. You must marry Paudie if that's what you want. Things will work out. We'll be alright.'

That afternoon Nessa cycled across the island to Killian's house What with pressure of work and everything else, she had seen very little of Killian during her last year in St. Imelda's, and was now looking forward to picking up where they had left off. The air was heavy with the scent of gorse and the sharp tang of the sea. For five years she had dreamed of being back on Inishbawn, with its emptiness and space and sense of freedom. How she had longed for it throughout those days in the classroom and those gloomy evenings in Ballymona. Her heart lifted as the wind whipped at her hair and whispered through the sedge grass. She stood up on the pedals and felt the surge of power as she cycled over the bumpy track.

She was home, and everything was going to be fine. On Inishbawn she was strong enough to cope with anything.

# CHAPTER EIGHT

The Doyles' place looked prosperous. Nessa couldn't help comparing the well- stocked fields and properly maintained farm buildings with the shabbiness of Derryglas. There was a time when the McDowell place had been the finest on the island, and when Owen McDowell had been the man who had set standards for the other islanders. Now, Doyles looked the better farm. Cormac had built on to the house, put in piped water, invested in machinery, and given the whole place an up-to-date, progressive appearance.

Killian was tinkering with the tractor in the yard when Nessa cycled in. He looked up, his face streaked with oil.

'Nessa, the scholar returns! How were the exams? Tough?'

'Awful.' Nessa threw her bike against the wall and sat down beside Killian.

'It's great to be back. I thought this day would never come. How's everything here? I see you're into the big machinery now.'

'Not me – Brendan. He's the man with the ideas.'

'He's doing well. The place looks great.'

Killian peeled off his blackened overalls, and wiped his hands on a rag.

'Yes, the father gives him plenty of rope, I'll say that for him. And Brendan doesn't spare himself. They make a good partnership. Anyway, come on, we'll walk down as far as the strand. I'm sure they won't miss me for an hour or so.'

Nessa fell into step beside him, her strides matching his. Once out of sight of the house, he took her hand in his.

'It's good to have you back, Nessa. I've missed you.'

'Have you? She was pleased. Killian had never made a fuss of her, though she knew he liked her. 'I've missed you too, and Derryglas, and Inishbawn, and Toby. Have you heard about Hannah?'

'About herself and Paudie? There's talk they're going to have the banns called soon. And about time too.'

'I never guessed. I mean ... they're so *old*. What on earth do they want to get married for!'

'Security?'

'Sure, Hannah will always have a home at Derryglas, and Paudie managed his place fine up to now. Why the sudden need?'

'Paudie is alone now. It's lonely for a man on his own. And isn't it only natural that Hannah would want her own place? Aren't there two women already in Derryglas?'

'And of course she hates my mother – always has.' Nessa sighed, then brightened up. She wasn't going to be sad, now that she was home.

They walked slowly, hand in hand, to the end of the white sand, their feet making deep impressions on its softness. When they came to the rock pools where they had fished as children they sat in companionable silence. Killian picked up a twig and traced a pattern in the water. The ripples distorted their reflections and broke up the darkness of the pool.

'What are your plans now, Nessa?' He didn't turn to her, but continued to stare into the water.

'If I pass my exams I've a good chance of being called to teacher training college. I did the exams for the Civil Service too, and the Bank, but only because we had to do them. I've no notion of taking them up. But, three years in teacher training could lead to me getting a place here in the school in Inishbawn. That's what I really want.'

'You mightn't always want to stay on the island. Now that you're educated you could go anywhere.'

She looked at him in surprise. 'But I don't want to go anywhere! I want to stay here. That's the whole point of trying for teacher training. So that I could stay here and teach.' She didn't add that after she and Killian got married, she could still continue to teach, part- time at any rate. And then eventually their own children would be pupils at the school. She could picture them. Sturdy small boys looking like Killian did when he was little. And solemn-faced, red-haired girls!

'It will be lonely for you – with Hannah gone to Paudie's place. And ... '

'And what?' she asked impatiently.

'Well, and I won't be around here much longer either.'

'You're going to America? You're going over to your uncles?'

Her mind raced ahead. It would be only for a few years. Two or maybe three years. Just like she would have to go to training college for a few years if she wanted to be a teacher. He'd spend that time in America, make lots of money and then come back for her. The money would be ploughed into Derryglas. Her father could take it easy. Killian would run the place and make it as prosperous as it used to be. Killian could turn his hand to anything. Then later, when ...

His answer stopped her in her tracks.

'No, Nessa, I'm not going to America. As a matter of fact I ...' he shifted uneasily, and Nessa suddenly became aware of a chill wind that had whipped up, of goose pimples that had risen on her bare arms and legs.

'I'm going away alright. I'm going away, but it's not to America. I'm going to Maynooth, Nessa. I'm going to be a priest.'

'You're joking me, aren't you? You couldn't be a priest. You're not even ... you're not even holy, for God's sake.'

Killian Doyle, Nessa thoughts ran, who had robbed the priest's fruit trees when he was nine, who had been caught whipping his spinning top across the smooth marble of the altar rails when he was ten, who – worse still – had, on one of his overnight stays on the mainland, tried to climb up the convent drainpipe to peer into the nuns' rooms! Fellows who did things like that couldn't be priests. And besides, there was no tradition of island boys going for the church. She couldn't remember one single lad from Inishbawn who had been ordained. There had been a handful who had joined the Brothers alright, but that was different. Priests, as she knew them, were sons of prosperous shopkeepers or business people from the towns, not sons of fishermen or island farmers!

'Don't be upset, Nessa.' Killian took her cold hands in his. 'This is something I've been thinking about for a long time.'

'You never said.'

'No, because I wanted to be quite sure before telling you. I didn't even tell my father and mother until a while back. I talked it over with Father Deasy, and he sent me to see a Father Broderick on the mainland. He thought there might be a bit of a problem because I hadn't done my Leaving Cert. and all that, but no ... they're willing to take me on and give me some extra coaching until I catch up.'

'You just want to get away from the farm, and Brendan, and the island. That's what it is, isn't it? This is just a way out for you. You don't really want to be a priest. You never wanted anything like that.'

Even as she said it, Nessa realized how petty and childish her remarks were. She felt cold inside, as if the wind now blowing in from the sea was piercing her bones.

'Ah, don't say things like that, Nessa. You know that's not the way it is. I thought you'd be glad for me. I thought you, of all of them, would understand.'

'I am ... I do ... Oh, Killian, but what about me? What about us? I'd always believed that you and me, that we'd get married one day. That you'd be taking over Derryglas. There's no man to take over Derryglas and help my father. It would be ours, Killian!'

Killian was silent. Nessa had always been very special to him. A sort of sister, a best friend ... more than that. He would be fooling himself if he didn't admit that he had often thought of what it would be like to marry her, to be farming Derryglas, bringing up his children on Inishbawn, handing on the island traditions to the next generation. But stronger than his love for Nessa, was this need to become a priest. He could pinpoint the very moment when the desire had formed in his mind, and that desire had grown stronger in the months that followed, haunting him until he had sought advice. He knew then that he would never join his uncles in America, just as he knew that he would never marry Nessa or farm on Inishbawn. They were the costs that he would have to pay.

Now a pang of guilt touched him as he looked at Nessa's bleak expression.

'We'll always be friends, Nessa. And when you get into training college you'll meet loads of fellows. You'll probably marry some rich business man, and just come back to Inishbawn on holiday.'

'And what about Derryglas?' She looked at him, and saw a Killian whom she had not seen before. A Killian who didn't seem to understand how much she had always loved him. Who didn't understand how deep her love for the island was, and how much she needed to be on Inishbawn. How could he think that she would chose to move away and make her life elsewhere? She had thought she knew everything about Killian, but maybe she had seen only what she had wanted to see. This Killian – this man who was giving his life to the priesthood – was someone she didn't know at all.

Nessa removed her hands from his, and got up. The tide was on the turn and the water was swirling in uneven movements around the rocks. Soon their footprints would be covered over, the waves licking and gulping until there was no trace.

'We'd better get back, Killian,' she said. 'They'll be wondering where I've got to.'

The joy of her first day home had been tarnished. Now there was just this awareness of everything changing. She had wanted Inishbawn to be the constant in her life. She had made this homecoming the focus of her longings. But it was all crumbling. First Hannah's news, and now Killian's. For five lonely years on the mainland she had carried this dream of returning to the unchanging Inishbawn of her childhood, and already on her very first day the reality was proving to be so different.

She avoided Killian that summer. When she told Hannah about his plans, her aunt showed no surprise.

'Didn't I hint as much to you? Sure the whole island knows that he's been up and down to Father Deasy's house for the past year. Mind you, they didn't let on to a soul, but people were drawing their own conclusions. Sinead Doyle must be the proud one - a son for the church. Isn't that every mother's dream? Still, there's many a slip betwixt cup and lip, and he's not there yet.' She looked sideways at Nessa. 'I used to think he'd be the right man to take over Derryglas. He seemed soft on you.'

'You can forget that, Hannah. Come September, he'll be off to Maynooth, and that's that.'

'Ah well, you have youth on your side, and time enough to look around.'

Preparations for Hannah's wedding to Paudie were low-key. She made daily trips across the island to Paudie's house, where she organised cleaning, painting and the moving of furniture. Nessa sometimes came with her to help, and would cook dinner for the three of them in Paudie's big old-fashioned kitchen. Paudie would sidle in shyly at one o'clock, nod to Nessa, and place his battered cap over the rung of the chair. Then he would sit at the table and silently down a plateful of floury potatoes. His grey hair sprouted wildly around his head, and his stubble- covered jaw moved in a slow and regular rhythm. Hannah, sitting opposite, would give him a list of complaints about the antiquated fireplace in the parlour, the worn linoleum in the bedrooms, the way the hens were allowed to perch on the half- door. Paudie would nod and masticate, and after he'd finished, he'd smile at Hannah and tell her to make any changes she wanted to. Then he'd put the cap back on his head, give Nessa a gap-toothed grin and disappear out the back door.

'You'd want to light a fire under that man to get him to move,' Hannah grumbled, but Nessa could hear the proprietorial note in her voice, and could sense the pride beneath the frown. Hannah was coming into her own. She had long enough been the daughter, the sister, the sister-in-law. Now, very shortly, she would have her own place. Not as grand as Derryglas had been in its prime, but a tidy farm. With the dowry which she'd bring with her, and with Paudie's hard work, they would make a comfortable living for their old age.

Nessa worked hard that summer. With Hannah busy about her own plans, most of the housework fell to her, and there was also the constant worry about her mother's behaviour. Nessa tried hard to establish some kind of normal relationship with Margaret, but with each week that passed Margaret was drifting further away. She became thin and gaunt, and her eyes burned with a fierce intensity in her white face. Her energy, though, seemed boundless. She slept no more than a few hours each night, neglected to wash or comb her hair, and her clothes hung about her shapelessly. She cycled for miles, pedalling furiously as though she had a purpose in her journey, heedless of rain or burning sun. And on returning to the farmhouse, she would throw herself on the bed and cry. Nessa was terrified.

'We must do something Dada. She'll injure herself, or worse.'

'Hush child. I'll look after her.'

Owen was beginning to appear almost as haggard as Margaret. Nights of following his wife on her wild jaunts and bringing her back, and days of trying to sooth and pacify her, were taking their toll. The farm was being badly neglected, and Owen was turning into an old man. He sold the cattle at the big September fair on the mainland, taking what price he could get, to guarantee Hannah's dowry, and when Brendan Doyle approached him about leasing some of his fallow fields to him, he did not hesitate. Hannah said nothing. For years she had seen this coming, but he wouldn't heed her. Now she was out of it. Soon she would be taking over the running of the Barrett farm with Paudie, and Owen could do what he liked with Derryglas. She was sorry for the child. If it came to it, herself and Paudie would have her live with them, but Nessa would be better off away from the island altogether – away from that mother of hers, and from the whispering tongues. Nessa should look to the future, and make a life for herself in some place where she would not be known, and where she would not have the stigma of being that woman's daughter.

# CHAPTER NINE

Hannah's wedding took place on a still October morning, one of those mornings when autumn slid into winter, and the last golden leaves hung shiveringly on the stunted island trees.

The best Sunday trap had been cleaned and polished, and the grey cob looked jaunty with a plume of foliage decorating his halter. Hannah sat beside Owen, a tartan rug draped across her new tweed coat and her hat pinned firmly on her tightly permed hair. She didn't look like a bride, but Nessa thought she was very smart and fashionable. Nessa had helped her to choose the coat and hat in Dan's Drapery on the harbour road in Ballymona, steering her away from the heavy wool that Hannah had favoured. Owen wore his Sunday suit, and the collar of his blue shirt was stiffly starched, making his neck bulge. Nessa and Margaret sat at the back of the trap. Margaret hadn't wanted to come to the wedding, but Owen was uneasy about leaving her alone, so Nessa persuaded her and promised her father that she would stay with her throughout the ceremony. Now she spoke softly to her mother, pointing out various cottages along the way, and trying to draw her in to conversation about the occupants. Margaret was mostly silent, but she turned her head, acknowledging Nessa's pointing finger, and smiled and nodded occasionally. She looked thin and frail.

At the church, Paudie was already seated, a neighbour beside him, a few cousins sitting behind him. In the church also were the Doyles, the Sheehys, the Brennans, all the neighbours. At the back of the church a bundle of shawl clad old women from the fishermen's cottages in the village huddled together, praying their beads and keeping an eye on everyone. Owen handed his sister over to a shiny- suited Paudie, barely recognisable with his hair brylcreemed to an uneven smoothness and his face shorn of its grey stubble. The new curate, Father Casey, presided over the ceremony, intoning the solemn Latin words in his soft accent. He was new to the island, still puzzled by these people who, though just across a stretch of water from the mainland, were so different: closed, suspicious and wary. He longed to be posted back to the mainland. One winter in this wild, wind-torn spot had been more than he could bear. Father Casey spoke the words of blessing and congratulated the newly-weds, then shook hands with the bride's family and the groom's relations. It was all over. In less than an hour the church was empty.

A fleet of horse-drawn traps, tractors and bicycles brought the wedding guests back to Paudie's cousin's house, where a lavish wedding breakfast had been laid on. Paudie and Hannah took their place at the top of the table, and pots of tea, fresh soda bread, salted bacon, black pudding and eggs were served up to everyone who could squeeze in. Bottles of whiskey and poteen, especially kept for the occasion, were then opened up, and the keg of black porter was tapped. Soon awkwardness and shyness gave way to loud, ribald talk, laughter and merriment. Somebody produced a fiddle. A few men began to sing. The women sprang to their feet to dance, first quietly, then with gathering exuberance. Tables and chairs were pushed back, someone arrived with a squeezebox, someone else with a tin whistle. The dancing gathered speed, the singing got louder. Hot, sweating faces, glasses raised and downed and replenished, the room throbbing and vibrating.

Outside, a cold October sun dropped behind the gathering banks of cloud. Evening gave way to nightfall. Impatient horses whinnied in vain, scraping at the remains of the fodder that had been left for them. The evening star glittered coldly, and was then swallowed by the cloud. The older women, leaving their menfolk to their revelry, gathered their shawls around them and crept silently away to their cottages. Tired children were wrapped and placed in the rooms upstairs, to drift into that half-state between sleep and awareness of the sounds beneath them.

Nessa sat by the door with a group of girls and wondered at the wildness of this ritual. The harvest festivals on Inishbawn were lavish and uninhibited, but this wedding feast was something more. Two island families merging in marriage was an occasion to bring about an almost pagan celebration. Nessa had never been at an island wedding. Men whom she had known to be shy and silent in their daily lives were now singing and laughing and dancing like young boys. Staid, sensible women were showing their legs and shouting to one another above the music. Sweat gleamed on excited faces. When the porter ran out, another keg was tapped, and with the second opening a maudlin exhaustion overcame some of the dancers. The music grew slower and more melancholy. When the bride and groom left for the Barrett farm, to spend their first night together, the singing changed to the sad, introspective songs of the islanders.

Nessa twirled the clear liquid in her glass. Someone had pushed a glass of poteen into her hand, and she savoured the burning immediacy of the drink. She felt a tearful nostalgia for something which she couldn't define, but which was bound up with her own sense of identity, and of her place with these people. Her father stood by the dying embers of the fire, surrounded by a group of men. Tight collars had long been discarded, shirt buttons were opened, jackets had been removed. The men talked across each other above the music, voices slurred, gestures clumsy, uncoordinated. She had never seen her father drunk. In drink, his quiet dignity gave way to an argumentative crossness, where he appeared to be taking umbrage at everything that was being said. As she watched, she saw him poke a finger into Con Mangan's chest. Mangan owned the biggest boat on the island, and was reputed to be a hard man. She hoped they weren't going to fight.

The crowd in the room had begun to thin out. Sinead Doyle had offered to drop Margaret at Derryglas on her way home, and had told Nessa that if she wanted to stay on longer then Brendan would bring her back. To her right, Nessa could hear Brendan discussing tractors and farm machinery with some of the younger men. His speech was clear and sharp, and those of his friends who weren't the worst for wear were listening attentively to him. After a while he detached himself from the group and sat beside Nessa.

'Great wedding, wasn't it?'

'A send-off to be proud of,' Nessa agreed.

'Your father is enjoying himself!'

Nessa looked over and saw Owen gripping Con Mangan's shoulder and pressing his face towards the bigger man, emphasising some point.

'A bit too much ... I've never seen him like this before.'

'Ah sure, why wouldn't he? Hannah took her time, but she got a good man in Paudie. Owen will have to work twice as hard now, to keep up Derryglas.' He looked sideways at her.

'Derryglas needs a lot of upkeep,' Nessa agreed.

'Your father isn't getting any younger. He needs another man about the place.'

'What are you trying to say?' Nessa felt slightly befuddled. The poteen was potent stuff, though she had only taken a little.

'Well, if Killian and yourself were ... you know ...' He shook his head. 'I'll tell you something. A priest is the last thing I'd have thought Killian would want to be. We couldn't believe our ears. I'd say you were disappointed yourself?' He moved slightly closer to her. 'I'd say you got a bigger surprise than any of us. Would I be right?'

Nessa felt a great sadness washing over her like a wave. Tears pressed against her eyes. Killian should be here with her, not Brendan. Since their First Communions, and even before that, it was Killian and Nessa, Nessa and Killian. He should not have abandoned her. He could have gone to America, or England, moved away from the island – anything. But as a priest he would be forever gone from her. He would always be someone apart. Never, ever there for her. She tried to stop the tears, but they began to flow, down her hot face, bitter and salty on her lips. Killian, gone forever.

'Ah, don't be upsetting yourself over him. Don't be crying now. Come on.' Brendan took her arm and pulled her up. 'We'll go outside, where they won't all be looking at you. We'll go for a stroll. It's too hot in here.'

With his hand on her arm, Brendan steered Nessa out through the back door. The cold air hit Nessa. Her head felt fuzzy and her feet seemed to have difficulty in placing themselves one in front of the other.

'Strong stuff, that poteen, hah?' Brendan laughed and tightened his grip on her.

'I only took a few sips.'

'That's all it takes when you wouldn't be used to it. You'll have a head like a drum in the morning. Look, we'll sit down here for a while ...'

He led her into one of the sheds behind the farmhouse. Hay and fodder were stacked on one side and the farm carts were on the other. The lamps from the house threw a dim light across the shed, making shadows and shapes up the whitewashed walls.

Brendan sat on a bundle of sacks in the corner of the shed, and pulled her down beside him. She was glad to sit down. The walk from house to shed had seemed miles, with her legs so shaky. Her body ached, and her head felt as if it was lifting out beyond herself. She shivered.

'Are you cold? Here, let me warm you.' Brendan leaned across her and she felt the warmth and comfort of his body against hers. She closed her eyes.

'Killian is a fool. With all his brains, he's a fool. You're a lovely girl, Nessa. I was always mad about you, did you know that? But you'd never give me a second look while he was around.'

She listened to his voice, and it seemed to be coming from away out beyond her. His hands were stroking her, and it was pleasant to be stroked. When his lips touched hers, she didn't pull away. She would have to forget about Killian. But when her fingers traced the outline of Brendan's face, it was Killian's face she was touching, it was Killian's mouth she was kissing, it was Killian's body that was warm and urgent against hers. Killian belonged to the church, not to her. This was wrong ... very wrong. But the emptiness, the sadness and the guilt were lost in the pleasure and excitement of this new experience, and the voice in her befuddled head became fainter and less insistent, caving in before the voice of the man in her arms.

'It will be alright Nessa. I promise you, I'll look after you. I've always loved you Nessa. Please, Nessa. Please ...'

Nessa dreamt that she was a child and was building sand-castles on the clean white strand. The tide was coming in, and each froth-topped wave licked closer and closer to her row of castles. Finally they reached them, washed over them and retreated, leaving behind shapeless bumps, which she kicked apart in a helpless fury. She cried out, and her cry woke her. She sat up, the blood thundering in her head. At first she couldn't remember where she was, or why she had been lying in this hay-strewn shed. Then she saw Brendan Doyle curled up in sleep beside her, and realisation flooded over her. It was still quite dark, and from the farmhouse she could hear the music, sad and melancholy, the plaintive notes of the tin whistle echoing the whine of the squeezebox. An intermittent wave of voices rushed across the farmyard as the door opened and shut, and revellers made unsteady footsteps across the cobbles. It must be nearly dawn, she figured, and here she was in this shed with ... with.... O God! What had she done? It wasn't Killian here with her. It was Brendan. She had to get home quickly. Panic-stricken, she wondered if her father had already gone. Or was her mother all alone at Derryglas? Why had she been so foolish? Hazy memories of what had happened between her and Brendan pierced the fog of her brain, and she shuddered. Without disturbing the sleeping form, she crept from the shed and ran out into the night, stumbling and slithering across the rough pathway from the farmhouse.

The night air was cold, and a white frost shimmered like icing on bare fields. A thin slice of moonlight gave her enough light to see her way across the island, and by the time she reached Derryglas, the sky was lightening, and the rim of a fiery sun was pushing itself up over the eastern horizon.

There was no sound when she entered the house. The fire was out, the brown ashes of the turf spilling across the hearth. The kitchen was strewn with the evidence of yesterday's wedding preparations – combs, hatpins, a bit of netting which Hannah had decided against wearing on her hat, Owen's spare shirt stud. Toby crept out from beneath the settle, stiff from the long sleep, and wagged his tail in welcome. Nessa patted his head and let him out into the yard. She went upstairs and opened the door of her parents' bedroom. Her mother lay on her back, her eyes fixed on the ceiling, the bedclothes thrown on to the floor.

'Oh Mama, you'll get your death of cold. Why didn't you keep the blankets on you? The room is freezing.' Nessa wrapped the quilt around her, and tucked her up. Margaret closed her eyes and turned her face to the wall. She made no reply when Nessa asked her where her father was.

'I'll make you a cup of tea and some porridge as soon as I get the fire going.' Nessa went downstairs to clear out the ashes and get the fire lit. She thought it strange that her father hadn't come home. It was out of character for him to stay away a night from Margaret, but then, remembering the amount of drink he had been taking after the wedding, she assumed he must have fallen asleep in some corner, and Paudie's cousin had left him there.

By nine o'clock the kitchen was warm with the peat fire. Nessa had made breakfast, and had fed a little bit to the reluctant Margaret. She had seen to the hens, and was tidying up the kitchen when she heard the sound of a pony and trap coming up the boreen. Running to the door Nessa saw that it was the Doyles' trap. The pony clattered into the yard.

Sinead and Cormac alighted from the trap, and when Nessa saw that Hannah and Paudie were with them, a coldness gripped her. Hannah's eyes were red and puffy.

'What's wrong? What's happened, Hannah? Is it Dada? Has something happened to Dada?'

Hannah's arms were around her, and Sinead and Cormac were half lifting her back into the kitchen. Paudie stood awkwardly, holding the pony's halter. Even before they told her about the accident, about Owen falling and striking his head against the sharp rock ... even before they told her that he was dead ... she knew. Her wickedness was being punished. Her father was dead, and it was her fault.

PART THREE


ORLAGH

# CHAPTER ONE

W
hen the ferry docked at the landing pier, Orlagh slung her rucksack over her shoulder and followed the other passengers across the gangway. Voices of elderly American tourists mingled with the guttural tones of young Germans and the confident, strident voices of French and Spanish students. Local farmers and fishermen shyly greeted visitors and tourists, and cast sly glances at bronzed legs and golden arms. A green and white bus stood by, to transport the holiday-makers and their baggage up from the port to the village, its running engine belching hot oily fumes into the air. This was not at all as Orlagh had remembered Inishbawn.

All along the horizon, white bungalows dotted the landscape, and new roads and paths snaked across the island. Garish advertising hoardings defaced what had previously been the narrow emptiness between the harbour and the village, and parked cars shimmered in an iridescent heat haze. Prosperity and better access to the mainland had made this part of Inishbawn little more than an extension of the harbour area of Ballymona itself, and Orlagh felt a pang of disappointment. When she was last here, some ten years ago, it hadn't been like this. There had been an emptiness about it then, a stillness and a bleakness, accentuated by the startling whiteness of the cliffs and the sand against the dark of the sea. There were no bungalows here then, no tourists, no cars. Just the gulls wheeling and shrieking above the heads of the fishermen, and a pony and sidecar to transport herself and her mother to the other side of the island.

Shaking her head at the offer of a seat on the bus, driven by a red-haired young man dressed in jeans and shirt, Orlagh walked slowly up through the village until she came to the church. She remembered this alright. This was where the funeral Mass had been held. She had sat in the front bench, her skinny frame pressed against her mother's body, her mouth dry with fear as the coffin was placed on the stand in front of the altar. Inside that coffin was her mother's Aunt Hannah, whom she had never met. The church had been packed. Old women in weird black shawls huddled in the side aisles, knots of men stood around the back of the church, women and young people filled the front seats. The priest had gone on and on about how this good Christian woman had fulfilled God's plan for her, and was now returning to her Creator. Orlagh had watched in terror, anticipating the lid of the coffin opening and the corpse emerging to soar heavenward through the arched ceiling. After the Mass, whispering groups had gathered in the church yard, people had shaken her mother's hand, and some had kissed her cheek. They had followed the coffin, shouldered by four men, to the graveyard, and had stood silently beside the widower, Paudie, a man stooped and twisted with rheumatism, until the priest had said more prayers and sprinkled the coffin with holy water. Then the first shovels of clay had been thrown down into the hole. It had been a terrifying experience, one which had surfaced in nightmares for months afterwards. They had spent the night in Paudie's house, where she had shared a bed with her mother in a small dark bedroom. People had called to the house for hours after the funeral, where they stayed to eat and drink and talk until the small hours. Orlagh had found it all very strange. She had been too shy and frightened to talk to anyone, and had longed to be back in Dublin.

Before returning on the ferry on the day after the funeral, her mother had zipped her into her jacket and told her that they were going for a walk. Orlagh had been frightened that they were heading back to the graveyard, but instead they had taken a dusty, stony road across the island for what seemed like miles. Cottages and farmhouses grew sparse, goats and sheep stared at them from scrubby fields. Eventually they had reached a gateway and followed an overgrown pathway until they came to a shabby-looking farmhouse. Mud-caked windows looked sleepily back at Orlagh, gangling shrubs waved at her from the chimneypots. Her mother had turned the handle of the front door, and pushed against it with her shoulder, but it wouldn't budge. They had walked around to the back of the house, and from there they could see the glittering and winking sea.

'This was my home, Orlagh,' her mother had said softly, her grip tightening on Orlagh's hand.

'This is Derryglas?' She had been surprised at how close it was to images she had formed in her mind, based on the stories her mother had told her about her childhood, and yet how different.

'Yes, this is Derryglas. It's all empty now, and run down and sad. But when I was a girl ... well, it wasn't like this.'

Her mother had sat on a rock and seemed to forget about Orlagh. She had stared out to the sea, and hadn't answered when Orlagh asked her where all the people had gone to.

'Are they dead, Mummy? Are all the people dead?'

Eventually she had tugged at her mother's sleeve.

'Mummy, Mummy, I don't like it here. I want to go home.'

Her mother had pulled her on to her lap and hugged her fiercely.

'Of course you do, pet. I shouldn't have brought you here with me. Of course you don't like it. It's a lonely, sad place.' She had kissed Orlagh, smoothing back her hair.

'Mummy wanted you to see Derryglas,' she had said. 'But you don't have to come back here ... not ever ... if you don't want to.' Her mother had risen abruptly, her arms still around Orlagh.

'Now that you've seen it, and we've buried Hannah – now we can go. Come on, pet. We'll have to hurry or we'll miss the ferryboat. We don't want to spend another night here, do we?'

Orlagh remembered hurrying across the island to collect their bag from the house where they had spent the night. They had shaken hands with the grey Paudie, and had then being taken down to the harbour in a very jolty cart, pulled by a large, bony horse. It was the one and only time she had been on Inishbawn ... until now.

Orlagh left the cool silence of the church and walked away from the harbour and the village. The sun was pleasantly warm, and the road became emptier and more desolate the farther inland she went. She had no idea which direction she was walking in, or where Derryglas was. But Inishbawn was a small island. She would find it, and maybe in finding it, she would discover the answers to all those questions. Somehow, everything returned to here. All her life, it seemed, she had been searching, trying to make sense of things, but always coming up against this barrier of silence from those around her. Now, before she could move on, she had to know. She had to be here in Inishbawn, by herself, away from her family and friends. Especially away from her mother. Her mother and stepfather had no idea that she was here on the island. As far as they were concerned she was backpacking in France with a group of friends, blowing the earnings of months of work, night after night, loading up supermarket shelves. She was glad to get away from everyone.

Once she had put some distance between herself and the village, Orlagh met few people. Occasionally a car passed her, slowing to allow curious eyes to size her up, then moving on up the hilly road, dust billowing around its disappearing image. Silence then settled once more. When she reached what seemed to be the highest point on the island, Orlagh had been walking for hours. Her feet were aching and hunger pangs were stabbing at her stomach. She climbed over a dry stone wall, and, finding a sheltered spot, removed her rucksack and sat down to eat her sandwiches. She looked with interest at her surroundings. From this vantage-point the whole of Inishbawn was visible. On one side the harbour, the gleaming white cliffs, the rocky fields. On the other side, in astonishing contrast, a rich green valley, grazing cattle, prosperous looking farm buildings, and a shingle beach of the same dazzling whiteness as the cliffs on the other side.

Down there somewhere in the valley was Derryglas, her mother's home. Orlagh knew that the house was still there, empty as it had been for years. She wondered why her mother had never sold the house. She was aware that the farmland had been sold years ago to a neighbouring farmer, but her mother would not part with Derryglas. When Orlagh had asked her about it, a vague and distant look had come over her mother's face, and she had muttered something about family and that her father would not have wanted it to go to strangers. Seeing that she was never going to live in it, and never even visited it, that seemed to Orlagh to be a very stupid reason. So many unanswered questions. Perhaps, she thought, when she'd been in Inishbawn for a while, things would become clearer.

Her hunger satisfied, Orlagh continued down the twisting road. Thick grey clouds were now rolling in off the sea, hiding the sun and threatening rain. The sound of the waves grew louder as she headed into the valley. She rounded a bend in the road, and there it was, unmistakably Derryglas. Orlagh remembered tightly clutching her mother's hand as they had walked up that dark pathway, with the eerie sound of the wind whipping up the shrubs. She remembered the neglected, crumbling porch and the heavy door that had refused to budge at her mother's push. Quietly now, her heart thumping, she approached the farmhouse. Most of the glass in the front porch was broken. Ivy clung to the walls of the house and crept across the windowpanes, almost obliterating the light. Orlagh tried the handle of the door, pushing her weight against it, but it was as firm and solid as it had been all those years before. She walked around the back, briars and nettles snapping at her jean-clad legs. The back door was also locked. A small window beside the door looked less secure, and sure enough it yielded to her shove, and opened up into what must have been a scullery or back kitchen. Orlagh climbed on to the windowsill, threw in her rucksack, and lowered herself into the room.

# CHAPTER TWO

By Christmas Nessa knew. Realisation of the full horror of her situation came slowly to her. Her father's death had touched depths of such sorrow in her that she wished over and over again that she too could have died that night. His death was a punishment for her, and a punishment that was also to affect her mother. Margaret at first refused to accept that Owen was gone. She attended the funeral Mass and reacted to the proceedings in much the same way as she had reacted to the ceremony of Hannah's wedding such a short time before. A confused vagueness curtained her features, and every now and then she would push away Nessa's restraining arm and try to leave the church.

'I have to get home, Nessa,' she interrupted once.

'Hush, Mama.' Nessa pressed her hand. And Margaret complied, lapsing once more into the inner life to which she had withdrawn so many years before. As Owen's coffin was lowered into the earth, Hannah had wailed and clutched at the sobbing Nessa. Margaret stood motionless. After the burial, Derryglas throbbed with the sounds of the islanders who had returned to the house to drink tea and whiskey and eat the food prepared by the neighbouring women. They talked about Owen and his place on the island, and how he would be missed, and they whispered about what would become of 'her', and what would Nessa do with what was left of the farm. Hannah stayed on in Derryglas with Nessa, and Nessa was grateful not to be left alone with Margaret and with her own guilt and sorrow.

'Will you be alright, pet? Will you be able to manage her?' Hannah was torn between staying on indefinitely with her niece, and returning to Paudie. She had spent a week with her, and Paudie was getting restless.

'I'll be alright, Hannah. Thomas will help me out. I'll just need to do the poultry ... and of course keep an eye on Mama.'

'There's enough in that, God knows. Dr. Whelan says you shouldn't have her here at all. You'll have to think of the future, Nessa. Without Owen around, you don't know what she'll get up to.'

'I know, I know. We'll think about it, Hannah. Leave her for a while – maybe she'll get better...'

'God help your innocence. She's gone too far down the road for that. Well, she's not my problem, but you know where I'd have her put, don't you? And Dr. Whelan agrees with me. Your poor father wouldn't hear of it, so signs on he was an old man before his time. And the farm has been so neglected these past years that you'd be sensible to think about Brendan Doyle's offer. You won't do better. Sure there's no one else on Inishbawn who'd offer a price like that for the fields. That Doyle lad has a cute head on his shoulders. Those fields would be a fine addition to his own land.'

'Would Dada have wanted me to sell though, Hannah? Would he have wanted the Derryglas land to go to the Doyles?'

'Wouldn't you still have the house and the biteen of garden? Paudie and myself would have no business with more fields, and who else could raise the cash to buy? You're going to need the money, Nessa. Mark my words, you're going to need it!'

Hannah didn't add that doctors and drugs and treatment came expensive, but Nessa knew that that was what she meant.

Nessa got a fair price from Brendan Doyle. The cash was lodged in her name in the bank on the mainland. A solicitor drew up the appropriate deeds, and the McDowell land passed to the ownership of the Doyles.

'Will we shake on it, Nessa?' Brendan reached for her hand and shook it vigorously, then let his fingers linger on her arm. Business completed, Brendan and Nessa were alone in the farmhouse kitchen. Nessa tried to feel detached. Memories of their intimacies had been submerged in the shock of her father's death. How could she have done that with him? How could she...?

'You're satisfied with the deal?' he asked now.

'I am, Brendan. You've been more than fair.'

'You'll stay on in the house?'

'For the moment, yes. I ... I don't know what I'll do yet. It depends on Mama.'

He moved closer to her. 'You and me, Nessa. We could .. you know. I meant what I said that night after Hannah's wedding. I wasn't just messing. You're a lovely girl – I was always mad about you, Nessa. I knew I didn't have a dog's chance, with Killian and all that. But now ... Would you think about it, Nessa? I'm sure we could make a go of it. Would you think about it?'

Nessa stood up abruptly. 'There's nothing to think about, Brendan. Our business is finished. I wish you luck with the farm, and I'm grateful you took the fields off my hands. But that's it, Brendan; that's as far as it goes.'

He flushed, dark red springing up from his neck to his forehead.

'Fair enough,' he said. 'That's spelling it out to me, loud and clear. But if you've nailed your colours to Killian's mast, forget it. You won't change his mind. You'd be daft to try to compete with the church, and especially now ... now that ...' He shrugged, leaving the implication hanging in the air.

Tears sprang to Nessa's eyes, and she turned away to hide them. Just then the clunk of the bicycle against the gable wall announced the return of her mother from one of her trips, and Brendan, pulling his cap firmly down on his forehead, left the room without another word.

'Who was that I saw leaving, Nessa?' Margaret asked when she came in. Her face was scorched red from the wind, and her dress clung to the sharp angles of her body.

'That was Brendan Doyle, Mama. You remember I told you that he bought the fields from us?'

'Owen won't like that. Where is he going to graze the cattle now? He always said those fields were the sweetest on the island, so why is he selling to the Doyles?'

'Oh Mama, I explained all that to you, over and over. Dada is gone ... he won't be back, Mama. He's dead. And Mama, why do you go out on your bike without your coat?' Nessa pulled her mother over closer to the fire. 'Don't you know it's winter? You must wrap up warm if you're going out. Can't you feel the cold Mama?'

Her mother stared at her, as if somewhere deep in the recesses of her mind she was trying to grapple with a question of her identity.

'Nessa,' she said. 'Nessa?'

Nessa hugged her. 'Yes, yes. I'm here. I'll look after you Mama. Don't worry. I'll always look after you.'

Sometime later that night her mother again left the house. She was still gone when Nessa rose at first light. Frantically, Nessa searched the outhouses and the yard. She rushed about, calling "Mama" at the top of her voice. Nessa grabbed her mother's bicycle, still thrown against the gable wall, and searched farther afield, her heart thumping in fear and foreboding. Three hours later, having enlisted the help of some neighbours, Margaret was located. She was huddled in the corner of a derelict cottage miles from Derryglas. Still in her nightdress, her body was blue with cold, and her bare feet were bruised and bleeding from her trek across the rocks and scrub. They took her to the mainland, where a waiting ambulance transferred her to the County Hospital. For weeks she clung tenaciously to life, but then her strength ebbed away, and she gave up the struggle.

Christmas came and went. Nessa spent some time over in the Barrett place with Hannah and Paudie, and except for the special trip to midnight Mass in the village church, there was little else to distinguish the festival. A year before, Nessa thought, she had been full of hopes and plans about the future, optimistic about her chances of being called to teacher training. Now both her mother and father were dead, Hannah had her own life to lead, Killian was gone, and she was alone and crushed with the weight of her guilt and sadness. What was more, the dawning realisation of yet another catastrophe was becoming more certain with every day. She spent a lot of time in her room, away from Hannah's sharp eyes. But surely Hannah would never suspect her of that? No, Hannah was just full of concern for her plight. Hadn't she lost both her parents, poor thing? Why wouldn't she be crying and mooching about half the night? Wouldn't anyone be the same? By January, though, Nessa sensed that Paudie was beginning to resent her presence. Since he'd married Hannah, he had been swamped with McDowell disasters. He was too kind-hearted to say anything, but Nessa knew that it was now time for her to move on.

Nessa returned to Derryglas, and tried to reach a decision about where her future lay. Marry Brendan Doyle? It would certainly solve problems. After all, it was his child she was carrying. She would have security, the child would have a family, she would be able to stay in Inishbawn — maybe even in Derryglas. But ... to spend the rest of her life with someone she didn't even like much? Marry Brendan, knowing that it was Killian she yearned for? How could she do that. No, that surely could not be the answer. There would be no question of her remaining on the island once her pregnancy became obvious, so the only option open to her was to leave. To go somewhere, Dublin maybe, where nobody would know her, and where she could get a job, and maybe a bed-sit or a flat. After all, she had the money from the sale of the fields, and even after paying off all the debts which had mounted around Owen's ears over the last while, even after giving Hannah and Paudie a generous share, and paying medical bills and funeral expenses, she would still have enough to keep her going until she found herself a job. After the baby came ... well, she'd cross that bridge when she came to it. Whatever lay ahead, Derryglas would always be there. She would never sell the house, no matter what.

Her mind made up, Nessa wasted no more time. Early in January, the doors of Derryglas locked and her suitcase at her feet, Nessa waited in the yard for Hannah and Paudie to take her to the harbour. Soon she heard the ring of the pony's hooves on the frosty road, and Hannah and Paudie came into view, with Toby sitting between them in the trap.

'I knew you'd want to say goodbye to the auld dog,' Hannah said, as Paudie put Nessa's suitcase into the back. 'He was that restless all morning, I'd swear he knew you were going away.'

Nessa hugged Toby's warmth to her.

'You'll take good care of him, won't you, Hannah?'

'You know I will! Sure he settled in grand with the other two. He found his own spot in the stall, and not a bother on him. And, anyway, won't you be back to see him – and us – as soon as you settle in to your new job? It will be the making of you. All the excitement of Dublin, lots of young people, and no one to answer to but yourself. It'll be the best thing in the world for you. Isn't that so, Paudie?'

Paudie nodded, then clicked at the pony to 'go on there', his eyes fixed on the road ahead.

The ferry rocked gently in the sheltered arm of the harbour wall. A trickle of people snaked across the gangway, bags and packages balanced precariously. Paudie went on ahead with Nessa's luggage, while Hannah held her niece in a last tearful embrace.

'You'll write, won't you? And you'll get the bus straight to your friend's house? Don't be talking to anyone you don't know – you couldn't trust them city fellows.'

'I'll be grand Hannah. Don't worry about me. I've plenty of money and a tongue in my head, so I'm not likely to get lost or nabbed or anything. It's only Dublin I'm going to for heaven's sake! You look after Paudie and Toby – and maybe you'd check on Derryglas now and again, would you?'

Nessa kissed the flaky skin and struggled to keep back the tears. She would not cry. She would not show the fear and sickness which clutched at her insides.

'Goodbye, Hannah. Goodbye, Paudie. Thanks for everything. I'll write just as soon as I get settled.'

Nessa hoped that they wouldn't wait until the boat moved off. She didn't turn around, but, pushing the suitcase into the baggage hold, she proceeded down the steps to find a seat in the dimly lit covered area below. There she leaned back and closed her eyes, shutting out last images of Inishbawn and of the people who had been her life for so long.

# CHAPTER THREE

Orlagh stood on her tiptoes to click open the back door. She closed it carefully behind her, then skipped down the flagstones that formed a path to the end of the walled garden. Each paving stone had a different shape, and she had to make sure that she didn't skip on the round ones. If she did, something bad would happen to her. At the end of the garden was the big willow tree that grew like a giant umbrella, and beneath this was her den. She had a box for a table, a small stool, a rug that the doctor had thrown out, and a plastic bag to hold her toys, books and colouring things. This was her own special place. Here she could draw, colour, read, and talk to her dolls. Through a gap in the stone wall behind the willow she could even watch Dr. Baily's patients coming and going, though all she could see of them was their legs and feet. Bare legs, legs in trousers, feet encased in clumpy working boots, feet strapped into high-heel sandals. Tiny feet in buckled shoes and old lumpy feet in bulging slippers. One morning she had counted one hundred feet, none of them looking the same. The sun shining through the leaves of the willow made strange dappled patterns on her own feet, and changed the faces of her dolls until it seemed as if they were talking to her.

Orlagh loved this place best in the whole world. She liked the big bed upstairs too, and the feel of her mother's back pressed up against hers, when she woke during the night. All her bad dreams faded as soon as she felt her mother there beside her. When she cried out, her mother would hug her close and whisper 'Hush, Orlagh, Mummy is here', and then everything would be alright. Orlagh liked living in Dr. Bailey's house. Even though she wasn't allowed around the house when her mother wasn't with her, she knew that it was a friendly house. It was brown and yellow and smelled of flowers. And she liked Dr. Bailey. He could move his teeth around, and sometimes he gave her apples to eat in her den. On sunny afternoons he had a habit of walking slowly down the zig-zag garden path, poking at weeds and nettles with his walking stick, and removing the dead flowers from the rose bushes. When he reached her willow tree he would rap on the path and say 'Anybody home?' Then, pulling aside the branch that made her front door he would say 'Good day to you Madam, and how is the family?' Taking a stethoscope from his pocket, he would examine all the dolls and teddies, and say 'ship-shape, ship-shape'. Then doffing his hat to her, he would continue his round of the garden. He was the only person, apart from her mother, who knew about her den. Sometimes a gardener came to mow the grass, but he didn't cut down near the willow tree. She could watch him through her tangled screen, and could hear him whistling as he pushed the heavy mower up and down the rough grass.

When winter drew in, and the days began to shorten, Orlagh had to abandon her den. She then collected all her toys and bits of furnishings and brought them indoors, where she placed them beneath the kitchen table in the flat. From there she could watch her mother's feet in their black slippers with the silver stars on the toes, as they moved from cooker to sink to table, and out into the hall.

Orlagh was a strange, silent child. Nessa puzzled about her quietness, but with her own life limping from crisis to crisis, she really hadn't given her daughter's behaviour much priority. It was in fact a blessing. She knew she could never have coped if the child had been troublesome, or noisy, or bad-tempered. Things were difficult enough as it was. Nessa removed her slippers and flexed her tired feet. The cup of tea in her hand was comforting. From underneath the table she could hear the sound of Orlagh's soft murmuring to her dolls, and the occasional rustle as she moved about. She was healthy – what more mattered? When she started going to school everything would be easier. She would be mixing with other children then and would soon find her voice. Nessa considered herself lucky to have a comfortable self-contained flat here in Dr. Bailey's house. Her work as a receptionist-cum-housekeeper for the widowed doctor was not too demanding, and it meant that she could keep an eye on her daughter, and not have to farm her out to cheap baby-minders, as she had been doing. Nessa shuddered as she thought back on the horror of these last years.

When Nessa had arrived in Dublin from Inishbawn on that wet Monday morning four years before, her first priority had been to find somewhere to stay. With no idea of where she was going, she had left the train station and headed across the city, her suitcase getting heavier by the minute. More to rest than to pray, she had gone into a big church facing the river, where she had sat in the dim silence, her mind a blank. On her way out she saw the notice on the notice-board. There was a name and a telephone number. She wrote down the number, and leaving the church she went to the first telephone box which she could find. She had dialled the number, but when a woman's voice had answered, her courage failed, and she had put down the phone.

Leaving the telephone box, she crossed over the bridge, and walked up along the quays in a state of numb indecision. Eventually she had gone into a cafe and ordered coffee and a cake, and had stayed there until the waitress began to clear the table around her. Out on the pavement once more, she was pushed and jostled by the rush of umbrellad figures running for buses and trains. Shops and offices were closing, and everyone was in a hurry to get home. The rain was heavier now, and Nessa felt a rising panic as the darkening streets began to empty. She found a dilapidated Georgian house with a Bed and Breakfast sign stuck in its front window, and here she booked herself in for three nights, cash in advance. The room was on the third floor, shabby but adequate, with a bathroom at the end of the corridor.

Nessa had unpacked her case, and hung up her crumpled clothes. All she wanted to do now was to sleep ... to shut out the misery of her situation, and the mess she had made of her life. She lay down on the narrow bed and closed her eyes.

In the morning realisation hit her as soon as she awoke. A watery sun searched for the gaps in the curtains, and when she looked out she saw that she was surrounded by rooftops glistening with the night's rain. Today she would have to look for a job, find a room or a flat, and set up some kind of a life for herself. However, as soon as she moved from the bed a wave of nausea hit her, and she had to rush to the bathroom. Afterwards, weak and shivery, she crept back under the covers, and lay there staring at the ceiling until she felt able to get up again.

The girl in the agency didn't hold out much hope for her. No qualifications, no training, no experience, no typing – what on earth was she fit for? However, she arranged two interviews for her. One was for a position as a junior in an insurance company, the second was in a clothing company. A new suit, with blouse, shoes and extras made a big dent in her money, but she had nothing in her suitcase which was formal enough for interviews. Taxis to the firms in question were also expensive ; there was no point in trying to find her way in buses, as she knew she would only get hopelessly lost. She did her best at the interviews, but she was floundering from the start, and wasn't really surprised when she was turned down twice. The agency organised two more interviews for her over the next few days, but again she was told that she was 'not really suitable for the position'. The agency assured her that they would let her know if anything else turned up.

Nessa booked a further three nights in the guesthouse, and scoured the evening papers for a flat. Anything that seemed remotely decent and reasonably priced was gone by the time she phoned. She was two weeks in the guesthouse before she finally found a bed-sit. Cramped and dark, it was on the top floor of a tall house in Rathmines, and she had to share a bathroom with three other tenants, but the rent was cheap and it was within walking distance of the city, so she would save on bus fares. She still had no job, and her money was dwindling frighteningly fast.

As soon as she had established an address, Nessa wrote to Hannah. She told her that she was having a wonderful time with her friend in Dublin. City life was exciting, with something new going on every day. She was having such fun that she hadn't got herself a job yet, but there were lots of things in the pipeline, and she was trying to make up her mind between the bank and the civil service. She hoped Hannah and Paudie were well and not working too hard, and that Toby wasn't missing her too much. Nessa stressed that, what with the new job on the horizon, it might be awkward for her to get back to Inishbawn for a while, but she assured Hannah that she had no need to worry – everything was fine. She sealed and stamped the envelope, brought it down to the post box, and then came back to her room and cried into the small hours.

Six weeks after coming to Dublin, Nessa finally got a job in a city centre restaurant. She was getting desperate at that stage and at least the salary would cover her rent. Her meals were supplied, which cut down on food expenses. She was now reduced to her last few hundred pounds, and her future seemed bleaker than ever.

By June it was becoming obvious to the rest of the staff in the restaurant that Nessa was pregnant. She had done her best to disguise it, with loose blouses and floppy cardigans, but the bulge defied her efforts, and she was becoming clumsy as she moved between the cramped tables. Following some weeks of pointed silence, her supervisor took her aside.

'How long more did you intend to deceive us, Nessa? You know we can't possibly keep you on.'

'Oh please ... I need the money!'

'I'm sorry, Nessa. You will have to finish at the end of the week.'

Nessa worked until the Saturday, when she was dismissed with two weeks' wages. She returned to her room in Rathmines, and calculated that she had barely enough to pay for one more month's rent and food, and after that she was broke. At the bottom of her purse was a slip of paper with a telephone number on it. It was the number she had copied down in the church on that first day when she had arrived in Dublin. It was either that or face returning to Inishbawn, to bring shame and disgrace on Hannah, and to be gossiped about in the community. She decided to phone the number.

The nuns were kind – well, most of them were. She was given a bed in a dormitory with five other girls in various stages of pregnancy, and was put to work in the laundry, folding and sorting acres of bed linen and napkins, running the sheets through the big pressing machines, sorting coloureds from whites. It wasn't difficult work, just monotonous and repetitive, and she got through the days by blanking out her thoughts and working like a robot. She made no effort to get to know the other girls, or to share any confidences with them. From their accents, she reckoned that they were from different parts of the country, but the less she knew about them the less she would have to get involved.

Her child was born on a steamy August night. All that day Nessa had felt strange. The heat was intense and her ankles had swollen so much that Sister Benedict would not allow her to work. Instead she had rested on a wicket chair in the convent garden. It was a garden very similar to the one in the convent in Ballymona, where she had walked with her mother on the day of her school entrance examination. There were orderly rows of vegetables and fruit, with everything structured and every corner earning its keep. Nessa stared down at her hands and wondered how she could have made such a mess of her life. Tears spilled from her eyes, and ran unheeded down her cheeks and on to the floral smock - convent property. She became aware of the pains, faint at first, then becoming increasingly urgent. This must be how it starts, she thought. She sat there, tensing with each contraction, gripping the edge of the chair, until the convent bell rang out the Angelus. Then she heaved herself out of the chair and walked slowly back to the Infirmary to present herself to Sister Mary, the midwife. She inhaled and exhaled, as she was told; she screamed silently but uttered no more than a whimper. She gripped and tore at the sheet. She bore down when she was ordered to. And finally, when she felt that she would die if she had to endure any more pain, the child was expelled into the waiting hands of the midwife and the nurse.

# CHAPTER FOUR

'Don't you want to see your little daughter Nessa?' Sister Mary pushed the tiny bundle towards Nessa's rigid form. Nessa closed her eyes and turned her face away. The pain had ended, and now she wished she could die; just to close her eyes and be no more. The emptiness and the sadness inside her was total, and she had no desire to even see what some of the nuns called 'the fruits of her sin'.

Sister Mary's voice took on a sharp edge.

'Sit up, Nessa, and take the baby. See ... she's perfectly healthy, and you must learn to feed and look after her until we get her placed. We won't have a bit of trouble finding adoptive parents for her. Healthy girl babies are always easy.'

Nessa kept her eyes closed, and eventually Sister Mary, with much tutting, put the bundle into the crib beside the bed. Nessa could hear the baby snuffling, and occasionally a tiny cry, but she kept her face averted.

She awoke to a cacophony of sound as the other babies in the ward were wheeled in to their mothers to be fed. There were four other new mothers in the ward, and Nessa saw them all pick up their babies, their faces becoming animated with love as they held the searching mouths to their breasts. The crying quickly subsided, to be replaced by contented suckling sounds. The nun approached her bed.

'Sit up! It's not a hotel we're running here you know. We've no time for tantrums. Now sit up and feed your baby like the other mothers, and no more nonsense out of you.'

Nessa pulled herself up. She was aching all over, but obediently she held out her arms and put the child to her breast, keeping her eyes on the blanket. If she didn't look at it, maybe they would take it away. She might wake up and find it had all been just a bad dream. The baby whimpered and began to cry. Not the loud indignant cry of the other babies, but a soft cry. Its body felt tense and stiff against Nessa's.

'We're not making much progress here, I can see. It will have to be the bottle for this one. Would you stir yourself and make a bit of effort, and not be feeling sorry for yourself? The child will have to be fed, whether you like it or not,Madam!'

The nun's rough red hands reached over, and tried to place the baby in a more comfortable position, but the soft crying continued.

'She doesn't want me, any more than I want her. Why don't they take her away?'

Nessa wasn't sure whether she mouthed the words or if they remained in her head, but eventually the nun returned the child to the cot with much tutting, and the muttered words 'wicked, unnatural, mother'. Nessa fell asleep, shutting out the sounds of her whimpering baby.

'Nessa, Nessa, wake up dear!'

This time it was Sister Benedict, and she had brought a bottle for the baby.

'It might be easier this way,' she said kindly. Propping up the pillow behind Nessa, she handed her the bottle and placed the baby in the crook of her arm. 'There you are now ... it's not so difficult, is it?'

The child began to suck.

'See, she's a hungry little girl. Isn't she pretty, Nessa?'

Nessa looked down at her daughter. Dark eyes stared steadily into hers. The hair was thin and wispy, her skin blotchy, the nose too big for the tiny, sallow face. She didn't look at all pretty.

'She'll be baptised on Saturday,' Sister Benedict said. 'Father Doran comes in every Saturday to do the new babies. He'll have five little souls this week, God bless them. Have you decided on a name, Nessa? There are two saints' feast-days around this time ... and of course there's the feast of the Assumption, if you want to call her after the blessed Virgin.'

Nessa had not given any thought to names. To name the child would have been to make it real.

'I'll call her Orlagh Mary,' she said. The name just came out. She knew nobody called Orlagh. It wasn't even a name she liked. But it was as good as any other, and it would stop Sister Benedict from pestering her.

'Orlagh Mary ... that's a grand name. A fine Irish saint, and of course the Blessed Mother to make it even more special. We'll make a Christian of her on Saturday, and then you'll have four or five weeks to look after her and get your strength back before you hand her over to her new parents. Will you stay on in Dublin, Nessa? Or will you return to the country? You told me your parents have passed on, so perhaps you'd be better off in Dublin. Meet some nice man who'll offer you marriage maybe. The father of little Orlagh ... is he in a position to marry you?'

Nessa felt her stomach lurch. 'No ... no, he's not.'

Sister Benedict did not pursue the subject.

The child was baptised, along with the other babies, on the following Saturday, and Nessa resumed her work at the laundry, returning to the nursery at regular intervals to feed and change her daughter.

Orlagh rarely cried. She slept a lot, and when she was awake she snuffled and whimpered and sucked her fist, but she seldom joined in the vigorous demanding cries of the other babies. When Orlagh was a month old, the nun told Nessa that there was a couple waiting to adopt her.

'You don't have to make up your mind immediately, but you must be conscious of what is best for little Orlagh. This is a grand Catholic couple; they'll give her a sound home life and she'll want for nothing. Are you happy enough with that?'

It was a statement rather than a question. It was almost unheard of that any of the mothers in the home would argue about the placing of her child.

'I suppose so, Sister.' Nessa just felt relieved that the decision had been taken out of her hands.

'I should think so. What could you offer her yourself? You should be very grateful that you're getting a second chance to start again, and know that your baby is not being neglected. We can vouch for this couple, that they'll cherish little Orlagh. They've been married for ten years and are longing for a family. Now, you can sign the papers during the week and then make a fresh beginning. The couple in question will be coming in to see the baby on Sunday, so you can dress her up in her best finery. I know they'll love her as soon as they set eyes on her!

On the Sunday, Nessa dressed Orlagh in a clean white nightgown, prepared enough bottles for the day for her, and after Mass got a bus from outside the convent gate into the city. She wasn't allowed to meet the couple, and didn't want to be around when they called. Nessa planned to walk around the city scouring windows for job offers. Then, when it was all over, she would find another bed-sit and a job, and maybe go to classes at night to gain some qualification. She might even go back to Inishbawn for Christmas. With some new clothes and her hair done, Hannah would believe that she was having a wonderful life in Dublin, and would never need to be told anything else.

Nessa returned to the convent in time to give Orlagh her six o'clock bottle. She didn't ask how the visit had gone, but she noticed that a little teddybear had been placed at the end of the cot. It was the first toy that Orlagh had received, and it was an expensive, beautifully finished one.

One morning, about two weeks later, Nessa was working in the laundry when Sister Benedict called for her. She told her that the papers were ready, and asked her if she would like to go to the nursery and say goodbye to Orlagh, who would be taken to her new home that afternoon. Nessa removed her overalls, and made her way to where the babies slept.

There were only three cots left in that particular section of the nursery. Already two of the five babies born around the same time as Orlagh had been taken to their new homes. Lucky babies, to be placed in nice, clean, respectable homes. Lucky babies. Mothers who didn't deserve it, getting a second chance. Lucky mothers. Best thing for everyone. Sister Benedict said so. So did all the other nuns. So did the priest who had come to talk to the girls. Girls who had done wrong, but through the grace of God and the goodness of the nuns were able to wipe the slate clean and make a fresh beginning, safe in the knowledge that their babies would be brought up properly. Lucky mothers, lucky babies, lucky everyone ... the right thing. Yes, yes, the only thing to be done.

By the time Nessa reached Orlagh's cot she was weeping uncontrollably, her tears running down her face, and soaking the front of her cardigan. She wiped her eyes with her sleeve and looked down at her daughter. Orlagh, sucking her fist in rhythmic silence, stared back at her. Nessa bent down and removed the child from her cot, feeling the tiny body first tense, then relax against hers. Her tears ran down on to her daughter's head, darkening the wispy hair. She crushed the child against her wet cardigan, feeling for the first time a rush of love and protectiveness, and of bonding with this little part of her own body.

'I won't give you away. I won't. I won't. I'll look after you. I'll give you the very best I can. There's nobody going to take you away from me, my beautiful, beautiful Orlagh. I'll take care of you.'

The baby stared up at her unflinchingly, then she began to cry: loud, demanding sobs, rising to a scream that set off all the other babies in their cots. Sister Martin, the nursery nun, came rushing in.

'What on earth are you doing, Miss? Upsetting all the babies like that? Isn't your baby going to her new home shortly, and you haven't even dressed her yet. You'd better get a move on, or she won't be ready when they call for her.'

'She's not going anywhere,' Nessa shouted. 'I am *not* having her adopted ... I'm keeping her. She's my baby and I'm keeping her.'

Sister Benedict and another nun now came running in from the chapel, and Nessa, still clutching the screaming child, shouted at them. 'You're not taking my baby. I don't have to give her away, and I'm not going to give her away. And you can't make me. Nobody can make me!'

Sister Benedict put her arm around Nessa's shoulders and led her out from the nursery down the corridor to her office, where Orlagh, cradled in her mother's arms, promptly fell asleep.

'Now Nessa,' the nun's voice was gentle and reassuring, 'of course we won't compel you to give your daughter up for adoption. We would never force you to make such an important decision against your will. But have you thought this through, Nessa? Have you considered what kind of a life you can offer your baby? Can you justify depriving her of the love of two parents in a stable Catholic home?'

'I can love her more than they can. I *do* love her, and I'm not going to give her up.'

All the arguments which followed failed to make any dent in Nessa's resolution. She was suddenly filled with the maternal love which had eluded her up to now, and nothing would persuade her to even consider signing the final adoption papers. After that, she was on her own. Her life in the convent was over. It was time to move on.

Nessa found a cheap bed-sit in a run down area of Dublin, and began her search for a job. Nobody wanted to take on a woman with a young baby. With Orlagh in the push-chair which Sister Benedict had provided, Nessa walked the city searching, but it was always the same answer. No, she wasn't suitable. No, she couldn't bring her baby with her. No, the job was no longer available. Finally, she had to take a risk, and she asked the young mother in the flat adjoining her bed-sit if she would look after Orlagh in the mornings while Nessa got a cleaning job. Six mornings a week in six different houses. It wasn't the ideal solution, as the woman, living in a very cramped flat, already had two small children of her own and an out-of-work husband. It certainly wasn't the life that Nessa had hoped to provide for her baby. However, the job gave Nessa a reasonable income. In the afternoons she would take Orlagh out in her pram, and walk around the parks and the open spaces, hoping that her child wasn't missing out too much from not having a proper family. At night-time, while the baby was asleep, Nessa would lie on the bed, reading or just listening to the comings and goings in the rest of the house : the shouting, the fighting, the children crying, the sounds of radios and televisions. And she would think of Inishbawn and of Killian, and of all that might have been.

Orlagh was slow to walk and slow to talk. She rarely cried. It was as if she had learned very early on that the less obtrusive she was, the better chance she had of survival. She followed Nessa around with her eyes, and when she became steadier on her feet, she clung on to her, one hand holding on to Nessa's skirt, the other stuck in her mouth, always sucking – her thumb, her finger, a piece of cloth, the teddy-bear's foot. Her baby-minder slapped her when she refused the food put in front of her, and she learned to be wary of the male presence in the house, who disliked what he called 'that weird brat', and who teased her to make the other children laugh. She would watch the door, waiting for her mother's reappearance, and only when she was back in their own room would she take food or fall asleep.

'How has she been, Mrs. Deegan?' Nessa would ask each day on getting home from work.

'No trouble at all,' Mrs. Deegan would reply, bundling Orlagh into her coat, and handing her over with relief. Nessa, looking at the wan little face, would wonder. But what was the use? It was the best she could do ... and maybe next week, next month, whenever, something would turn up. In the meantime her priority was earning enough money to pay for rent and food and heating.

Eventually, something did turn up. One afternoon while taking Orlagh for her walk, Nessa heard her name being called. Sister Benedict looked genuinely pleased to see her.

'Nessa, how are you? And how big Orlagh Mary has grown. You know, I have been trying to trace you – to satisfy myself that you've been able to cope. How have things been, Nessa?'

It didn't need her observant eye to see the stress in Nessa's face, and the pale, worried look of the child.

'Alright, Sister, thank you. It's been hard to find a job – with Orlagh I mean. I have to get someone to look after her while I'm working. But we're coping fine.' Nessa was not going to let the nun think that she couldn't look after her daughter.

'Well, maybe I can help you there. A friend of mine approached me only last week to ask if I knew of anyone who would help out her brother. He's a doctor, a widower, and he urgently needs someone to answer his phone and take appointments, and maybe do a light meal for him in the evening.'

'I couldn't possibly leave Orlagh all day, Sister.'

'But that's the beauty of it. You wouldn't have to. There's a self-contained flat going with the job, and I'm sure the doctor would have no objection to a child. If you're interested, it would be ideal for you, and I think the salary would be quite generous.'

If she was interested? Nessa could hardly believe it wasn't a dream! Oh yes, she was more than interested.

'That's settled then.' Sister Benedict looked relieved. She had had a bad conscience about this young girl.

'The doctor's sister will interview you as soon as you can call round to her.' She handed Nessa a card with the address on it. 'Phone her as soon as you can ... and remember, Nessa, even if you don't get this job, you can always come back to the convent. We'll find something for you. Now, let me know how you get on, won't you?'

Nessa assured her that she would, and having said goodbye, sailed back to her bed-sit on a cloud of optimism. Things were going to change now. At last Orlagh would get a proper home; maybe a home with a garden and space to run around and play in, and with a real bathroom. And as soon as she was settled in and had found some kind of normality, Nessa decided that she would write to Hannah and tell her about Orlagh. She didn't have to know anything about the father – just that there was a child and that the relationship hadn't worked out and that she was bringing her up on her own. Hannah would be shocked – more than shocked. She would probably keep it a secret from the neighbours – even maybe from Paudie. But at least she would know. Hannah was entitled to that much. For Nessa herself, this would be an important step in putting the past behind her and beginning anew. Nessa and Orlagh. From now on it would be just the two of them, and she would do her very best to ensure that Orlagh was compensated for not being born into a proper family.

# CHAPTER FIVE

'Is today the day, Mummy?' Orlagh pulled back the corner of the quilt, and crept into Nessa's bed. Every morning, as soon as the first chinks of light broke through the shutters, Orlagh would feel free to climb into her mother's bed.

'You're too old for this!' her mother would protest. 'For heaven's sake, you're almost five years old. When are you going to stop being a baby?'

'But I like being a baby,' Orlagh would answer. And she did. She often awoke during the night, and lay rigid with terror, as the memory of some bad dream surrounded her, making the darkness full of menace. She would stare into the blackness, probing it for shapes that she could identify : the washstand with the faint glint of marble top, the big wardrobe, whose heavy doors hid some awful presence. As soon as the blackness turned to grey, and she could see her mother's bed by the door, she would creep across the carpeted floor, and climb into the bed's familiar safety. There all her fears disappeared, and she would fall back into a deep sleep.

'Is today the day, Mummy?' she said again.

'Yes, love. Today is the day.' Nessa rolled over on her side. 'But it's far too early to get up ... go back to sleep, there's a good girl.'

Orlagh was much too excited to sleep. All week there had been a frenzy of activity in the doctor's house. From her den in the garden, she had seen large white vans, adorned with blue writing, pull up by the gate. She had watched as men in white, paint-spattered overalls and shoes dotted with white made their way to the front door, armed with tins, buckets and brushes. During the day a group of these workmen would sit near her den, smoking and drinking from cans. She watched them from behind the swaying curtain of greenery, and held her breath as they sometimes threw the cigarette butts and the empty cans in her direction.

'They're the decorators,' her mother explained. Dr. Bailey is having guests, and he wants the house to look nice. It's going to be all done up.'

'Will there still be room for us, Mummy?'

'Course there will, lovey. Haven't we got our very own little place? Nobody is coming in here – not even decorators.'

Orlagh was relieved. She didn't want to go back to where they used to live. To the woman who slapped her, and that man who ..... No, she liked being where they were, and having her mother around .

'Dr. Bailey's son is coming home to help him in the practice,' her mother explained. 'The doctor's son will be living here now, with his two children. He's a doctor too, and he's going to take over the practice from his father, so that Dr. Bailey can have a rest.'

Later that day Orlagh heard the taxi pulling up, and saw watched Dr. Bailey's feet hurrying past her hideout. She heard the whine of the front gate and shouts of greeting, laughter and shrieks of 'Granddad, Granddad'. Peeping through her green screen, Orlagh saw a tall man, who looked like Doctor Bailey, except that he was thinner, and two girls in pretty blue dresses. They looked like the princesses in Orlagh's story book, with golden hair falling in waves down their backs. Their shoes seemed so soft that Orlagh longed to reach out and touch them. The girls came by her den, dancing and twirling around their grandfather, both talking at the same time in high-pitched, musical voices. Dr. Bailey slowed down as he passed by the hidden Orlagh. She held her breath as she waited for his usual greeting of 'Anybody home?' but he walked past, followed closely by his son, whose shoes were brown, with stitching all along the sides. Orlagh stayed quite still until she heard the thump of the front door. Then she ran around the side of the house and in the door to their apartment.

'The visitors have arrived, Orlagh.' Nessa was flushed with excitement. ' Did you see them coming? Go and wash your hands and comb your hair quickly. The doctor might want us to meet them. You don't want to frighten them off with the cut of you. All those bits of bush stuck in your hair!'

Orlagh did as she was told. Looking at her reflection in the mirror, she wished that she could be as pretty as the doctor's granddaughters. She wished that her hair was golden and thick. She combed the thin, black strands back behind her ears, and carefully washed her hands and face, then joined her mother in the kitchen, where she was busy filing papers for the doctor.

After tea, when surgery hours were over, Orlagh was introduced to the new arrivals. The beautiful blonde girls had now changed into matching dungarees, their hair caught back in ponytails, tied with ribbons of the same colour as their eyes. They sat on either side of their father on the big sofa in the doctor's sitting room.

'Come and meet my granddaughters, Orlagh. Come now, don't be shy.' Dr. Bailey took Orlagh's hand as she stood by the door, paralysed by shyness. He had to prise her other hand from the door.

'Ruth and Rebecca, this is Orlagh. The twins are seven, Orlagh – just two years older than you. I'm sure you'll all be great friends when you get to know one another.'

The two girls got up from the sofa. Their smiles were broad - lots of white teeth. They looked at one another and giggled, as Orlagh lowered her eyes to the floor. 'How do you do, Orlagh' they said, hands outstretched.

'She's a bit timid,' she heard Dr. Bailey explain.

'Why won't she shake hands with us, Granddad?' one of the girls asked. 'Does she live here? She's not very friendly!' the other girl added.

Orlagh stared at their shoes ... white with thick blue laces. She could feel tears coming, burning behind her eyes. She mustn't let them see her cry. They would think she was a baby, and now she didn't want to be a baby. But she couldn't stop the tears. Down they plopped, leaving wet stains on the cream carpet, and causing the girls to giggle again. Dr. Bailey scooped her up in his arms, and with his handkerchief which smelled of pipe tobacco, gently patted her eyes.

Her mother was cross with her when they got back to their apartment. Two red spots flushed her cheeks, and her eyes were angry.

'I'm so ashamed of you Orlagh. You were bad-mannered and rude. And in front of those nice girls. Why, Orlagh? Why did you make such a show of me? What is Dr. Bailey's son going to make of that behaviour – when his children are so well- mannered? Why did you act like that, Orlagh?' Nessa shook her daughter by the shoulder, which caused Orlagh to burst into tears once again.

'I don't know, Mummy. I'm sorry Mummy.'

'So you should be. Don't you ever behave like that again – do you hear me? When you see Ruth and Rebecca tomorrow you'll shake hands with them, and you'll play with them. That is, if they'll want to play with you, after the babyish way you carried on. Now, get off to bed before I say anymore! Go on ...off with you.'

Orlagh crept into bed, her eyes sore from crying. She had never seen her mother so cross. She was hardly ever angry with her. It was all their fault. Ruth and Rebecca, with their beautiful long hair and their silly giggles. She wished they had never come to Dr. Bailey's house. Everything was spoilt now. When the bad dreams came that night, Orlagh clutched her teddy to her, and let the tears slide silently down her face. And when the blackness turned to grey, and she could make out her mother's shape in the bed by the door, she turned on her side and stayed in her own bed until it was time to get up.

For Nessa, life now moved on to a new plane. Robert taking over the practice brought many changes. Old Dr. Bailey more or less retired, and now his days were spent reading and writing articles for medical journals, in between entertaining his grand daughters. Robert Bailey was a very different kind of doctor, and soon acquired a much wider clientele. Nessa was kept busy, ushering patients in and out, filing records, answering the phone. Robert involved her in the day to day running of the practice. He discussed changes with her, even asked her advice. Nessa felt herself opening up like a flower after rain. The tightness and tension, which hadn't left her since she had sailed away from Inishbawn, now began to loosen. She was suddenly a person who was needed and valued. She had something to give. Robert came to depend on her, not only for her help in running the practice, but also for the practicalities of dealing with two young daughters. He spoke little about their mother. Nessa knew that she had died when the girls were young, and that their maternal grandmother had helped to look after them. Dr. Bailey's housekeeper, who did the cleaning and some of the cooking, soon made it clear that looking after children was not part of her duties, so when it came to buying clothes for the girls, or taking them on outings, it was to Nessa that Robert turned. He would stand there, looking surprisingly awkward. His sharp, professional manner unpeeled, to reveal a father unsure of his role.

'I think the girls need sandals. And their hair could do with a trim. Do you think ...could you possibly find time to go along with them Nessa?'

Nessa would smile at his diffidence. She would be delighted to help out. Robert would hand over what seemed to Nessa to be an enormous amount of money, and ask her to buy whatever she thought necessary. The girls knew exactly what they wanted, and shopping with them was a pleasure. Orlagh would trail along behind them on these trips. She would watch silently as Ruth and Rebecca pirouetted in front of the store mirrors, their golden hair swinging as they twirled in their new shoes. She would sit on her mother's lap, as the hairdresser trimmed the girl's beautiful locks, and made admiring comments. When it was her turn to get her hair trimmed, she was told what a good little girl she was. So quiet. She longed for hair like Ruth's and Rebecca's, but beside them, she seemed to become almost invisible.

'But you are beautiful, Orlagh!' Nessa would reassure her. 'You're Mummy's beautiful little mouse, and I wouldn't swap you for anyone in the whole wide world.'

Orlagh didn't want to be a little mouse. She wanted to be like a princess.

Soon after the twins had come, they had discovered Orlagh's hiding place beneath the willow tree. Orlagh had gone down the garden to find Ruth and Rebecca setting up some of their own toys on the box that Orlagh used for a shelf.

'Come on in, Orlagh', they called, as she lifted the greenery aside. 'We're going to play hospitals. You can be the patient. We'll be the doctor and the nurse.'

'I don't want to.' Orlagh's anger at finding them in her special place spilled over into her voice, which came out with a wobble. Ruth and Rebecca giggled.

'She never wants to do anything, does she?' Rebecca said. 'She's such a baby! Let's play Mothers and Babies, Ruth. Orlagh can be the baby. Let's put her into the cot with the dolls.'

When they reached out to Orlagh, she sprang at them, grabbing handfuls of silky hair, and pulling as hard as she could. Their screams brought Dr. Bailey's housekeeper running from the house.

'Bad girl! Look what you've done!' She pointed to the hairs wound around Orlagh's fingers. The twins sobbed loudly behind her. Soon the young doctor arrived on the scene, followed by a frightened-looking Nessa. The two girls rushed into their father's arms, screaming. 'She

**180**

attacked us, Daddy. She attacked us, and pulled out our hair. And we did nothing to her. We just wanted to play with her.'

Orlagh shrank from the accusing eyes. She turned to her mother, but Nessa's fury was written all over her face.

That night Nessa sat on the edge of Orlagh's bed. She looked sad, and distant. That was even worse than when she was angry. Orlagh reached up to twine her arms around her mother's neck, and press a kiss on her cheek. Her mother sighed.

'I don't understand you, Orlagh. When I think how good Dr. Bailey has been to us, and then you do something like that to his little granddaughters. They only wanted to play with you, and you go and pull their hair like that.' She shook her head, dislodging Orlagh's arms.

'But they were in my special hide-house, Mummy! They didn't even ask me. They were just there, playing with my things.'

'But it's their garden too, love. You have to remember that. They've come back to live here with their Daddy and Granddad, so the house is theirs, and the garden is theirs, and ...'

'The hide-house is mine, Mummy. Dr. Bailey says so. It's mine. I fixed it up, and nobody ever goes in there except me!'

'That's just selfish. You'd have lots more fun if the three of you played there together, wouldn't you?'

Orlagh was silent. It would be no fun at all. Her secret den was special because it *was* secret ; because it was just hers, where she could put her toys, and from where she could watch without being watched. If Ruth and Rebecca were going to play in her den, then she didn't want to go in there ever again.

Nessa sat by her daughter's bedside until the child fell asleep. I have to give her time, she thought. She's not used to mixing with other children. That was it. It was only natural that she should be wary and on the defensive. But give her time and she would learn to love Robert's girls. It would be almost like having sisters, wouldn't it? And doesn't every child want a brother or sister? An image flitted across her mind of a small mound on a distant hillside. Of a little unknown brother. Of her mother's vigils. She dismissed it quickly. That was another life, over and done with now.

Nessa kissed her sleeping daughter, and left the room.

Early the next morning Orlagh crept from the apartment, down the garden path to her special den. A soft morning breeze lifted the greenery, making it sway with whispering sounds, and forming jagged patterns of light on the ground. She took a black plastic rubbish bag, and into it she put her dolls, her teddies, her books, and any other bits and pieces which she had gathered there. She looked around, making sure that no trace of her occupation remained. Then she dragged the bag back up to her bedroom, and shoved it beneath her bed. After that, she slept until breakfast-time.

Summer merged into autumn, and with autumn came school. Nessa had already put Orlagh's name down for the local convent school, and now Ruth and Rebecca were also enrolled. Robert was happy to leave most of the arrangements in Nessa's hands.

'The girls have been through enough trauma, what with the move to Ireland and leaving their friends and everything. I want as little upheaval for them as possible', he told Nessa.

As Dr. Bailey had already recommended the convent school, and had spoken to the nuns about his granddaughters, it didn't need much persuasion from Nessa for Robert to make his decision.

'Orlagh will be starting – I know the twins are two years ahead, but still, won't it be nice to have the three of them in the same school? It will make it much easier for bringing and collecting them too.' Nessa saw the worry lines ease on Robert's forehead.

'What would I do without you Nessa?' He smiled.

'It makes sense Robert, for the moment at least . They'll get to know all the local children, and make new friends. And I know the nuns will love them. They're such good girls.'

Robert shrugged. 'I've done my best with them ... they miss a feminine presence though. You being here has made such a difference, Nessa. And Orlagh too of course.'

Nessa thought of Orlagh's closed expression when in the company of the twins. Maybe school would create a bond between her and them. Sharing these new experiences would surely bring them closer. It felt good to know that Robert relied on her where the girls were concerned. It felt good to be valued. And there was something else too – a tenderness towards another human being. She hadn't felt this way for a long time. Some nights she lay awake thinking of Robert : of his strengths; his weaknesses; what his life must have been like before he came back to Ireland. A world apart from the life that she had been leading, that was certain. But now he was here, and he had come to depend on her ... and that felt good.

In no time at all Ruth and Rebecca settled into the routine of school. They were popular with teachers and pupils alike. The other children were awed by their confidence and their easy familiarity with the teachers. They had none of that fear or shyness which most of their classmates felt, and had charmed the nuns from their very first day.

Orlagh slid into her place in the junior grade without fuss. She gave no trouble to her teacher, and drew no attention from her fellow pupils. A year or so later she accompanied her mother on the long journey to the Island of Inishbawn, to the funeral of her mother's Aunt Hannah. It was a disturbing and a frightening experience, but it was also very special, because she had Nessa all to herself for the few days. Just her mother and herself on that windswept island, wedged together in an intimacy and a closeness which felt warm and safe to Orlagh. Memories of those few days were amongst the most powerful images formed in Orlagh's consciousness. They were images which would remain with her all through her childhood and into her teenage years.

# CHAPTER SIX

The trip to Inishbawn for Hannah's funeral was a defining moment for Nessa. It was as if she had stepped across a bridge linking her past and her future. She had stepped back to a time of sadness and loss, to re-enter a self, raw with pain, fear and insecurity.

Memories which had been blocked off now pushed forward. Her stomach churned, not just in grief for Hannah, but also in grief for the child she once was. She cried for Hannah, and she cried for the mother whom she had never really known. The woman 'touched' by an obsession with a dead child, to such an extent that she had nothing to offer the child who was living. Self-pity now overwhelmed her, and made her angry. Why did her father not do something about the situation? And after his death, why was she burdened with looking after the woman who had never nurtured or cared for her? Nobody on Inishbawn had given a thought to her life, or to what she was going through. Even Killian had rejected her. They could have had a good life together, but instead he had abandoned her for some ideal. In their different ways they had all abused her. She owed them nothing.

With Hannah's death, Nessa severed her emotional link with Inishbawn. She would make sure that Orlagh would never have to suffer as she had suffered. Her child was going to have every opportunity open to her. Nessa would see to that. The past was finished, and it was the future which mattered. Her future, Orlagh's future.

Nessa returned to Dublin strong in her determination, and when Robert Bailey asked her to marry him, as she knew he would, she didn't stop for reflection. She didn't ask herself if he loved her, or indeed if she loved him. She had had her fill of fear, poverty, rejection. Needing no reflection, she accepted him.

Business was prospering. Robert took rooms in a private clinic in the city, and as a consultant he commanded large fees. Less and less of his time was spent in Dr. Bailey's old surgery. Eventually, when the old man died, Robert decided to concentrate on his private consultancy. Nessa was fearful of the change, but said nothing. Robert was dynamic and positive about their future together, and utterly confident that the decisions he made were the right ones. It was exciting living with a man who could cut his way through most obstacles, but it was also frightening. Nessa sometimes felt that her personality was being obliterated, when things were not so much discussed with her, as presented to her on a plate. Occasionally a surge of anger would rise up in her, but then she would remember the past years, and the misery she had lived through, and she would quickly stifle it.

Robert had no desire to probe into her past.

'Life is too short', he would say. 'I have no time for people who are constantly looking over their shoulder at what was or what might have been. We're married. You're my wife, and Orlagh is my legally adopted daughter. And I don't want to know what you did in a previous life, or what her natural father was like. Why make things any more complicated than they have to be, Nessa? I'm more interested in making a good future for us, and for our girls, and to do that, we have to shed our hang-ups.'

He would listen to no reminiscences – 'sentimental tosh' – and he went about his work exuding confidence and dynamism. Nessa learned to keep her doubts and worries to herself, and to let herself be carried along on the tide of his positivism.

They sold the old house after Dr. Bailey's death, and moved to a sleek, modern house, all open space, light and whiteness. There were no hidden corners in this house, no space for clutter, useless items, or oddities for memory to reflect on. It was on the outskirts of the city, out of earshot of its one or two other equally expensive-looking neighbours. Each of the girls had a room to herself. Clean lines, sliding wardrobes which concealed clothes, shoes and toys. Narrow, white-covered beds, timber floors, long windows that flooded the rooms with light. Ruth and Rebecca gasped with delight at theirs. They were now eleven years old and had already developed into teenagers, but without the awkwardness of early teens. Tall, beautifully rounded, with skin that glowed and hair which now more than ever drew admiring glances from all who came in contact with them, they were the nuns' pride and joy. Children who were always polite and alert and who assimilated knowledge effortlessly. They were the children who sat in the front rows, to draw the attention of visitors and inspectors away from their duller companions. The twins were popular with the other children too. Their bubbly humour made them easy friendships, and their earlier bossiness had now developed into what the nuns called 'leadership qualities'.

Orlagh, at nine, was still 'the baby'. Her step-sisters teased her, and bossed her, and laughed indulgently at her attempts to keep up with them. Orlagh soon stopped trying. She stayed within her own group – the average students, who gave no particular trouble to their teachers, but who never shone either. The nuns would shake their heads sorrowfully, and say 'Orlagh Bailey, you're not trying. When your sisters were your age they produced twice the work that you do. You're lazy, that's what you are. What are you, Orlagh Bailey?'

'I'm lazy, Sister.' Orlagh always found it easier to agree. That way the spotlight would be switched off her, though sometimes she was suspected of being sarcastic, and that would bring out the fury of certain teachers. Sarcasm was far from Orlagh's mind however. She knew that she could never measure up to Ruth and Rebeccas' standards, so what was the point of trying? After school the twins stayed on to play tennis, basketball, or hockey – all of which they excelled at. Orlagh took the bus back home, hoping that her mother would be there. She would sit in the kitchen, and watch Nessa prepare dinner. Nessa was always busy and rushed. Robert liked to entertain at home, which threw a lot of extra work and strain on Nessa, as Robert liked everything to be just so. As Nessa was rushing about putting finishing touches to the table Orlagh would open her school-bag and ask 'Will you help me with my sums, Mummy?'

'Not now, love.'

'I can't do them, Mummy, and I'll be in big trouble tomorrow.'

'For God's sake, Orlagh, can't you see I'm up to my eyes?'

'It won't take you long, Mummy.' Orlagh would persist, seeing the red blotches breaking out on Nessa's neck.

'If you won't help me, will I ask Daddy when he comes in?'

'You'll do no such thing!'

They both knew how cross it would make Robert to have Orlagh moaning about her homework as soon as he came in the door.

'So, will *you* help me then? You never help me! And I have to get them done. You're *always* too busy.' Orlagh's voice would take on a whining tone, and eventually Nessa would capitulate. She would sit with Orlagh, her body taut with nerves, and show her how to do her sums. Orlagh knew she was furious with her, but for those moments she had her attention, and that was enough.

When the twins were twelve, they went away to boarding school. For weeks before their departure, Nessa was preoccupied with organising their uniforms, labelling their clothes, ordering their books, shopping with them for bits and pieces. The air of excitement in the house rubbed off on everyone, even Orlagh. Ruth and Rebecca talked of nothing else but what life would be like in Saint Angela's College for Girls. They would be able to participate in so many different sports, they would have art lessons, piano lessons, dance classes - even horse-riding lessons in the stables adjoining the College. Orlagh listened in awe. Sometimes she wished that she was going to boarding school too, but mostly she hugged to herself the thought of reclaiming her mother. She would show her mother how helpful she could be; she would even make a big effort to work harder at school, so that her reports would read 'Excellent', instead of 'Could do better' and 'Disappointing'.

When the morning of the twins' departure came, Orlagh watched excitedly as the cases and trunks were lined up on the gravel driveway, then loaded into the boot of Robert's car. Ruth and Rebecca looked very grown-up and elegant in their new cream gaberdine coats, their hair pulled back softly from their faces.

'Bye, Orlagh.' They kissed and hugged Orlagh. 'You'll be joining us in a year or two, and we'll be able to show you the ropes, and introduce you to all our friends, and bring you round the college.'

Orlagh kissed her step-sisters, and stood waving as the car slowly drove down the driveway, Nessa and Robert in the front, the two girls and lots of extra luggage in the back seat. When the car was out of sight, she went back into the silent house. The woman who helped with the cleaning was in the laundry room. She looked up when Orlagh came in.

'Do you want me to do anything?' Orlagh asked. She knew that the twins often helped Chrissie to sort out the clothes, or to hang things on the line.

'Not a thing. Just be a good girl, and let me get on with my work - I'm going to miss those sisters of yours. They're lovely youngsters. You'll be lost without them now'

'Yes, I'll miss them too ...' Orlagh hesitated. Would she miss them? Or was she secretly glad? Surely that was a horrible thing to admit to. Everybody said how lucky she was to have such wonderful sisters.

Orlagh went upstairs and opened the door of Ruth's bedroom. The bed was neatly made, its white cover without a crumple On the desk were some books and pens and a photograph of Robert. Orlagh slid open the wardrobe door. She took out a soft white blouse, with tiny red rosebuds embroidered on the collar. She had always liked this blouse. She tried it on. It looked all wrong with her jeans, so she selected a long, pale green skirt of Ruth's, which on her, trailed down beyond her ankles. She posed in front of the mirrored doors, turning this way and that, trying to make her hair swish, as she had seen Ruth do. Orlagh then went in to Rebecca's room. On Rebecca's dressing-table was a make-up case, a present from one of her friends. Orlagh opened it. Maybe she needed to put on some make-up to do justice to the blouse and skirt. Perhaps that was why they didn't look right on her. She squeezed out the creamy pink foundation and rubbed it around her face. Some of it dripped down the front of the white blouse. With a tissue, she tried to scrub it off, but the stain just got bigger. Horrified, she pulled off the blouse, and hid it beneath the mattress on the bed. In her hurry to get out of the room, she stepped on the trailing hem of the skirt, and heard a loud rip. The jagged tear ran halfway up the skirt, slicing the delicate material. Orlagh pulled off the garment, and stuffed it in beside the blouse, and then raced down the landing to her own room.

She felt sick. Her hands were shaking, and her knees wouldn't stop shivering. She stared out the long window at the chiselled lawns and the manicured hedges. Maybe they'd never find out. The car might crash, or something might happen, or ... oh, the teachers were right – she was a bad girl. She could never, ever be like her sisters. She had, as she had heard someone say of her once, a bad streak in her.

That was the first time that Orlagh ran away. Pulling on her jeans and anorak, she took out all the money she had in her moneybox – about six pounds – and crept down the stairs and out the back door. The driveway seemed endless, as she tried to minimise the sound of her shoes on the gravel. When she reached the gate, she hesitated, wondering whether to turn left, from where she could catch a bus which would take her into the city, or right, heading out towards the country. She decided to go towards the city. She stood at the bus stop for a few minutes, wondering how far the bus which passed her school would take her. When the bus came, she got on, and handed the conductor her usual fare.

Orlagh stayed on the bus until most of the passengers rose to leave, and then she stepped off, to find herself in the city centre. She was frightened now. What had seemed like a good idea an hour earlier now seemed threatening. She walked for a while behind a group of women, loaded down with shopping bags. They crossed a bridge, and now she was in totally unfamiliar territory. People were looking at her. A man came up to her and stopped.

'Are ye lost, girlie? Where's yer Ma gone?' He bent down to her, his arm outstretched. She noticed he had a front tooth missing. Twisting away from him Orlagh ran back the way she had come, but couldn't see the street where the bus had stopped. She was on a narrow, cobbled street, hemmed in by tall buildings on either side. Loud music poured out from upstairs windows. Crowds of young people gathered in noisy groups along the footpaths. They took no notice of Orlagh. She walked around for what seemed like hours, going deeper and deeper into the maze of small streets. When it started to rain the crowds thinned out, and soon the shops began to be closed up. Orlagh stood in the doorway of a shop that sold masks, their twisted grimaces leering at her from the barred window, and wondered what to do. She was hungry, she was wet and she was frightened. When the Ban Gharda approached her, she burst into tears, and made no protest when she was led away.

Robert came to collect her from the Garda Station, and Orlagh had never seen him so angry. As soon as he had got her into the car, he started on her. Why had she done it? Why did she put her mother through that worry? And what about Chrissie – had she any idea of the fright she had given her? Finding Orlagh missing like that and not a word of explanation?

'Where's Mummy?' Orlagh sobbed from the back seat. 'Where's Mummy? I want Mummy!'

'Your mother has pandered to you too much, Orlagh. That's half the trouble. You seem to expect her life to revolve around *you*.. All our lives, in fact. You don't see your sisters constantly looking for attention, do you?'

'I want Mummy'.

'You have everything you could wish for. A lovely home, the best of care ... but that's not enough for you. You have to take yourself off without a word to anyone. Without a thought of what you're putting people through! What kind of a child would do that? Eh? Answer me? What kind of a child?'

Orlagh was about to say 'a bad child'. Was that the answer he expected? Or would it only make him more angry? She decided to say nothing.

They continued the journey in silence. When Robert pulled up outside the house a tear-stained Nessa appeared at the front door. Orlagh ran into her outstretched arms. As Nessa led her up the stairs to her bedroom, Orlagh could hear the angry slam of first the car doors, and then the front door. Robert did not follow them upstairs.

Nessa found the ruined clothing a week later. She had been dusting Rebecca's bedroom, when she noticed the bulge beneath the mattress. She pulled out the blouse and skirt and wondered. Would Rebecca have hidden them? Surely not. It didn't seem in character for Rebecca. Then she remembered Orlagh's silence when asked why she had run away. She had just shaken her head and let the tears trail down her cheeks. Nessa, the offending garments over her arm, went to Orlagh's room. Orlagh was sitting at her desk, her books open in front of her. She turned when Nessa entered. Her expression froze when she saw the blouse and skirt.

'Well? Is there something you want to tell me?'

Orlagh shook her head.

'Talk to me, Orlagh. Don't just shake your head. Was it an accident? Tell me what happened.'

'It wasn't me, Mummy. I didn't do anything.'

'Did you go into Ruth's room and take her clothes? Did you damage her blouse and skirt, and then hide them under Rebecca's mattress? Tell me the truth Orlagh.'

Orlagh shook her head, and Nessa's heart contracted at the sight of the small, sulky figure in front of her. For a moment her face had that expression which her own mother had worn, when, back in Inishbawn,

Hannah had harangued her. Defensive and secretive, and yet vulnerable.

'Don't tell me lies, Orlagh. Who else would have done this if not you?'

'Maybe it was Chrissie?' Now she looked shifty, and Nessa didn't like what she saw in her daughter's face.

'Oh, Orlagh, how can you land the blame on poor Chrissie, for something you know you did yourself? I'm very cross with you. Lies and meanness and spite ... I can't believe you can behave like this. I'm just too disgusted with you to say any more!'

She threw the clothes on Orlagh's bed and left the room. Orlagh rushed after her.

'Mummy, Mummy, I'm sorry. It *was* me. I didn't mean it – it just happened! The stuff just spilled all over the blouse, and I couldn't clean it, and then the skirt got torn and I hid them, and I'm sorry, Mummy ...'

But Nessa had turned away. It was as if she hadn't heard Orlagh, and didn't want to hear her.

That night Orlagh ran away again. She waited and waited in her room for Nessa to call her down to supper, but Nessa didn't call. She could hear the clink of cutlery in the dining room, and smell the food from the kitchen. Then she heard the gush of the dishwasher. Her stomach rumbled, but she was too frightened to go downstairs and get something to eat. She sat on her bed until the room became shadowed and the sky outside the long window turned from pale grey to navy, but Nessa didn't come to kiss her good night. Her mother always kissed her good night, no matter how busy she was. Orlagh hands were cold. Her head ached and her mouth felt dry with fear and sadness. When she heard the sound of the television being switched on in the living-room, and the living-room door being closed, she put on her coat, crept down the stairs and out the back door.

This time she turned right, away from the city. Once she moved out of the circle of light thrown by the house, the countryside became inky black. She kept walking and stumbling blindly, just putting one foot in front of the other. She heard the sound of a car behind her, and suddenly was flooded with an arc of light. Robert stopped the car, and bundled her roughly into the back seat. When they got back to the house, she was locked in her room. For two weeks after that she was locked in her room every evening after supper. Ruth's ruined clothes were never mentioned again.

# CHAPTER SEVEN

Orlagh wheeled the bicycle around the rose bed, past the herb garden, and down the pathway to the workman's hut. The moonlight was sharp and clear, throwing shadows across the convent lawn, and giving a mysterious aura to the grim building. Having dumped the bicycle amongst the sacks of fertiliser and moss peat, Orlagh returned to the residential area of the convent, clambered up the rough brick wall, and climbed in through the dormitory window. She had been going through this procedure every Friday night since the autumn term began, and by now it was almost effortless. All that was needed was the complicity of her room- mates, and they were so awed by her nerve that there was no danger of them dropping a hint to anyone in authority.

It had been a good evening. All the usual crowd had turned up. She had gone pillion passenger with Paul, and the thrill of speeding along dark, empty, night roads, the wind in her ears, and her face pressed against his leather-clad back, had been exhilarating. The club afterwards had seemed almost tame in comparison, but that too was exciting, with its noisy, smoke-filled interior. She didn't know half the people there, but it made no difference. There was a warm sense of camaraderie, a feeling of acceptance, tinged with danger. The beat of the music was hypnotic, and Orlagh wished that she didn't have to return to the school.

'We're all going back to Leo's place', Paul shouted, his lips pressed against her ear. 'Give the school a miss, and come with us.'

Orlagh shook her head. That would be pushing her luck, and luck had been with her these past Fridays. She wanted to keep it that way.

Paul had dropped her off at their usual meeting-place, and with a casual 'Be seeing you', had roared down the road, back towards the city. Sometimes she wondered what he did during the day. She knew nothing about him – not even his second name. She just knew that he liked her, that he asked no questions, and that being with him was excitingly different.

'You're going to get caught one of these nights.' Loreto's sleepy voice had a sharp edge to it.

'Shut up, and go to sleep'.

'If you get caught, we'll all get into trouble.'

'I'm not going to get caught.'

The possibility of getting caught added an extra whiff of danger to the thrill of those Friday expeditions. Orlagh had met Paul and his friends during the summer holidays, when she had been doing some part time work in a city fast food restaurant. They had hung around together throughout the summer, and when he had suggested meeting her on Friday nights after she had returned to the school, it had added a new dimension to the relationship. What had been just a casual way of passing time was now the exciting high point of her week. She found the boarding school stiflingly dull and stodgy. Only two more years to go and she'd be out of it for ever.

Orlagh settled down in her narrow bed and closed her eyes. Loreto had already gone back to sleep, and her nasal breathing mingled with the snores and snorts of the other four girls in the dormitory. This school – St. Gobnait's – was much shabbier and less pressured than St. Angela's had been. More suited to the 'less academically inclined', as it had been politely put by one of her former teachers. Following Ruth and Rebecca to St. Angela's had been a disaster for Orlagh. They were already the shining stars of the school when Orlagh started, and remarks like 'Are you really Ruth and Rebecca's sister? You look so different' soon became 'Why can't you be more like Ruth and Rebecca? Such hard workers. So good at sports. So popular with the other girls.' There was no point in even trying to compete, and Orlagh found herself switching off. Discipline was strict, and twice in that first year Orlagh ran away. She didn't know where she was running to, and when she was found and brought back, life was even more unpleasant.

In her second year in St. Angela's the twins complained that she was 'disgracing' them with her bad behaviour, and so it was agreed that she would be better off somewhere else. Her hopes that she would be sent to a local school, where she could return to Nessa every evening, were soon dashed. Nessa informed her that she would begin the new term as a boarder in St. Gobnait's, and that she had better buckle down, because Robert was getting more than tired of her carry on.

Orlagh was now fourteen, and it was around this time that she began to feel uncomfortable calling Robert 'Daddy'. She started to question his place in her life and in her past.

'I don't want to go to that kip,' Orlagh yelled at her mother, on hearing of the plan to send her to St. Gobnait's. 'Why should I have to go there? He just wants to get me away from you, and as far away as possible from the two perfect princesses.'

Nessa glared at her.

'You are an ungrateful girl, Orlagh. When I think of how patient Robert has been with you. You've never made any effort to please him, have you?'

'Why should I? He's never liked me anyway, and he's only sending me to boarding school to get me out of the way. He hates me being a blot on his perfect life. St. Gobnait's is a dump – everyone knows that. It's for stupid people or people who can't afford anywhere else. You won't see him sending Ruth or Rebecca there, will you?'

'Can you hear how illogical you sound? How downright spoilt and childish? You got your chance to go to St. Angela's! And what did you do? Ran away, and made life as difficult for everyone as you possibly could! Robert could wash his hands of you, you know. But he isn't. He's giving you a fresh chance now. He's being more than patient, Orlagh.'

'Oh yeah, I'm sure. And of course you'll go along with whatever he says.' She muttered 'Mrs. Stepford' under her breath. Nessa gave no indication of having heard.

'What do you want Orlagh?' Nessa made to put her arms around her, but Orlagh pulled away angrily. 'Why do you go out of your way to be so difficult? We're doing our best for you, you know. I just can't understand why you always act like this.'

'Maybe it's because I've got a bad streak in me. Maybe it's because I'm like my real father, whoever he is ... maybe that's why!'

Nessa flinched as if she had struck her.

'What do you mean?'

'Nothing. Just leave me alone. All of you. Just leave me alone.'

Orlagh had rushed out of the room and down the stairs to the garden. The garden gave her no place to hide, so she kept running until she reached the roadway. She wished she was a little girl again, and could hide beneath the soft greenery of the willow tree in the old doctor's garden. She needed to think. How could she have been so naive? So innocent? She had always known that she was different, but she had never given it much thought. Robert had been around almost as long as she could remember. Up to recently she had called him 'Daddy', just like the twins had. The twins had grown up with her - Ruth, Rebecca and Orlagh Bailey ... only she wasn't a Bailey! Awareness of that had begun to dawn on her very gradually, and now her mother had not tried to deny it. Orlagh wondered was she half-witted as well as everything else, to have reached fourteen years of age and not to have asked questions? And if she wasn't Orlagh Bailey, then who was she?

Orlagh walked for miles that evening. She didn't notice the rain. She didn't notice the heavy traffic. She was deaf to all sounds around her. When it began to get dusk, she turned and walked back. It was only when she let herself into the house that she noticed that she was soaked through. Throwing her wet clothes on the polished floor, Orlagh got into bed, and fell asleep dreaming of the bad blood that must be flowing through her, making her do all those hurtful things to her mother, and making her so different from normal children.

It seemed like hours had passed, but the clock on the bedside table said ten o'clock, when Orlagh felt herself being gently shaken awake. Nessa was sitting on the edge of the bed, with a mug of cocoa and some biscuits.

'I heard you coming back. You missed supper.'

'I don't want anything.' Orlagh pulled the covers over her shoulders.

'Sit up and drink that. I want to talk to you.' Nessa put a dressing gown around Orlagh's shoulders, as she sat up sulkily.

'Maybe I should have talked to you sooner. I should have realised that you would have questions to ask. But ... we've always been a family. Robert, me, and our three girls. We're a proper family. Robert is your legal father – you're just as important to him as Ruth and Rebecca are. So, I didn't think it necessary to go into any details. Not yet anyway. Not until you were a bit older. Maybe I was wrong. Are you listening to me, Orlagh?'

Orlagh was listening. She was listening, but now she didn't want to hear. She turned her head away. Her throat felt as if it had sealed up, and she could feel the cocoa dribbling out of the corner of her mouth.

'I did what I thought was best ... best for both of us,' Nessa continued. 'How could I have managed to give you any sort of decent life on my own? I tried, but ...'

'Is he dead?' Orlagh's voice sounded as if it had come from somewhere else.

'What?'

'I said, is my father dead? If Robert is not my father, then is my father dead? It's a simple enough question, isn't it? Is my real father dead?' She waited for her mother to say 'don't be cheeky', or 'how dare you speak to me like that'. If they were angry with each other, it would be easier. Anger would dampen the tears which she could feel welling up. If they came, she knew that they would overwhelm her, and then all she would want to do would be to rush to the comfort of her mother's arms – like she had done when she was a little girl. If that happened, she would be defeated.

Nessa was silent for a few seconds, then said 'No, Orlagh. No, your father is not dead.'

'Well, where is he so? Why didn't he want me? Why did he dump me on someone else?'

'It wasn't like that at all, Orlagh. I was very young when I became pregnant with you. I wasn't ready for marriage. I wasn't ready to settle down – and we weren't right for each other, your father and me. I knew the marriage would be all wrong. So ... I left. I left without even telling him that ... that I was pregnant. But I had no idea how difficult it would be – to bring up a baby on my own I mean. To give you some kind of a future. And then Robert came along. He's a good man, Orlagh. He loves us both, and he's giving us the chance of a good life together. But you have to give something too, Orlagh. You must ...'

'You didn't answer my question. If my father is not dead, then where is he? I have a right to know, haven't I?'

Nessa hesitated. ' Yes, yes ... you have that right. Your father is in Inishbawn.'

It wasn't the answer Orlagh had been expecting. She didn't know what she had been expecting, but not Inishbawn. Inishbawn was a place for old people, funerals and graveyards and death. Her memories were vague, but they were of people swathed in black, a graveyard on a windswept hillside, her mother's sadness. Was that why she was sad when she had she had to leave the island? Because of what had happened to her there?

Nessa got up, taking the cup from Orlagh's hand. She kissed her daughter on the forehead. 'We'll talk again. But remember, we're a family now. There's no point in digging into the past. It's the future that matters, and a good education will secure your future, Orlagh. Don't jeopardise it.'

Orlagh stared up at the ceiling. Her real father, living on Inishbawn! If he had been dead it would have been easier to accept it. But to know that he was out there on the island. Maybe she had even seen him that day of the funeral. He could have been one of those stooped old men. Or maybe he ... But her mind refused to examine what was hovering on the edge. She would find out. As soon as she was old enough, she would go to Inishbawn and see if she could discover who she really was.

Orlagh said no more to her mother. She went along with the arrangement to send her to St. Gobnait's. Her couldn't care less attitude made Orlagh the scourge of her teachers' days, but for the first time in her life she found herself hugely popular with the other girls. When she had tried to establish friendships, she had failed. She had made no real friends in junior school, nor had she made any in St. Angela's. But from her first week in St. Gobnait's girls seemed to gravitate towards her. Instead of putting people off, her surly, indifferent attitude seemed to attract them. She rebuffed any attempts at close friendship, but was happy to mingle with the crowd, and it was a relief not to have to compete. In St. Gobnait's there was no one to measure her achievements against those of Ruth or Rebecca. No one who would look at her and say 'why can't you be more like your sisters?' She discovered that she was good at art, and she whiled away time – time that was supposed to have been spent at maths or science or other subjects at which she was weak – sketching and drawing. This caused much amusement among the other girls, and added to her popularity. But Orlagh was indifferent to the reactions of either the teachers or fellow pupils. She had decided that she would just get through the school years with as little effort as possible. And as soon as she could, she would leave, and find out about her past.

Two years later, when she met Paul, her Friday night outings with him added a bit of spice to her life. Paul was alright. Maybe he'd still be around when she finished school. Maybe not. It didn't matter. But in the meantime, the skirting with danger – the thrill of the forbidden – gave her weeks a focus, and helped her through the boredom of the classroom.

Paul's blank indifference to her background, and hers to his, allowed Orlagh the freedom to put a shape on her own insecurities. When she had told him what she had discovered from her mother, he replied with a shrug. 'So? I don't see the big deal. Your old man is not your old man, and your real old man doesn't want to know. Happens all the time. Nothing to get uptight about.'

Orlagh had sipped her drink, and looked at Paul. His eyes were half-closed and he was leaning back in the chair. She had just poured out all her bottled up venom – venom at the way her mother had deceived her, venom at how her stepfather saw her as a duty, venom at being left in ignorance of her true identity. She had opened up about things which she had never discussed with anyone. Could Paul really be that cool about what she had told him? She had been seeing him every Friday night for almost a year - how could he be so indifferent? Anger battled with disbelief. She wanted him to react ... but then she would never have told him such intimate details if she had expected a reaction. She wouldn't have told any of the girls in school. They would have been agog with excitement. They would have offered indignation, advice, warnings, sympathy. But Paul marched to a different beat. He never showed any curiosity about her, never asked questions. It was as if her life before their meeting had been non-existent. She didn't know all that much about him either, but she did know that he was one of a large family, and that he lived in a house packed so tight that his bike was his escape. In a way, it was his blind acceptance of her which had drawn her to him – that and the element of risk in their meetings – so why was she narked now?

'How can you say that? All my life I've felt different. How can I be a real person if I don't know who I am. And *she* won't tell me anything. Only that my father is from this island where she used to live. And that he's probably still there.'

'What's a real person? You are who you are. And if you want to know more about your old man can't you go and find him?'

'Don't be so stupid. How could I do that? Stuck in St. Gobnaits with those creeps breathing down my neck.'

'You'll be finished next summer, won't you? And then who's to stop you? If that's what you want. Seems to me you're O.K. as you are though. I wouldn't bother snooping around if I were you. You'd never know what you might turn up.'

It was a valid point. It was something which lurked constantly at the back of Orlagh's mind. If what she found was something she'd rather not have known, would she be able to live with that? Would it be better or worse than existing in this limbo in which she now was? But she had to find out. The seed was planted, and she had to follow it through. Paul was right. She'd be a free agent once her final exams were over. She'd make up some excuse – a trip with some school friends – anything. They wouldn't care anyhow. They'd be glad not to have her knocking around for the summer months, getting under everyone's feet. There would be relief all round if she had her own summer plans. Orlagh decided that she would get a summer job to top up her savings, and then head off to Inishbawn and see what she could discover.

Making up her mind was the impetus for Orlagh to get on with her studies. She put a bit more effort into her final year at St. Gobnait's. She pulled out all the stops for the weeks before her Leaving Certificate exam, and sat the exam with a certain amount of confidence that she would pass. Then she got a summer job in a supermarket near the city, and worked such long hours that she barely saw Nessa, Robert or the twins from one end of the week to another. At the end of July, having ensured that Loreto and another of her class-mates would vouch for the lie, she announced her plan to go on holiday with school friends. Nobody raised any objections –Nessa's fears being allayed by Robert who said 'Give the girl her head. She'll come back older and wiser. It will do her the world of good.' And so the path was cleared.

# CHAPTER EIGHT

I t was dark in the room, the tangled overgrowth obscuring most of the light. She waited until her eyes had adjusted, and then, picking up her rucksack, proceeded to explore the rest of the house. The scullery led into a large kitchen. There was a big open fireplace, scattered with twigs, soot and dirt. Mice droppings formed dark patterns all over the table and the wooden dresser, and she heard the scamper of their retreat as she entered. On the other side of the stairway was what must have been the parlour. The furniture here was heavy and dark. A gate-legged table and high-backed chairs, all thick with dust, and a glass-fronted cabinet with its door hanging drunkenly on one hinge. It must have been filled with china at one time, but now all it contained was some faded newspapers, and more mouse droppings. Upstairs the rooms were filled with light. The windows had escaped the greenery which engulfed the lower windows. Even their griminess could not dim the clarity of the light which bounced off the sea and the white shingle of the strand in the distance.

Orlagh gasped as she pushed open the window of one of the bedrooms and gazed out. The sky and the sea seemed to blend into a canvas of aquamarine, fringed by white and framed by the explosion of scarlet fuchsia which banked from the yard of the house right down to the sea edge. She dragged herself away from the view to explore the other rooms. She found what she guessed must have been her mother's bedroom when she had lived there. It was smaller than the other rooms, right at the top of the house, and with the same wonderful view, and Orlagh decided that this was where she would sleep. The iron bed was topped with a sagging horsehair mattress which had been nibbled in patches by the mice, which seemed to have colonised Derryglas, but cleaned up, it would make a base for her sleeping bag. On the bookshelf opposite the bed was a dog-eared photograph of the young

Nessa. A confirmation photograph of a very beautiful twelve year old. Orlagh felt a lump in her throat. Nessa's face, open, smiling, innocent ...her clothes old-fashioned and frumpy, the pose obviously a studio one. Orlagh touched the spines of the books on the shelf, and wiped off the dust to read some of the titles. Books by Canon Sheehan, Annie M.P. Smithson, Graham Greene, Francois Mauriac, Ernest Raymond, Dickens, Edgar Wallace ... Orlagh was surprised by the variety of the writers, and even more surprised that her mother would have been reading books by authors, some of whom she herself could now relate to. She tried to picture Nessa sitting in that window seat, lost in her reading, the soft hum of the sea in the background. She had never before thought of her mother as a child, as a teenager, as a young woman with her own dreams and hopes. Had she been happy there? How could anyone be otherwise, surrounded by such beauty.

Orlagh opened some of the books, and read the inscriptions on the fly leaves. A book of Shakespeare's sonnets had 'From Mama and Dada with love'. The Annie M.P. Smithson said 'From Hannah'. The Graham Greene said 'Love from Killian'. Orlagh wondered who Killian was – a school friend maybe? A neighbour? There were so many things she didn't know about her mother's life. Nessa had always side-stepped any questions about her past. She would always refer to the present, how great it was to live in the city, how lucky they were – it was as if the past was a closed door, which, if opened, would release some terror. Orlagh herself had her own closed doors. She had vague memories of rooms where she had been while her mother was out at work, of shouts and arguments,of a woman screaming at her, and a man who ... But that door was closed, and safety was her mother returning, was her snuggling up to her mother's warm back, was hiding beneath her screen of greenery in the doctor's long garden. Orlagh wondered what lay behind her mother's closed doors – maybe now that she was here she could understand more, and by understanding she would then learn about herself? Orlagh blew her nose and set about clearing a space for her rucksack and her sleeping bag.

Orlagh slept soundly that night. She had cleaned up the bedroom as best she could, and had blocked off any holes from which mice could emerge, and now the vague rustlings from behind the skirting board didn't disturb her too much. The soothing, swishing sound of the sea lulled her to sleep. The sun shining through the uncurtained window woke her early. She lay, snug in her sleeping bag, and wondered at the silence all round – no traffic, no voices, no snorts and snores from slumbering schoolmates. Hunger eventually got her up. There was no food in the house, and she had finished her own stock the night before. She would have to go into the village and get some provisions. She found an old bicycle in a shed behind the house, and after spending some time pumping up the tyres and fiddling to get the chain back on, she rattled her way out of the driveway and on to the road. It took her twenty minutes to come within sight of the village, but rather than take the brakeless bike down to the shops, Orlagh hid it in a ditch, and walked the rest of the way.

'You must be camping around here?' It was a question rather than a statement. The woman's eyes darted at her curiously, as she clocked up the beans, bread, tin opener, milk, torch. Orlagh hadn't thought of herself as camping, but she nodded.

'You're from Dublin? We get a lot of Dublin people here since they opened the hostel and the camping site. We see loads of people from all over the world really; they seem to love it here.'

'Well, it's a very beautiful place.' Orlagh felt an affirmation was expected, but the woman just continued on, ignoring her reply.

'Oh yes, we meet all sorts of people here. I could tell you some stories of what goes on. Still, it's all money in the till, isn't it? They have plenty to spend, the foreigners who come here, and it's only for the couple of months. The rest of the year is long and dreary enough. Will you be staying long? Was it the hostel you said you were staying in?'

The woman had packed her purchases into a plastic bag, and was settling down for a longer chat, when a group of Germans came in, so her attention was diverted, and Orlagh made her escape. The little village was by now dotted with locals, dark-clad and mostly elderly, and holiday-makers, colourful, young and ebullient. A signpost pointed the way to the hostel and camping site, and Orlagh was relieved to see that they were on the opposite side of the island to Derryglas. Here there were also some guesthouses and a small hotel, as well as two pubs, an old fashioned grocery store, and a shop selling 'Ladies' Fashions'. Farther down she came to a fishing tackle shop, a boat yard and yet another pub. The ferry from the mainland was already disgorging its first bunch of day-trippers, tumbling on to the quayside in a gaggle of transistor radios, picnic baskets, rugs, swimming gear. It would be a noisy day in the little coves around the harbour.

Orlagh turned back through the village, past the church, and up the hill to where she had hidden the bicycle, and on the way back to Derryglas, the only sound was the clank, clank of the bicycle chain, and the occasional call of the gulls as they swirled across the sky.

Orlagh ate her breakfast sitting on the dazzling shingle, her back to Derryglas, the sea stretched out in front of her. Then, lying back, she dozed for a while. Afterwards she swam, the cold of the water making her gasp. There was not another soul to be seen. It was as if she was alone on the island, and yet she didn't feel lonely. Orlagh felt content and complete. It was almost as if she had found home.

When she returned to the farmhouse she sensed that something was different. Making her way around the back, she climbed in the window, as she had done the night before. All was silent, but there *was* something different. She crept up the stairs, and tiptoed to the bedroom where she had left her gear. A dark-haired teenage boy was sitting on the window seat. He was engrossed in one of the books, and it was a few seconds before he became aware of her standing in the doorway. He looked up, dropping the book in his confusion.

'What are you doing here?' he said. 'Do you know you're trespassing on private property?'

On the precept that attack is the best form of defence, Orlagh retorted, 'Well, I could say the same to you. You obviously don't live here, so what are you doing poking about with those books? And you had no business messing with my things.' She pointed to the rucksack which had been pulled out from under the bed, and was now in the middle of the floor.

His face flushed, spreading a deep crimson across his sallow skin.

'I didn't go through it ... I wouldn't do that. I just pulled it out to see if there was a name on it.'

She strode across the floor. 'Well, there isn't. So keep your hands off it.'

'You're very aggressive, for one who's in the wrong. You could be arrested for this you know. Breaking and entering. Squatting on private property. Damaging a window ...'

'Oh yeah? Let's phone for the police then. Where do you keep the phones? Oh ... and is there a garda on the island? I'm sure I'll be dragged away screaming, for committing this terrible crime!'

They stood now in the centre of the little bedroom, glaring at each other. Then his face crumpled into laughter.

'You're a brazen one, I'll say that for you. I wouldn't like to be the person who crossed you too often!'

Orlagh relaxed.

'Well, you asked for it – going for me like that.' She picked up her rucksack, and the book which he dropped – noticing that it was Graham Green's *The End of the Affair*, the book with the inscription from Killian on it.

'You are on private property though.'

'What's it to you?'

'Well, my father owns the land around here. We graze cattle on it.'

She looked at him more closely now. He was about her own age, maybe younger, but had a weathered look about him ... like someone who spent all his time out of doors. His wiry frame was muscular, without being bulky, and he was clad in a thick jumper and trousers, in spite of the heat of the day. He had that sallow, dark, appearance that she had noticed was a feature of many of the islanders. He wasn't good looking, but he had a nice smile, and suddenly she felt glad that he was there.

'I suppose I should explain myself so. My name is Orlagh – Orlagh Bailey. I'm from Dublin, and I came over to Inishbawn on the ferry yesterday. I was just sort of wandering around, and I saw the house – saw that it was empty. Thought it would be a good place to kip down for the night, so here I am'.

'Why here? There's a camping site on the other side – near the harbour. You must have seen the signpost.'

'Yeah, well. The last thing I wanted was to be in the middle of all those tourists. Besides, I wanted to see this side of the island. And I fancied the look of this house!'

'I don't know what my dad would say if he knew you were dossing here.'

'I won't tell him if you don't!'

He laughed again.

'Done!' he said.

They went back downstairs, and out into the fuchsia-drenched garden, where the tang of the salt air bit into the heavy perfume of honeysuckle and dog roses, all growing in wild abandonment .

'It must have been lovely here ... once,' Orlagh said.

The boy, who had introduced himself as Ronan, shook his head.

'It's been a wreck as long as I remember it. I used to play here as a child – around the garden I mean. I never had the cheek to break a window and actually go in to the house. But it was a great place for exploring as a young lad. So many nooks and crannies. They say the person who lived here went bonkers, and then the family moved away. That's why no one has lived here since. Bad memories I suppose.'

Orlagh decided to say nothing about her real reason for being there.

'Does your father come here often?'

'You mean – are you likely to be spotted? No. He never comes near the place. The nearest he'd come would be to the field down there where the cattle are, and that wouldn't be very often. I usually get that job.'

'So your house must be that farmhouse over there?' She pointed vaguely in the direction of the only other house to be seen.

'Yep. Most of the land on this side of Inishbawn belongs to us.' He lay back in the overgrown grass of the garden, shading his eyes against the now slanting rays of the sun. 'We're the monarchs of all we survey. Kings of the island – my Dad and me. At least, he thinks he's the king. And I'd better toe the line, or else!'

She looked at him, and wondered. But she wasn't here to interest herself in someone else's problems, and she made no answer.

'What's it like to live in Dublin?'

'It's O.K. I've been in boarding school, so I don't get to live the high life much.'

'Me too – boarding school I mean! I finished this year. I'd have liked to travel for a year or two, but ...'

'But what?'

'Duty calls! The king needs a crown prince, and since I'm the one, well, my future is well and truly mapped out'.

'If it's not what you want, then why should you toe the line? You should live your own life!'

The boy stood up abruptly. 'Who says anything about not wanting it? I like it here. It's just ... I don't know. Anyway, I'd better be getting back.'

She watched him until he was out of sight, then turned back into the house. Already this house had a stamp of home about it. She went from room to room, touching, examining, thinking what it must have been like for her mother when she lived there. The boy had said that somebody here had been 'bonkers'. Maybe it was her father. Maybe he was locked up somewhere right now. More secrets. More mysteries. But there was no sense of evil in Derryglas. It had a benign atmosphere, an atmosphere that wrapped itself around Orlagh, and brought her an inner peace which had eluded her for a long, long time. She sat in the window seat of the little bedroom, and read Graham Greene's *The End of the Affair* until the light faded and the room became swallowed up in shadow. The moon rose, and traced a path of silver across the sea, so calm it seemed like it was holding its breath, waiting. The book fell from Orlagh's hand. A great tiredness overwhelmed her, and pulling the sleeping bag around her, she rolled on to the squeaky little bed and fell asleep.

The days followed a pattern. She would cycle into the village most mornings to collect groceries and talk to the woman in the supermarket. Some time, in the future, she might ask questions of this woman. Not yet. For now, it was the woman who did the asking, and Orlagh surprised herself at the agility of her lies. She told her of the friends she had in the Hostel, of the noise at nighttime, of the babble of different languages to be heard over breakfast. She told her of the fun and the music and the talk. The woman listened and nodded and added bits of her own about boisterous beach parties which had got out of hand, and camp fires which had set the gorse alight, and thefts which had taken place in broad daylight. Still, as she said, it was 'money in the till', and who'd want to go back to the old days of isolation and poverty? Not her at any rate. Not when they could now afford to spend the harsh winter months on the mainland, and enjoy the comforts of restaurants and cinemas and big stores.

If the weather was fine enough, Orlagh would swim and loll about on the strand, reading or just day-dreaming. She would walk and cycle around every corner of the island, keeping to the lanes and paths, and avoiding the road, which lead from the village to the hostel. Her side of the island was another world, a valley separated by the steep hill from the village and its surrounds. This side was sparsely populated. Just the big farmhouse, Derryglas itself, and a couple of dilapidated cottages, now used for storing fodder and bits of machinery. Orlagh wondered about the families who used to live in these cottages. Would they have known her mother? Or maybe they were already deserted when her mother was a child. They seemed so tiny – how could they have been home to families, she wondered.

When the days were wet, and the relentless rain rolled in from the sea, gulping up the fields and the paths and the animals until all became as one grey blanket, Orlagh stayed in the house, reading and sketching. Some day, these sketches would be the inspiration for paintings which she knew she would produce. Some day, but not yet. She also cleaned more of the house, making the kitchen area habitable. She would have liked to light a fire in the big open fireplace, but she daren't risk that. The smoke would be seen. Someone would be sure to investigate.

Ronan came by on the second week she was in Derryglas. She found she had been looking forward to seeing him again, to his easy banter, his big smile. This time he brought her a chunk of meat pie, still hot from the oven, and she was amazed at how good it tasted. Sandwiches, crisps and beans were becoming so monotonous – she longed for a home cooked meal. They sat at the scrubbed kitchen table, and shared the pie in companionable silence. When she had drunk three cups of tea from the flask, she asked him about his family. Had they always lived in the farmhouse? Had he any brothers or sisters? Did he like his parents? He laughed at this latter question.

'What a daft thing to say! Of course I like my parents. They're stodgy and old- fashioned, and my Da thinks he knows everything, and my two little sisters are a nuisance, and my mother worries too much. But they're alright. All of them. They're not the worst.'

He asked her about her parents, and she listened as the lies tripped from her tongue. The wonderful holidays abroad. The visits to exotic lands with her father, who was devoted to her. The death of her mother in a plane crash in the Alps. Money tied up for her in trust, until she was twenty-one ...

'I don't believe a word you're saying.' He cut her off mid-sentence. 'You don't have to tell me anything about yourself, but don't expect me to believe that nonsense.' His smile was still there, wavering at the edge of his mouth, but his eyes told her that he wanted her to be straight with him.

She shrugged.

'Believe what you want,' she said. 'It's not important.'

He didn't press the point, but she knew he was curious. He wasn't like Paul, indifferent. She could see that he was fascinated with her background –how a girl on her own could be wandering around and sleeping rough in a remote abandoned farmhouse. Because she sensed his interest, she could not bring herself to tell him anything. Anyway the less people in Inishbawn knew about her the better. Then, when the time was right for asking her own questions, they would be off their guard and more open. She liked the feeling of blankness around her since she came to the island. It was like a protective coat, shielding her from the need to search. Here, she had no identity. She could be anyone she wanted to, and take on any personality she needed to, and when she did find answers, that coat could be shrugged off like a snake shedding a skin.

They swam together that afternoon, running down the crunchy shingle, and plunging, gasping, into the cold blue sea. They turned their backs to the incoming waves, and bobbed and swayed on the frothy tips, until they were thrown together in a heap on the shoreline. Out they swam, farther and farther each time, their shouts drowned in the roar of the sea, and the shrill screams of the gulls. Then they floated back, and lay breathless on the white sand, until the weak August sunshine had dried them. Orlagh couldn't remember a time when she had been so happy.

She had one more week to stay on the island, and then she knew she would have to return to Dublin, and resume her life as Orlagh Bailey. Her mother would be cross that she hadn't kept in touch more. She had phoned once, from the box outside the Post Office in the village. She had muffled her voice, and led her mother to believe that she was in France with Loreto and the other girls. Her mother's questions were easily waylaid, and then they were cut off. She felt mean, deceiving her, but when she returned, she would make it up to her. Now, with one week to go, she still hadn't decided whether to tell Nessa where she had really been. It might be better if she knew nothing of her trip to Inishbawn. It would only upset and worry her, and it would get in the way of any future trips to the island. Orlagh fully intended returning. Whether or not she found out who her father was, she knew she would still return. She was drawn to this island.

'Will you come down to the farmhouse for a meal on Sunday?'

Ronan didn't meet her gaze. His eyes were fixed on some distant point.

'Will your folks be there?'

'Of course they'll be there. They live there! But they'll be delighted to have you visit. It gets lonely for my mother sometimes ... and she loves to cook.'

'Won't they ask questions?'

'I've already told them a bit about you. That you're here on a camping holiday, that you're from Dublin, that we've been swimming together a few times. You know ... the usual.'

'Not that I've taken up residence in Derryglas?'

He laughed. 'No, not that. I think the idea of a girl kipping down in a deserted farmhouse, miles from anywhere, might be inclined to shock them!'

'We wouldn't want to shock them, would we?' She laughed with him, then said 'Why not! A real, hot, home-made dinner is exactly what I'd love now. In fact there's nothing I'd love more. Name a time, and I'll be there ... and thanks Ronan.'

She met him outside the church after the twelve o'clock Mass that Sunday. It was a still, heavy day, when the clouds hung low over the island, blocking off the views and giving a vague air of isolation and abandonment to the landscape. There hadn't been very many at the Mass, just the stragglers who hadn't made it to the earlier one. The church was dark and silent, and the old priest droned through the prayers with the ease of his fifty years experience. Orlagh loved the quietness and the calm in this harbour church. In spite of the changes on the island, and the throngs who spilled in here from the ferry boats day after day, in this church, time seemed to have moved not at all. Everything was as she remembered it from Hannah's funeral, as it must have been when her mother was a girl. If she asked to see the Baptismal Register she knew that she would find records of her mother's family, going back through generations, their family as much a part of the island as the rocks and the land. Maybe she would find generations of her father's family too – it was an awesome thought. Roots so deeply embedded in this patch of land so far from anywhere.

Ronan looked a little nervous. He was wearing new jeans and a cream coloured jumper. She had never seen him spruced up ... he was better looking than she had thought. His smile broadened when he saw her.

'I was afraid you wouldn't come.'

'I said I'd be here.'

They walked together up the hill, to where she had dumped the bike. Ronan's bike lay on top of it, wheels entwined, and the spikes of the bull rushes shooting up through the double spokes. They pulled up and dislodged the bikes, and cycled in silence in the direction of the farmhouse.

It was Orlagh's first time seeing Ronan's home close up. It was a prosperous looking farmhouse, well maintained, lighting up the dull day with the dazzle of its whitewash and the bunched colours of the cottage garden to the side. The out-offices were well stocked with all sorts of farm machinery, and a spacious silver-coloured car was pulled up on the gravel in front of the farmhouse.

Ronan's mother was in the kitchen, a huge room dominated by a dark green Aga cooker. The long pine table was set for lunch, and smells of cooking made Orlagh's stomach rumble in anticipation. The television was blaring in the room off the kitchen, and two girls of around nine and eleven were sprawled on the floor in front of it. They waved casually at Ronan and Orlagh, and then resumed their viewing. Ronan's mother was a large woman, round faced and frizzy haired, with a smile as big as Ronan's and surprisingly blue eyes. She juggled saucepans and dishes deftly around on the cooker, moving with the sureness of one who spent much of her time in this kitchen, and greeted Orlagh as if she had been coming to lunch every Sunday.

'Brendan will be in at two o'clock, and then we can eat,' she said. Orlagh wondered whether she should offer help, but decided against it. Instead, she joined the two girls in the television room.

At two o'clock they all sat around a table weighed down with so much food that Orlagh wondered how they could possibly get through it.

'Eat up, girl – don't be shy.' Brendan Doyle sat at the top of the table, looking slightly uncomfortable in his Sunday shirt and tie. He looked like a man who was happier out of doors. Orlagh didn't need to be urged to eat. Vegetables fresh from the garden, potatoes floury and crumbling, beef that melted in her mouth, home-made apple tart surrounded by pools of thick, yellow cream – it was a feast. Appetites were big, conversation was casual, and Orlagh's place within the family circle was more or less unquestioned. She wondered how often stray guests turned up for the Sunday lunch.

**210**

Afterwards, they slumped back in their chairs, relaxed in the afterglow of good food. Brendan had removed his tie, and had opened the top button of his shirt. There was a sharp division between the redness of his face and neck, and the pallor at the top of his chest.

'You're doing a bit of relaxing after your Leaving Certificate I take it?'

'Something like that,' she replied. She was conscious that they were all looking at her now.

'And how did you find your way to Inishbawn?'

'Oh, I was on the mainland, liked the look of it from afar, so here I am.'

'Ah yes. It looks quite exotic from the other side of the bay, Inishbawn does. I often think it looks far more enticing than when you actually land on it.'

'Don't you believe him,' Ronan said. 'He wouldn't live anywhere else in the world.'

'And what about you, Mrs. Doyle,' Orlagh asked. 'Have you always lived here?'

'Always.' She was poised to clear the table, but now she sat back once more into her chair. 'I was born and raised in the village – knew nothing about farming until I married Ronan's father.'

'It was a whirlwind romance,' Ronan chipped in, 'and she took to the place like a duck to water!'

'And now that you have the studying behind you, what will you do? Plenty of opportunities these days for young people – you don't all have to be sent off to the States like the youngsters in my day.' Brendan Doyle shook his head.

Orlagh laughed. 'They can't get the visas now, even if they wanted to. I think I'll go on to art college.'

Even as she said it she realised that that *was* what she would do. She hadn't voiced it before – not even to herself. But since coming to Inishbawn she had discovered that something in the artistic line was what she was cut out for. Fine art, or maybe photography, or some kind of craft work. She didn't know. But yes, something in that field.

'Well, when you're a famous painter, you'll have to come back here and paint some scenes on Inishbawn.'

'There'll be loads more exciting things to paint up in Dublin,' Maria, the youngest of the two sisters chipped in.

'Yes,' added Sheila, 'like huge buildings and big shops, and lots and lots of people. I wish I was living in Dublin!'

Her brother was just about to retort to this, when the sound of a car on the gravel diverted attention. Maria rushed to the window.

'It's Uncle Killian. Mam, it's Uncle Killian, and I'll bet he'll want his dinner!'

Ronan's mother rose from the table. She seemed unflustered at the idea of an extra guest. Orlagh felt that this was a house where food was always at the ready. The front door clicked shut, footsteps could be heard in the hall. The kitchen door opened, and Orlagh's heart missed a beat. The man in the doorway had the Doyle eyes, but none of his brother's bulk or ruddiness. His face was lined, and his once dark hair was streaked with grey. In spite of his years, Orlagh had no difficulty in recognising the young man in a photograph which she had found stuck between the pages of one of Nessa's books. The serious faced teenager astride the black bicycle, Derryglas in the background. The boy who had written 'Love from Killian' on the back of the photograph ... in the same handwriting as that other 'Love from Killian' on the fly leaf of Graham Greene's novel. The man stood for a moment in the doorway, smiling at the gathering around the kitchen table. He was dressed in a black suit, and wore a roman collar.

# CHAPTER NINE

The train back to Dublin was crowded and noisy. Lots of young people returning to city jobs, lots of back-packers, some tourists. Orlagh sat in the seat and stared out at the damp landscape. Her last few days on Inishbawn had been ones of isolation, shored up in Derryglas while the island was battered by a wild Atlantic storm, which seemed to spring up from nowhere, and which spread its fury across the valley, slapping the old farmhouse with salty gusts, and whining and moaning in the chimney. She was cold, and wished she could light a fire. Instead, she wrapped herself in her sleeping bag, and read her way through all the books in the bedroom, breaking off for food, and sleeping when the light grew dim. She saw no sign of Ronan, and only made her way to the village when the storm had spent itself and she could risk cycling, without being blown off the road. She could have made her way cross country to the Doyle farm, to sink into the comfort of a warm house and good food. She knew her presence would be accepted without question. But she felt the need to distance herself.

That Sunday had disturbed her, and made her feel uneasy. Afternoon had eased into evening. They had played cards, drank more coffee, stoked up a fire in the sitting room, and sat around it, flushed and sleepy until darkness began to creep through the windows, and it was time for Brendan and Ronan to see to the livestock, and for Fr. Killian to catch the last ferry back to the mainland. She could think of no excuse when he said he would drive her to the hostel.

'Just bung your bike into the boot of the car, and I'll have you there in no time.'

Alone with him, she had dreaded his questions. He was more astute than his brother, and something had crossed his face when he had looked at her. Maybe he had just picked up her own shock at seeing him. Maybe he was tuning in to the disturbing thoughts which raced through her mind. The car was small and cramped, creating an intimacy which she could not ignore.

'You won't be locked out of the hostel, will you? It's a bit late, you know. We don't keep city hours around here!'

'I'm not staying in the hostel.'

He slowed the car down, and looked across at her.

'Oh? You're staying with friends, are you?'

'I'm staying at Derryglas.' It was out of her before she had time to consider. In any case, this was not a man she could lie to, and she sensed that he would have a crucial role to play in her search. The words hung there in the darkness. She wished he would say something, but all his attention seemed to be focussed on the twisty road ahead. Finally he broke the silence.

'Derryglas has been empty for years. Why would you be staying there?'

'I'm not doing any harm. I'm not bothering anyone, and anyway, Ronan knows I'm there.'

She heard the aggressive tone in her voice – the tone she had perfected over the last few years, and she waited for his riposte about trespassing and danger and all the rest. They had reached the gateway leading up to Derryglas. In the car headlights she registered the drunken slant of the gate, and heard the tap of the overhanging trees on the roof. The place had a forlorn and neglected and slightly eerie look about it. The priest pulled up in front of the house.

'Do you need money? Is that why you're staying here?'

'No. I've enough money. I just *want* to stay here. Only until the end of the week.'

'You've been here before, haven't you?'

'Once, years ago.'

'I thought so. You're Nessa's daughter, aren't you?'

When she didn't deny it, he went on. 'I knew there was something familiar about you. When I walked into Brendan's place something twigged. It's been nagging at me all evening, but I couldn't pin it down. Now I can see it. You're not much like her, but yet, there's something.'

'Well, you'd know, wouldn't you!' She wasn't quite sure why she said that. She pulled her jacket around her and lurched out of the car, into the chill and the freshness of the night air. He leaned over to shout 'Will you be alright? Are you sure you don't want me to take you back to the hostel, or to Brendan's?'

'I'll be fine, and please Father ... please don't tell Brendan that I'm here? I'll be gone by Friday. Promise.'

She ran around to the back of the house, her torch drawing a dim pool of light ahead of her. She waited until she heard the sound of the car moving off, and then went up to the bedroom, where she placed the photograph of the gauche teenage boy into her bag. The years had traced deep lines on his face, and had peppered his hair with grey, but otherwise the face was the same. There was no doubt in her mind that the boy who had written 'love from Killian', and the priest who had driven her back to Derryglas, were the same person. Orlagh felt that there was a lot more he could have told her, but she wasn't ready to hear it. She buried herself deep down into her sleeping bag, rubbing her toes together to warm them, and fell asleep to the rising groans of the wind, as the storm approached.

A rucksack full of dirty clothes, shoes cakes in mud, a sodden jacket. They offended the virginal whiteness of the kitchen. Orlagh had showered and changed into clean dry clothes, and was sorting out washing for the machine, when her mother returned. Orlagh noticed the flicker of distaste at the mess in the kitchen, before Nessa rushed to embrace her.

'Why didn't you let me know you were coming? I would have come to meet you. How was the trip? You look thin ... you haven't been eating properly. And those bags under your eyes. Where have you been spending your nights?'

Orlagh laughed at all the questions. She felt a warmth towards her mother, a warmth which had long been lacking in their relationship. Three weeks of living in Nessa's past had brought her close to her. She wasn't just Robert's wife any more. Not just the step-mother of Ruth and Rebecca, or the woman who kept this streamlined house in perfect order. Orlagh now saw her as the girl who had grown up in Derryglas, as the teenager who had spent long hours in her room, losing herself in reading, as the young woman who had kept the photograph of Killian, as the likely owner of the old bicycle which Orlagh had been using these past weeks.

Orlagh fobbed off questions regarding her trip as best she could.

Robert was pleased at the new serenity about her.

'There, what did I tell you?' he said to Nessa. 'Having to fend for herself has been the making of her. I told you she'd come home a new person.'

Nessa agreed, smothering uneasy feelings about her daughter's time away. She knew Orlagh too well not to know when she was lying. She was hiding something, but Nessa knew better than to quiz her. Orlagh would clam up, and the old barrier would be put between them. Right now, it was nice to have her daughter back safely, and to have her without her usual anger and aggression.

The leaving certificate results came out. Orlagh had passed. She had even got high enough marks to gain her a place at one of the art colleges. Nessa was pleased.

'Get your degree, and you'll be able to teach. You'll have a qualification which will give you security, wherever you go. Teachers are always in demand.'

Orlagh knew she would never be a teacher. Becoming a teacher had been her mother's dream. It was not hers. But she loved the college. Maybe she would never see out the four years to degree status, but she loved the colours and the tactile sensuousness of the materials she was working with. She loved the vision of her lecturers, the way they 'saw' things in a way that she herself saw them. She loved the sense of excitement among the other students. Here, nobody cared whether she worked or not. Nobody questioned her if she didn't turn up for lectures. It was all up to herself, and she discovered that she drove herself harder than anyone else could ever have done.

Robert made it clear from the start that fees would be a joint responsibility. If Orlagh had to find part of the money, she would appreciate the course more. Nessa was fearful – she would get discouraged, she would give it up, she would drift. But Robert was right. Orlagh ploughed what was left of her summer earnings into her first year's fees. She would work again next summer, and maybe even pay the full fees herself. That way, she would be in control. She could opt out if she wanted to. She could decide on her own future. The Bailey home was not conducive to artistic experiment, so Orlagh found herself spending longer and longer hours in the college. At weekends she helped out in the galleries, gaining much valuable experience.

The following winter, Orlagh made an unplanned trip back to Inishbawn. Nessa and Robert had gone abroad following a hectic round of socialising over the Christmas period. Ruth and Rebecca were away. Only Orlagh remained in the house. The Art College was still closed for the holiday, and she felt restless and unsettled. One morning on impulse, she threw a few things into her rucksack and decided to head for the island. Having made the decision, she didn't stop to think about it, just hurried in to town, caught the first train to Ballymona, and four hours later she was standing by the pier waiting for a ferry to take her across to Inishbawn.

Except for the crew and herself, the ferry was empty, with rows of rain-soaked seats, and water swirling around on the floorboards, dancing to the vibration of the engine. Orlagh went down below to escape the biting wind. Here the smell of diesel made her feel nauseous, and she was relieved when the ferry tied up at the harbour in Inishbawn. This time there were no tourists, no bustle, just a few fishermen standing in the sheds on the quay, smoking and waiting. She wondered what they were waiting for. For the weather to improve so that they could take their boats out? For evening to draw in so that they could go home? They stared at her as she walked past them, up towards the village. She felt conspicuous. The hostel was closed for the winter. So were most of the guesthouses. People didn't visit Inishbawn on bleak January days. She strode purposefully past the shops, and up the hill towards the church. She stopped briefly to look in on the church. The sanctuary lamp glowed before the altar, and a few candles flickered in the candelabra. It was dark and comforting. When she left the church to tackle the long walk to the other side of the island the wind stung her face and found its way through the loops in her gloves and her knitted hat. With its damp saltiness it seeped through her jacket and jeans, and made her limbs feel numb. She walked faster and faster to keep her circulation going, and the gloom of the day was melting into the dusk of evening when she finally reached Derryglas. She went around the side of the house. The broken window had been boarded up.

Orlagh tried all the windows. She pushed and shoved at the doors, back and front. She climbed up the ivy until it snapped beneath her weight. There was no way she could get in. The outhouses were bare, no straw, no hay, nothing that would give her shelter. The light was fading fast, so she decided to walk on to the Doyle farmhouse. She could not be any colder, so she might as well keep moving. With any luck Ronan would be at home, and he would know what to do.

The farmhouse was flooded with light. Smoke curled up white against the black sky. The soft hum of animals settling down for the night carried from the sheds. As she approached, two collies rushed out from one of the sheds, barking furiously, teeth bared. They skidded to a halt beside Orlagh, tails now wagging, tongues licking her outstretched hand.

'Well, well ... who have we here? What in the name of God are you doing out on a night like this. Is it Orlagh? It is Orlagh, isn't it?' Brendan Doyle appeared in the doorway, his face flushed from the fire.

'Come inside, come inside. Kathleen,' he called, 'look who we have here. It's Ronan's friend from Dublin ... Orlagh.'

Orlagh followed him into the kitchen. She was ushered into a seat by the fire. Her damp outer garments were removed from her, and a mug of tea and some cake were pressed on to her. From the television room the girls appeared, pleased at this diversion from their homework. Kathleen Doyle fussed and clucked around her, and then went to the bottom of the stairs and called up 'Ronan! You have a visitor.'

Ronan came clattering down the stairs. He smiled his pleasure at seeing her. Orlagh felt enveloped in an aura of acceptance and welcome. Being in this house was like sinking into a familiar bed, whose curves merged with one's shape.

'The hostel is closed', she said, by way of explanation.

'Well it would be! It always closes from October to Easter.' Brendan shook his head at her ignorance. 'You'll stay here ... we have plenty of room. Isn't that so Kathleen?'

Kathleen nodded. 'I'll make up the bed in the back room, and put on the electric blanket for you.'

'Oh, are you sure? I don't want to be any trouble.' Orlagh exchanged looks with Ronan. She wondered who had boarded up her window. Had Brendan suspected? He certainly didn't seem to know that she had been using Derryglas during the summer.

Orlagh had no chance to talk alone with Ronan that night. Next morning they walked together to Derryglas.

'My father found the broken window,' Ronan explained, as soon as they were out of earshot of the farmhouse. 'He was furious. He blamed the day-trippers – thought they must have been looking for something to steal. He's been keeping an eye on the place since. I don't think you're going to be able to camp out there again, even if you wanted to in this weather.'

'He didn't know I had been there, did he?'

'Of course not. I said nothing, and they assumed you'd been in the hostel.'

'Your uncle knew.'

Ronan looked at her. 'Uncle Killian? How would he have known. I certainly didn't tell him!'

Orlagh explained about the lift back that night, and how she had told him to drop her at Derryglas.

'And he just left you there? And said nothing to my dad? That seems strange. It doesn't sound like what Killian would do!'

'I persuaded him. You see...' Orlagh hesitated, then blurted out 'you see, there's something you don't know, Ronan. My mother used to live in that farmhouse. She grew up there. Lived there all her life until she went to Dublin.'

He stared at her, his open mouth, giving him a comical appearance.

'My God ... you must be Nessa McDowell's daughter so? My dad often talks about Nessa McDowell. About the hard life she had in Derryglas, looking after her mother, and what a brave woman she was ...'

'Brave?'

'Well, you know...'

'I don't know. That's the trouble. I don't know anything about her life on Inishbawn. She never talks about it.'

'And your Dad? Is he not curious? Surely she's talked to him!'

'My Dad ... yes, well. I don't think my Dad wants to hear about her past. Don't be looking over your shoulder. Move forward. Be positive. My Dad is a man of the here and now. Maybe that's not such a bad thing either. Anyway, he's not my real father. He's my stepfather.'

Ronan leaned forward. He had an islandman's curiosity – an eagerness to empathise with other people's lives. Orlagh thought of Paul's off-handedness. Paul had no desire to delve into the past – maybe he was a little bit like Robert in that way. She had never thought of that before. Ronan watched her, waiting for her to continue. When she remained silent he prompted her.

'He's dead, is he? Your real father?'

'No ... I don't think so. But I don't know who he is or anything about him. All I know is that my stepfather appeared on the scene when I was about three – with two ready-made sisters for me!'

'Did he treat you badly? Give you a rough time?' Ronan's eyes deepened with sympathy. His family background was so secure that he could not visualise what hers must have been like, but it had to have been bad. Otherwise why was she dossing around, staying in derelict farmhouses? That explained so much about her.

Orlagh suddenly felt guilty. Robert might not have been her real father, but she had to be fair to him. He had been no ogre. He had always been a kind father to her and a good husband to Nessa. And as for Ruth and Rebecca ... well, the truth was, she had been jealous of them from the start. She had resented her mother's interest in them and couldn't bear the competition. Maybe that was the real barrier between them. She would have liked to have wallowed in Ronan's sympathetic interest, but it would not have been right.

'No', she replied. 'He's never treated me badly, and he's been good to my mother. And my sisters are O.K.'

'But it's not like they're your real family.'

'No, I suppose not.'

Orlagh suddenly felt exhausted. She didn't want to pursue this conversation any further. They walked back to the Doyle house, where she gathered up her things. Kathleen Doyle pressed her to stay for another night, but Orlagh, thanking her, declined. She was grateful for the offer, but she could not stay. She had to return to Dublin and to her family.

Brendan drove her to the harbour. He accepted her decision to return to the mainland as quite natural.

'Sure, what business would you have here in this weather? Inishbawn isn't a great place for young people in the winter. Come back in the summer. Plenty of jobs in the guesthouses and shops in the summertime. You could make a bit of money for yourself during those long holidays you get.'

'I'll do that', Orlagh assured him. She wondered whether Ronan would have told him who she was by then. Most likely he would. Ronan had been deeply affected by her story. They were a close family, and she couldn't imagine that they wouldn't talk about her when she was gone. Brendan would be angry that she had deceived them. Kathleen would feel that she had abused her hospitality. And then Fr. Killian would reveal that he knew all along. The tangled web of her lies was getting more dense. The longer the deception went on the more explaining she would have to do eventually.

As they drove past the entrance to Derryglas, she decided, on impulse, that it would be better if Brendan heard it from herself now, before she left the island.

'My mother lived there,' she blurted out, pointing at the farmhouse. 'That's what draws me back to Inishbawn. It was where my mother's family lived.'

Brendan looked stunned.

'I know all the land is yours,' she went on. 'Ronan has told me that only the house belongs to the McDowells now. And he told me that you keep an eye on that. My mother would be glad to know ... that someone is looking out for it, I mean.' She felt that she was blabbing on.

Brendan stopped the car. Beads of sweat gathered under the band of his cap. He removed his cap to wipe them away with the back of his hand.

'Nessa McDowell's daughter!' he said, and it was almost a whisper. 'Well, well, well.' He shook his head, looking closely at Orlagh.

'And tell me ... how is Nessa? Did she make a happy life for herself? She never came back, you know. Never came back, except for Hannah's funeral. And even then she avoided us all. All those years. Cut off her roots, she did ... 'twas like they were poison to her.' He sighed deeply. 'And maybe they were at that,' he went on. 'Hard times they were. Hard times.'

'Why? Why were they so hard for her?' Orlagh felt as if she were probing into some private world of his.

'Ah, you wouldn't understand.' He started up the car. 'Poor Nessa. No young girl should have had to cope with the life that she had. She did right to get out, and head for the city.' He smiled across at her. 'We'd better get you to the harbour, or you'll miss your ferry. Tell Nessa I was asking after her. And tell her that herself and her husband have a lovely daughter. Yes, she made the right decision. I dare say she's had a far better life in Dublin.' He patted her hand, and as the car drew up by the harbour she saw the ferry bobbing impatiently on the choppy sea.

'Come back in the summer,' he said. 'Inishbawn will look more inviting then.'

She waved goodbye to him, and felt a lump in her throat as she watched the car drive off. Soon the engines of the ferry started up and the boat faced out to sea. The cold salt wind stung her eyes and whipped her hair around her face. The other passengers looked at her curiously. A young woman with a baby smiled at her. The baby was swathed in layers of tartan blankets. The woman looked as if she was going to talk to Orlagh. Questions flickered in her green eyes. Orlagh huddled down in her seat, and turned away. She couldn't face talk just now. She couldn't face any more questions.

# CHAPTER TEN

Robert was away at a medical conference. Nessa had opted not to go with him. She would touch up the paintwork in the bedrooms – white on white. Orlagh's room especially needed touching up – she could do it when Orlagh was out. Orlagh was out most of the time, so she would have a clear run. Before starting on the paintwork Nessa had to move mounds of bags and storage boxes out of her way. Library books, old school books, magazines, paperbacks, academic books – the place was so cluttered! It was no wonder Robert always insisted that Orlagh close her bedroom door. The mess she created around her always offended his eye. He loved the spartan minimalism of the rest of the house, but had given up trying to convert Orlagh to his taste. He now settled for a closed door, and didn't want to know what was going on behind it.

Nessa pulled out one of the boxes from under the bed, and felt a shock of recognition. The box was full of dog-eared, orange Penguin paperbacks, their pages thick with damp, their spines crumbling. She lifted the top one, and turned to the fly page. '*Nessa McDowell, Christmas 1956*'. Neat, looped lettering. Black ink, slightly faded. Two Jane Austens, with '*School Prize to Nessa McDowell*' printed on the inside covers came next, then some anthologies of short stories and a bundle of well thumbed novels. She picked up the faded copy of Graham Greene's *The End of the Affair*, and flicked it open. The inscription, in spiky, rushed lettering, said '*To Nessa. Love from Killian*'. Killian she remembered had never been a great reader, not like she had been. But he had often brought her back library books from the mainland. He knew the authors she liked. He knew Graham Greene was one of her favourites. She recalled how thrilled she had been when he had bought her that paperback. Crisp and fresh, straight from the booksellers in the town. She had stroked it, smelled the exotic newness of it, quivered at

223

the thought of reading it, of plunging into the grown-up world of love affairs and disillusionment and despair. She had been touched by Killian's thoughtfulness, and surprised that he had taken the trouble to write on the fly-leaf. She had reached up and kissed him shyly. His face had flamed in embarrassment, but she could see his pleasure. Love from Killian. Hadn't it always been Killian? Killian and Nessa. Nessa and Killian. She had put all that away from her. Like someone stuffing an offending item to the bottom of a trunk, she had deliberately, for all those years, steered her thoughts away from that direction. Now the sadness welled up in her and overwhelmed her in pain. She flicked through the book, and something fluttered on to the floor. It was a photograph. A young Killian astride his bicycle, his eyes connecting directly with the camera. Such an open, trusting, solemn look. Nessa sank on to the floor, all thoughts of paint forgotten. She went through the rest of the box. Yes, all her books. All of the little library which she had kept on the bookshelf in her attic bedroom in Derryglas. At the bottom of the box was another photograph. This was of a boy and a girl emerging from a wave-tossed sea, on to the shimmering whiteness of a beach in the foreground. The girl was Orlagh – her Orlagh. The boy was someone called Ronan. And there was no doubt about that beach. Even without reading the scrawled 'Orlagh and Ronan. Summer on Inishbawn' on the back of the photograph, Nessa would never have mistaken that white sand for anywhere else in the world.

Nessa sat on the floor of the bedroom for almost an hour, staring at the books, at the photographs, at the box. A chill of fear had gripped her, making her incapable of movement. So Orlagh had been back to Inishbawn. She had been to Derryglas. She had to have been in Nessa's bedroom to have taken these books. She had been swimming with this boy Ronan. Ronan? Ronan who? Was he someone who had gone to the island with her ... or was he ...? Had they been together in Derryglas, when she and Robert believed her to have been in France with her school-friends? The implications of what might be, what could be, seeped through her. Shivering, Nessa got up, carefully shoving the box back beneath the bed. She would have to think. Confrontation with Orlagh was inevitable. But first, she would have to think.

Nessa was sitting at the kitchen table, coffee cup clasped between her hands, when Orlagh returned. She had forgotten to make lunch, or to prepare dinner. Any thoughts of touching up paintwork had been completely discarded. Orlagh dumped her bag and the scrolls of paper she was carrying on to the kitchen floor. Since Robert was away, she didn't feel the need to take all her stuff straight to her room.

'Join you in a coffee?' Orlagh put the kettle on, and then noticed the slumped demeanour of her mother.

'What's up Mum? Is something wrong? You look awful.' She sat down beside her mother at the table, taking the cold coffee cup from between her fingers. Nessa looked at her. Orlagh could see that she had been crying.

'You weren't in France at all, were you.'

It wasn't a question. It was a statement. Orlagh immediately went on the defensive.

'What if I wasn't.? Does it matter? It's water under the bridge at this stage anyway!'

'You were in Inishbawn, weren't you? Why didn't you tell me? Why did you have to go behind my back? And how did you come to be in Derryglas? Who let you in there?'

Seeing Orlagh's startled look, Nessa went on. 'Yes, I know all about it. I wasn't prying. I just found the books in your bedroom when I was clearing space for painting. My books. My books from my bedroom in the farmhouse. You could not have got them anywhere else. So, what have you to say for yourself?'

She stood up, her face now flushed with emotion. Orlagh stared back angrily at her.

'You're a fine one to talk, aren't you? Haven't I got a right to know about the past? About who I am? You've always just closed the door on whatever went on in your life before you came to Dublin. You wouldn't take me to Inishbawn ... so I had to go myself. And I did. Last summer I spent three weeks on the island. Three weeks dossing in a derelict farmhouse, reading your books, and trying to piece together what all the mystery is about!' She was shouting now, steaming with anger at being wrong-footed once again.

'And what did you find out? What did your snooping reveal to you?'

Orlagh slumped down on the chair. 'Very little. When it came to it, I was afraid to ask too many questions.'

'Who's Ronan? Is he someone from college?'

'No, Ronan is a boy from Inishbawn. His father owns all the land around Derryglas ... that's how we met. He discovered that I'd been sleeping there, and ... well, we sort of hit it off, and messed about together after that.'

She wasn't aware of the colour draining from Nessa's face, but she registered the change of tone in her voice.

'The land around Derryglas you say? Then he must be ... what's the boy's surname? Ronan what?'

'Ronan Doyle,' Orlagh answered sulkily.

There was silence in the kitchen. In the distance Orlagh could hear a dog barking, the hum of traffic. Outside this room, life continued as normal.

'You and this boy.... did you? I mean ... was, is, there anything between you?'

'Oh, for God's sake Mum. Isn't that just typical of you. Don't be so stupid! You don't have to worry. We haven't been sleeping together, and I'm not pregnant or anything daft like that.'

Ronan and herself? It had never crossed Orlagh's mind to think of Ronan in that light. He was just a nice lad, who was good to her while she was on the island. A young fellow, younger than herself. Wasn't it just like her mother to jump to conclusions!

All the fight had gone out of Nessa now. She was crying softly, her head in her hands. Orlagh put her arm around her shoulders.

'I loved the house Mum ... I read all your books.'

Nessa squeezed her fingers.

'Killian was asking about you. Father Killian.'

'You saw Killian?'

'Yes – he recognised me. Would you believe that? He knew I was your daughter. Isn't that strange Mum? Don't you think that's very strange? When he hasn't seen you for about twenty years?'

She waited, watching her mother's reaction closely. Her mother was silent.

'He said I didn't look at all like you, but yet there was something familiar about me. I thought that was very odd!'

Nessa looked up at her. Her face was streaked and puffy.

'You're wrong, you know Orlagh. I know what you're driving at, but you're wrong! It wasn't like that at all.'

'Then, for God's sake what was it like, Mum? Will you tell me. What was it like?'

Orlagh pressed her face close to Nessa's bowed head. Darkness had now crept across the manicured garden, and curtained the long elegant windows of the breakfast room. The white units stood out, ghostlike, against the encroaching blackness. Orlagh could hear her mother's breathing, coming from deep down, as if she were drawing on some hidden reserves of oxygen. It was some time before she spoke, then her voice, low pitched, almost childlike, came flooding out, spilling the memories that had been banked up for so long. She told of her mother Margaret, a young girl from the town, marrying an islandman against the wishes of her people. Of her difficulty integrating with the islanders. Of her first baby, stillborn, taken away in the night to be buried in some bleak place for the unbaptised. Of her depression, and her eventual insanity. She told of how she, Nessa, had craved for the mother's love that never came her way. How she had poured all her love on to Killian, but that his love was promised elsewhere. She described how lonely she had felt, and how frightened she had been of what the future held. The awesome burden that had been placed on her, and she only seventeen. And then that night. The night of Hannah's wedding. When a man had made her feel beautiful and desirable and wanted. When she felt that the burdens that had been too heavy for her to carry could be laid on someone else's shoulder. The music, the excitement, the sympathy. She wasn't blaming him. How could blame be apportioned? They were both young, both foolish.'

'Who was he Mum?' Orlagh's voice was barely a whisper. To speak too loudly would be to break the spell. 'Tell me ... who was he?'

'He was Brendan Doyle. Killian's brother, Brendan. But he never knew, Orlagh. He never knew that I was pregnant. He wanted us to marry. He loved me – he said he loved me. And if he had known that there was to be a child ... you know how strong family ties are on Inishbawn! He would have insisted – they would all have insisted – on us marrying immediately.'

'But you didn't want that?'

'I didn't love him. I loved Killian. I was frightened and confused and ashamed. I just wanted to get away from the island. Go away to some place where nobody would know me or judge me.'

She looked up into her daughter's face. Orlagh could see the glisten of her eyes.

'I've wronged you, Orlagh. I've wronged you terribly. I've deprived you of what was your right. But everything I've done since has been for you. Everything. Even marrying Robert ... in a way. I wanted you to have a father, a family, security. To make it up to you.'

Orlagh barely heard her. The low voice continued, but now it floated past her conscious mind. She was thinking of Brendan Doyle. Her father ... It was surreal. It was like something from a dream, where everything is mixed up and jumbled. She had suspected Killian – ever since she had seen that photograph, she had thought that ... maybe Killian. But Brendan? Ronan's father? Married to the cheerful Kathleen. How could she grasp that? No, it couldn't be. She couldn't be Brendan's daughter. Ronan's half sister? It was grotesque.

She let go of her mother's hand and stumbled up the stairs to her bedroom. She fell on to the bed, and lay there, her eyes burning, her head pounding. She had wanted to know. She had been determined to know. Well, now she had all the information that she had craved. Orlagh McDowell, Bailey, Doyle ... it was all there for her now.

Orlagh felt as if she was an observer, standing on a height watching her own life and Nessa's life unfolding. She was having difficulty connecting with reality, and yet time moved on. Robert returned from the conference. He took charge of all the happenings within that white house. Orlagh guessed that he had been told the full story, but he gave no indication. She had never been very close to him, so now it wasn't difficult to keep her distance. Nessa had dropped the mask of cheerful compliance, and there was a frightened, anxious depth in her eyes. She skirted around things, avoiding people as much as possible, doing her work mechanically. She was like some hurt animal, longing for a place to hide and be alone with her wounds. Orlagh saw all this with a clarity that surprised her, but she saw it in a detached way, like someone watching cinematic images rolling on, without sound. College life continued. She plunged herself into the projects she was working on, and the work she produced, according to her tutors, was close to brilliance. She had never before excelled at anything. Now she was shaping up to be the most promising student of the year. Some evenings she met up with Paul. He never asked her whether she had returned to Inishbawn ... whether she had found her roots. She never spoke to him about it. She liked his acceptance of her in the here and now. It was comfortable being with someone like Paul. He had no urgent ambitions, yet he could turn his hand to most things, and was making a lot of money she knew in the flood of building projects engulfing the city. He had moved into a flat, but she had no curiosity about it, or about his life away from her. She felt that her life was being lived in compartments, all separated from one another, and that to try to interconnect the compartments would be fatal.

One day in early spring, when a haze of green was beginning to ooze from the suburban trees, and people were fearfully removing the heaviest of their coverings, like butterflies emerging from their long winter, Orlagh returned from college to see an unfamiliar car in the driveway.

He sat in the formal drawing room, dressed in casual clothes, and looking more like a business man than a priest. She had only seen him in black, with his collar, and it took her a minute or two to register who he was. Opposite him sat Nessa and Robert. Robert had Nessa's hand clutched firmly in his.

'Come in, Orlagh.' Robert indicated to her to sit down. She shrugged herself out of her jacket, her rucksack, her papers, and sat down. Killian smiled at her, and suddenly she knew that it was going to be alright. Something had happened, but it was not the ominous scenario that had galloped through her mind when she saw the three of them seated there looking so solemn.

Killian spoke, looking at her, his eyes sympathetic but his tone matter of fact.

'Nessa wrote to me, Orlagh. After your last visit to Inishbawn, she wrote asking for my advice, and we have been corresponding since.'

Orlagh's glance flickered towards Nessa and Robert. Nessa sat composed, her eyes averted. Robert met her glance and said, 'Nessa has told me everything, Orlagh. We have no secrets from each other – no more secrets. We have to move forward. But there are things to be done first.' He looked at Killian, and Killian took up the cue.

'Brendan will have to be told ... and the family. It was all a long time ago, a different age. I'm not saying it's going to be easy, but I believe it's the only way.'

Nessa got up and moved forward to put her arm around her daughter's shoulder, tentatively, as if afraid of rejection. Orlagh was glad that she didn't say anything.

'I have asked Brendan to meet us here, in Dublin, first,' Killian went on. 'It will be up to him to decide about Kathleen and the girls, and Ronan. How to tell them, I mean. They have all met you, Orlagh, and they all like you. That's not going to change. Kathleen is a very down to earth woman, with a good heart. She's not going to be thrown by this.'

Robert moved closer to Nessa. The three of them formed a unit, with Killian opposite them. He was now the outsider.

'It will be alright, Orlagh.' Killian stood up. 'It should all have been cleared up a long time ago. If I had known ... if any of us had known. Your mother would not have had to suffer so much anguish, and you would have been spared all this. I will arrange things with Brendan, and we'll take it from there.'

Killian let himself out, and soon they heard the slow hum of the car going down the driveway, and turning towards the city. The three sat in silence for a few minutes, then Orlagh gathered up her stuff from the floor, and went to her room. She trusted Killian. He said that everything would be sorted out, and somehow she knew that it would be. She wondered at her own sense of calm. All the years of turmoil and anger, and now when she was confronted with her ghosts she felt this strange serenity. Maybe it was the sense of handing over her problems and all the baggage which had weighed her down for so long, to someone who was stronger and more capable. Or maybe it was that knowledge banishes fear – what terror could be as bad as the unknown one?

The meeting was arranged. Brendan, and Nessa. Orlagh would be included later, but for this meeting it was to be her father and mother only. How strange it seemed, that her mother and father should be together, for the first time in twenty years. Orlagh spent that afternoon in the cinema, huddled deep into the plush red velvet, her head resting on Paul's shoulder, feeling the comfort of his closeness. He knew about this meeting. When she had told him, he immediately suggested the cinema, and now she had immersed herself in the frothy world of make belief, and connected her emotions to those of the characters on the screen. To the treacherous hero, the scheming side-kicks, the glamorous female. The plot was thin, the characters were cardboard. If asked, she wouldn't even have been able to remember the title of the film. But for those two hours their world was hers, and the real world was suspended.

When Nessa returned from her meeting, her face was netted with exhaustion and strain. Orlagh gave an excuse that she was working that evening. The inevitable talk would have to wait. She took a bus into the city, and walked aimlessly until her feet ached. Then she sat in some dark pub and lost herself in the noise and the clatter, and the voices rising as the night went on. She caught the last bus home. The house was in darkness. She lay on her bed, fully clothed, until the first fingers of dawn poked their way through the curtains. Then she slept, waking only when she heard Robert's car turning on the gravel below her window. When she came downstairs Nessa was at the kitchen table, and the smell of percolating coffee gave a reassuring normality to the scene. Orlagh poured herself a mug of coffee, handed another mug to Nessa, and sat down.

'Well?' she said.

Her mother smiled across at her. Her face was smooth, as if the night had ironed away her exhaustion, and provided her with a fresh start.

'Killian had prepared him well. It wasn't as terrible as I thought it might be. He was so different from my memory of him.' She reached over and touched Orlagh's cheek.

'He had no idea, Orlagh. Absolutely no idea. I have to take the blame ... I should have told him. Now he just wants to make it up to you. He thinks you're a wonderful person, and he's so proud that you're his daughter...'

'And what about you, Mum? What are your feelings in all of this? Where do you fit in?

'It was all such a long time ago, love. Another world ... a place apart. Brendan, Killian – they were part of my childhood, of my growing up. We can't turn the clock back. My life now is here, in Dublin, with Robert. Robert says that I should visit Inishbawn in the near future, to lay my ghosts as it were. And he's right. I think I need to. There are so many things from my past that I have been blocking off. Will you come with me, Orlagh? Please? This is something we need to do together.' She squeezed her daughter's fingers. 'I need your courage, Orlagh. You're a far stronger person than I ever was, and I badly need that strength now. Will you come back with me to Inishbawn, Orlagh?'

# EPILOGUE

A cluster of small, white crosses stand on a bleak hillside. A slab of weathered limestone bears the inscription 'To the Memory of the Little Children'.

The priest intones a brief blessing, his voice merging with the whine of a westerly wind blowing in from the Atlantic. The women stand in silent groups, heads bowed, figures silhouetted against the skyline. Nessa draws comfort from the touch of her daughter's hand on her arm. In this place, she is conscious of a long forgotten presence. She is conscious of the sighs and tears of Margaret, and of her pain as she grieved for her dead baby. Now at last, Nessa feels that the circle is complete. This she will do for her mother, and in doing so she will free her daughter to move forward into her future.

It had been Killian's idea that all those islanders who had connections with babies who had been buried, secretly and without recognition, here in this killeen, should come together and participate in a ceremony of blessing. Each family brought a little cross to commemorate a child, and flowers and crosses were placed on the mounds that indicated an unidentified burial place. Now the cruelty of the past was overridden by the loving words of the blessing, and Nessa felt that at last her mother could be at rest.

When the ceremony was finished the other women nodded to Nessa and Orlagh, and went their various ways. Nessa shook hands with Killian, and thanked him. It was unlikely that they would meet again. What she had come back to Inishbawn to do was now finished. She would return to Dublin that evening, to her husband and her home. There she would weave together the threads of her life, into a strong and durable pattern. The great burden of secrecy and guilt had been lifted, and Nessa felt at peace.

Orlagh stood alone on the incline leading down to Derryglas. She could see the sturdy chimney pots, and the shimmering slate of the farmhouse roof. This was her house, her inheritance, and one day she would return to live there. She felt the quickening, the growing eagerness, as of one who was returning after a long, long absence. The pull of the island was getting stronger. Now she had no need to deny her island blood, and she knew that very soon she would reclaim the past, and come to live in Inishbawn, in Derryglas, where generations of McDowells had lived. The squally wind spat pebbles of cold rain against her cheeks. She wrapped her scarf around her and hurried back to where her mother and her father waited in the car.

'Are you alright Orlagh?' Brendan turned round and touched his daughter's arm briefly as she got into the back seat. Orlagh nodded.

Brendan drove the two women to the harbour, and as the rain lashed the island, they boarded the ferry and headed back to the mainland.

# Selected Titles from Wordsonthestreet

**Liar, Liar**
Alan McMonagle
ISBN 978-0-9552604-5-2
168pp RRP €12.99 pb
**Online Price! €11.99**

**Unconquered City**
Diarmuid Scully
ISBN 978-0-9552604-8-3
200 pp RRP €13.50 pb
**Online Price! €11.99**

**Décollage New and Selected Poems**
Patricia Burke Brogan
ISBN 978-0-9552604-6-9
100 pp RRP €11.99 pb
**Online Price! €9.99**

**The Man Who Was Haunted
By Beautiful Smells**
Jarlath Fahy
ISBN 978-0-9552604-3-8
76 pp RRP €11.99
**Online Price! 9.99**

**Calling the Tune**
Maureen Gallagher
ISBN 978-0-9552604-7-6
80 pp RRP €11.99
**Online Price! 9.99**

Log on to our online bookshop and buy at a special online price at:
**www.wordsonthestreet.com**
or order from:
Wordsonthestreet, Six San Antonio Park, Salthill, Galway, Ireland